# Stories
## for Jamie

*by*

## Kathy Sinnott
## &
## friends

edited by
## John Scally

**BLACKWATER PRESS**

Editor
*Margaret Burns*

Design
*Melanie Gradtke*

Layout
*Paula Byrne*

Cover Design
*Melanie Gradtke*

ISBN
1 84131 588 5

Produced in Ireland by
Blackwater Press
c/o Folens Publishers
Greenhills Industrial Estate
Tallaght
Dublin 24

*F99,758*
*€12.99*

# Contents

# Dedication

To Adam Patrick Minogue

# Preface

Most disablement is avoidable. Early and appropriate integrated intervention can minimise or even eliminate a primary disability, while maximizing potential. It keeps secondary disablement from developing. Timely intervention can also prevent a developmental difficulty from becoming a disability.

La Pilar Early Learning Research and Training Centre is designed to be a one-stop shop where a family can bring their child to get the right help.

La Pilar will have a primary medical clinic that will maintain links with the child's hospital consultant and a health and nutrition centre that can monitor special diets and work to improve the child's health. A wide variety of therapies will be available in specialised facilities like the Sensory Integration Gym and the Audio and Visual Rooms. Intensive teaching will be carried out in specially-designed classrooms. Family counselling and family training are vital for the child's successful development. Family apartments onsite will accommodate families who come from a distance. A library and conference room will facilitate staff training and research.

La Pilar will have a comprehensive menu of treatment, therapy and teaching so each child's needs can be met with an individual cocktail of services. Why? Because nothing less really works. Special needs are just that ... special. Each child is so different that to limit the help means that many needs will go unmet. Each child is so precious that that would be unthinkable.

La Pilar will offer three services:

First Response – An urgent and immediate response to a disablement or suspicion of a developmental difficulty. A child born visually impaired needs immediate help to maximise development. A Down's syndrome newborn needs to start treatment to balance his or her extra chromosome immediately in order to avoid intellectual impairment. A child in the early stages of autistic regression if appropriately helped can be normalised.

Early Intervention – Following First Response, some children will need to remain in a sustained, individualised program to keep development on track.

Transition – The aim of La Pilar is full inclusion. For children with special needs, successful inclusion, like successful development, must be planned and aided. La Pilar features an onsite Steiner kindergärten where children from the early intervention service can learn with their normally-developing peers to develop the skills needed to make a permanent transition from special services to mainstream.

What about expense? Early intervention is the only approach to developmental challenges that makes any economic sense. €1 spent early is worth €7 spent later.

The capital costs of La Pilar will be about €10m. To put this figure in perspective, La Pilar will be built and equipped for less than half the building costs of the new Oireachtas car park and for the cost of the toilet facilities in the Bertie Bowl.

La Pilar Integrated Early Learning Research and Training Centre is non-profit. It will be built and run by La Pilar Integrated Learning Centre, a registered limited charitable company founded by the Hope Project. All donations to La Pilar are tax-exempt.

All the proceeds of this book go to La Pilar Integrated Early Learning Research and Training Centre.

Thanks to John Scally who conceived this collection, the writers who contributed, Blackwater Press and to you for buying it. Enjoy!

*Kathy Sinnott*

# Foreword

There's a presumption that when people have to endure extreme difficulties, they are somehow inherently equipped for it – that their optimism levels are higher, that their sensitivity levels are lower – but that's so rarely the case.

Misfortune is random, but sometimes ordinary people manage to find the ability to respond to it in an extraordinary way: Kathy Sinnott is such a person.

She was a normal mother of three when her baby son Jamie suddenly began to scream non-stop. Her response was the usual one – Jamie had to be hungry, cold or in pain. At no point did she think the situation was anything other than temporary. But after he'd screamed day and night for three months, her father pointed out the obvious: this wasn't a phase. Something was very wrong with Jamie. That something transpired to be autism – and the diagnosis signalled the end of normal life for the Sinnotts forever.

Autism is a complex condition, made all the more complex by people's lack of understanding – even the experts are guessing. You can be autistic to such a mild degree that you lead an entirely normal life, but may be regarded as slightly eccentric, as is the case with many with aspergers, a cousin of autism but less severe. Or you can be autistic to the degree that you have severe social, communication and behavioural problems.

Many people think of Dustin Hoffman's portrayal of an autistic man in *Rainman* as an example of what it is like to be autistic. But the scenario in *Rainman* exists only in a small minority of cases – i.e. having brilliant abilities coupled with an inability to survive unassisted in the world. The fact is that for most severe cases there are huge learning difficulties and there may or may not be aggression and self-injurious behaviour. Usually there are rituals and compulsions as well as strange obsessions – often concerned with plumbing!

After the initial diagnosis Kathy was told to take Jamie home and 'watch his autism develop'. Instinct told her the last thing she should do was watch this regressive condition affect her son even further. But when she sought treatment for him, she discovered that Ireland had zilch in the way of special-needs services. And there wasn't much tea and sympathy either. A psychiatrist told her that children were made autistic by cold unloving mothers – 'refrigerator mothers'. He urged Kathy to give up on Jamie because she was young and attractive and he was going to ruin her life.

Instead Kathy took Jamie to Loyola Hospital in Chicago where the sensibility was very different. A team of professionals – educational psychologists, developmental psychologists and physical therapists – began to work with Jamie. Their attitude was that there was no time to lose and when Kathy and Jamie returned to Ireland three months later, Jamie no longer even looked autistic. But once home, without any treatment, he regressed to his earlier state. What it came down to, Kathy said, was a belief in Ireland that nobody who had a profound mental disability could learn.

The best that could be done for Jamie was to offer him two hours twice a week in the family and child clinic. But when Jamie turned five, Kathy was told – with brutal breeziness – not to bring him any more. No suggestion was given as to what should be done with Jamie: he simply wasn't to turn up there again.

Kathy approached another department and managed to secure another two hours twice a week. This new service made no pretence to provide any kind of help for Jamie – they were 'babysitting' him so Kathy could go shopping, they told her. This was funny, Kathy said, as she was penniless. She had no income and wasn't entitled to social security, so she spent those two hours twice a week sitting in the Franciscan church in Cork. She went to half-ten Mass, then, as soon as Mass was over, there was a small scramble as the local homeless community jostled with Kathy to get the seats with the heaters under them. 'Maybe I should have let them have them,' Kathy said, 'but I was underfed and stressed and very cold.'

It's very hard to imagine how she kept going. Being shunted from one inappropriate service to another, then having help abruptly withdrawn must have been utterly soul-destroying. But nothing compared to the terror of watching her beloved son recede further and further into himself.

But in the face of official indifference, even hostility, she kept showing up and being awkward. Even when a health board official in Cork told her that, 'There's no point in educating these kids because they're only going to die.'

Day after day after thankless day she got up and started afresh the struggle to persuade the health and education authorities to recognise autism and provide appropriate education and training for those with it. Though the official attitude was that Jamie and his ilk were unfixably faulty, Kathy would not agree because she had seen how Jamie had responded to intensive therapy in Chicago.

She never gave up and at some stage her struggle transcended the personal and became the general. She challenges how the authorities in Ireland view those with all disabilities – not just autism – and she gives those less abled a voice. She runs a helpline from her home and provides comfort for people like the man who has had to ring a government department so many times that now the staff simply hang up on him.

But, despite Kathy's years of campaigning, it's too late for Jamie now. Early intervention is the key and Kathy believes that if the care that Jamie first got in Chicago at eight months had continued, all that would be apparent now would be a slight clumsiness. As it is, at the age of twenty-four, he has recently learnt how to open the doors in his home. Kathy has just discovered that her third child is left-handed.

But despite all the doors slammed in her face, all the procrastination, the humiliations endured and the heartbreak of watching her son become locked into himself, Kathy is neither bitter nor beaten.

Anyone who has met her will attest to her extraordinary presence. She exudes a powerful air of serenity and she's great fun. In 2001 she won the *Irish Tatler* Women of the Year, Special Achievement category and no-one who was there can forget her immense charm, as she – in the nicest possible way – tried to embarrass Mary Harney into making an on-the-record commitment for funding. As Ms Harney presented her on stage with her prize – a crystal half-moon which she turned so that it suddenly resembled a make-shift crystal ball – she proceeded to 'foretell' all kinds of good things: funding to train special teachers, money for new units and allowances for equipment.

Autism is on the rise and for twenty-four years Kathy has campaigned to ensure that no more young people will ever have to 'share the scrapheap with Jamie'. She wants to avoid another generation of human beings locked inside themselves and another generation of ordinary families carrying superhuman burdens.

By buying this book you're helping her.

Thank you very much.

*Marian Keyes*

# Introduction

I don't often get very angry but I did the first time I met Kathy and Jamie Sinnott. For over twenty years theirs has been a world of pain, bewilderment, courage and perseverance. Kathy is a personification of 'Mother Courage'. For twenty-four years Kathy has campaigned to ensure that no more young people will ever have to 'share the scrapheap with Jamie' and, like him, arrive at the age of eighteen uneducated.

Meeting Jamie made me realize that we have condemned a generation, indeed generations, of Irish children with learning disabilities to lives where all the layers of their potential are not developed. The idea for this book was born to raise money for La Pilar, an early intervention centre for children with learning disabilities which Kathy is currently developing.

This book has no pretensions to literary greatness. It is intended to be an enjoyable read. There is a great divergence of styles and themes and my hope is that there will be something for everyone. Inevitably this means that we cannot be all things to all people all of the time.

It seemed indeed right and fitting to begin the collection with a story from Kathy. What could be more appropriate than for her to write a true story, 'The Summons' the story of La Pilar? Suzanne Power's 'Meeting Luke' is a wonderfully uplifting story of a very special friendship. Brian Leyden's story 'Special Needs' is a beautifully sensitive piece on a difficult subject which steers well clear of shallow sentimentality.

Micheal O'Siadhail provides a lovingly crafted poem, 'Parkinson's', which is worth reading for the last line alone.

Marisa Mackle is one of the rising stars in Irish fiction. Like Jane Austen in *Emma*, she enters the world of matchmaking in her charming story, 'Blind Date'. A tale for all true romantics and those who believe in serendipity.

Joseph O'Connor takes a more wry look at love in a typically humorous commentary on the Ireland of the Celtic Tiger in his story, 'Two Little Clouds'.

In the Ireland of the Celtic Tiger, house-hunting is said to be the new sex. Kate Thompson's 'On the Market' documents one woman's love for her house.

Kevin McDermott's 'The Bee Box' offers solace for all those who have loved and lost and provides a timely reminder of the triumph of the human spirit in the face of adversity. Martina Devlin's 'Flood Warning' also charts the stormy waters of good love going bad but with a light touch. John MacKenna's 'A Day in April' is set in Castledermot in County Kildare or in what is now known in the canon of Irish literature as 'the MacKenna Landscape'. MacKenna's characters always know the secrets of pain and his journey through an Ireland of the past deals with the universal search for warmth, affection and love. The main protagonist in PJ Cunningham's 'A Moment Beyond Paralysis' is also on a mission to reclaim lost love, but with a difference, in a story suffused with humanity.

Dermot Healy echoes the Beatles in his *cri de cœur*, the thoughtful and provocative 'Help!'.

All of us at some stage are confronted with the death of a loved one and have learned the hard way why 'Goodbye' is the most painful word in the English language. Parting is no sweet sorrow. That is why I was very anxious to include John Quinn's letter to his late wife, Olive. It is a work of incredible beauty and passionate intensity, which may bring some crumbs of comfort to those coping with a bereavement.

Anthony Glavin's story 'Treasure Island' recalls the beginning of his love-affair with Ireland, which happily continues to the present day. Meeghan Piemonte continues the American influence with her lyrical story, 'Snow House'. Peter Woods is the best writer I know on sport or a sense of place. He continues the cosmopolitan connection by taking us on a unique journey in his story, 'Roadkill'.

Arnold O'Byrne became a household name in the 1980s as the public face of Opel Ireland, particularly through his association with the Irish soccer team. He makes his literary debut with a delightfully comic story, 'A Tale of Two Tickets'. As befits a keen hurling fan from Tipperary, 'the home of hurling' (his words not mine!), Leo Cullen's story 'The Sand Dance' detours into sporting matters while exploring the good old days of the Music Hall variety show.

All of us at some stage dream of having a protective presence, greater than ourselves, cocooning us from harm and plotting our destiny with a hidden hand. Cathy Kelly's 'The Fortune Teller' opens a window of wonder to take us into such a world.

Maura O'Neill's voice will be known to many people from her work on RTÉ radio. This book showcases her writing talent for the first time. I am absolutely certain that she will go on to climb to dizzy heights as a writer both of fiction and non-fiction. Her story 'Liam' takes us right into the enchanting world of children.

Award-winning children's writer Catherine Ann Cullen's reworking of an old fairytale 'Golden Feathers' will lift the spirits of the hardest heart. To conclude a very simple fairytale, as befits its author, which will hopefully appeal to children of all ages.

This book was inspired by Kathy Sinnot's towering spirit, courage and rich vein of humanity. I will forever remain in awe of her.

I am eternally grateful to all my wonderful contributors: Leo Cullen, PJ Cunningham, Martina Devlin, Anthony Glavin, Dermot Healy, Cathy Kelly, Brian Leyden, Marisa Mackle, Kevin McDermott, John MacKenna, Arnold O'Byrne, Joseph O'Connor, Maura O'Neill, Micheal O'Siadhail, Meeghan Piemonte, Suzanne Power, Kate Thompson and John Quinn. Special thanks to the marvellous generosity of Marian Keyes and Catherine Ann Cullen. As always I am deeply thankful to my good friend Peter Woods, for his practical support. I am particularly appreciative for the moral support of Roddy Doyle.

I would also like to record my appreciation for my 'Nasty Nick' players: Siobhan O'Grady, Aisling Rodgerson, Owen Graham, Alistair Harvey, Marc McCabe, Jeff Taylor, Stephen Buckley, Tim Ryan, Roisín Watson, Katy and Lisa Dobey and my very own voice squad Samantha Brownlee, Darren Gill, Richard Pollock and Sarah Palmer. You're simply the best.

Thanks to Claire Hennessy and Ciarán Folen for their efforts; Rebekah Cornwell for her technical assistance and to Kate O'Neill for being an ongoing source of inspiration. I am indebted to John O'Connor, and all at Blackwater Press for their help and encouragement.

*John Scally*
October 2002

*For children with learning disabilities early intervention is essential if lasting damage is to be prevented. La Pilar will provide an early response for infants and children experiencing developmental delay.*

# The Summons

*Kathy Sinnott*

*I loved* my sleep. I flitted in and out of it hoping that the need to use the bathroom would wait till morning. Silly because of course it wouldn't and of course I would get up. But foggy brained and restless, I would still hope, wasting the very sleep I was trying to secure.

When I was finally sufficiently awake and desperate, I would plan the transition from warm blankets to cold night air. When I eventually slipped out of the blankets, I would open my eyes only the slightest bit to delude my body into thinking it was still asleep so there would be no time lost in returning to that blessed state when I got back into bed.

If and when I got back, there was one obstacle. To avoid it, I had to move quickly and very very quietly. The risk was great.

'Kaky.'

Don't move.

'Kaky.'

Wait.

Maybe she will stop.

'Kaky.'

'Yes Megan.'

'Drink of water.'

'Just a minute.'

The big family room where Megan lay was lit with stars and moon, but the adjoining kitchen where I went for a cup of water was dark and treacherous with darker shapes – broom, mop, chicken bucket, vegetable bin. I would not turn on the light because I was still pretending that I was going back to bed soon.

I also didn't want Megan to be more wakeful.

When I sat next to her bed I could see that she was wide awake and delighted for my company. The water, she only pretended to sip. I stroked her head and asked if she'd had enough. She said she needed more and pretend to sip again.

It was impossible to be anything but tender with Megan. I sensed her need for my company; I tried not to rush her. I even felt privileged to be with her in the quiet dark. But after a few minutes, my body was aching to be horizontal and warm and my mind to be oblivious. I made one more attempt to excuse myself and, undemanding, Megan let me slip away to bed.

I did not know she was soon to die. I would have stayed and kept her company. Or would I? The spirit is willing but the flesh is weak.

The spirit was willing – during the day.

I loved Megan. She had been my special baby sister when I was a teenager. I stayed with her in hospital when as a little girl she had her neck rebuilt. In those days, it was my lap she chose at the table and my bed she crawled into at night until I left her for college. Then she was largely out of my life. We got to know each other eight years later when as a mother of two I came to live in Mount Lodge.

It wasn't the same, I had my own babies and she had other favourite sisters, but I had a special way of making her laugh. And laughing was very important because her successful neck surgery was years later being undone by her teenage growth and she could no longer walk, dance, make chocolate chip cookies and be free of pain as she slipped into paralysis.

To make her laugh, I would make a noisy and dramatic entrance into the middle room where she sat propped in the big chair, accusing her of messing it and bemoan the task of tidying. I would then tie an old anything around my head, put on a big apron, grab a broom and start chasing offending rubbish around the room. 'Get out of there quick,' I would demand of a dust whorl that preceded the bristles behind the couch. 'Take that,' I would chide crumpled paper as I tossed it towards the bin. 'Where do you think you're going?' I would ask the same paper if it missed the bin and 'don't try to escape again' when I finally managed to get it in the bin. The scene would get louder and wilder as I addressed a sock and asked after its mate or shook a coat and told it to get lost and never be found lying around again or else. Eventually the room would be clean and Megan, exhausted from laughing, ready to nap.

But that was during the day. Heading back to bed quickly, I would tell myself that she'd had a drink and now she was grand. I wanted to be warm and asleep before the thought of her loneliness and my desertion kicked in.

Especially because I was leaving for Spain soon.

The year before, I heard the story of Saragossa. It was a traditional Spanish story in which Mary is transported by angels to console James, the apostle, who was camped outside the Roman walls of Saragossa. Mary tells him of his future martyrdom and prepares him for the long hard road home to meet it. She consoles him and prays with him. Before leaving she gives him a jasper pillar, which now stands in the church which was erected on the spot where they spoke.

I wanted to go to Saragossa. It was a strange wanting; there was no enthusiasm just inevitability. I didn't do anything about it like look at maps, ring travel agents, I just tucked 'that I go to Saragossa' into my night prayers. My sisters thought this amusing because I was not a traveller. I was not even pushed about going down the road. I was quite content to be at home, wherever home was at any given moment. In praying to visit Saragossa, I felt no urgency, I knew I would go, time and purpose did not even enter my mind. I was in no hurry and gave it only the passing evening mention.

Months later Dec, my husband, rang from Germany where he was gigging with the Cork band, Sunwheel. I was out of the house and my sister took the message. Dec had a surprise that Máirín mustn't tell me: Sunwheel had signed a contract to play for the American military in Spain and Joady, Brigid and I were going with him. I was not even in the door when I heard.

We got out the encyclopaedia and looked up Spain. For the first time I had my doubts. My impression of Spain had been Irish, everywhere within distance of everywhere else. Spain looked different. The map was full of cities and placenames. We finally located Saragossa. It was in the middle of the country far from the coast, where I assumed military bases to be.

A few days later Dec arrived and told me the surprise. I asked him where in Spain we would go. He thought hard and eventually remembered that one of the two places had an odd name, Saragossa. I told him I had been praying to go there – he didn't believe me. He was as surprised at my desire to travel as he was at the destination. He asked me to stay where I was. He went off and asked my sisters if I had said I wanted to go anywhere.

Late April he left for Spain in the band's purple van. The children and I were to follow by boat and train ten days later. He rang from Saragossa the night before we were to leave and gave me a trail of placenames to follow. 'I hope you can get to your precious cathedral, this is a big city.'

At the last minute, we discovered a problem with one of our passports. On the morning of departure, I took the early train to Dublin to the US Embassy. I completed the necessary paperwork and had it ready to process when the embassy closed for lunch. Disappointed, I sat outside for the hour watching the motionless marine just inside the embassy's glass door. I replanned the route to the train station, mentally rehearsing and refining it, hoping to shave minutes off the journey. All going well, I could just make the train back to Cork and the boat.

After lunch I was first in line, I flew through the next step and then was told that I had to see the consul. I was left in a little waiting area. Five minutes, ten minutes, a half an hour … the train was gone. The boat would be gone. I was not angry, or panicky, just incredibly sad. I had missed Saragossa. I began to cry.

Everything happened quickly. I was rushed into the consul, who was kind and quick. Someone hurried me out the door and told me to have a wonderful trip and I was blinking in the Ballsbridge sunlight wondering what to do now. I grabbed a bus for the quays, got off and then leapt on a bus for the Naas Road and for once CIE ran like clockwork.

I was seriously praying. I jumped off the bus and ran beyond the intersection. Turning to face the traffic, I asked for a fast car. The lights changed, I put out my thumb and a red sports car pulled up. I opened the door and hopped in. The driver smiled and said, 'I hope you like speed.' I laughed and said, 'I love speed.' We laughed for the short time it took to get to Cashel. Looking at my watch, I calculated. I could feasibly make it if I got an immediate lift from someone who knew where the boat was and would take me there. The first truck stopped. He often delivered to the Tivoli ferry and would drop me at the gates.

I ran the long drive from the gates to the boat. Dad, Mom, Joady, Brigid and bags were waiting by the gangway. They were very relieved to see me. A quick hug, up the ramp and we were pulling away.

Three days later we arrived into Bilbao, the taxi to the train was expensive. The train was cheap. I had no Spanish, no sense of where we were and no way to gauge the demands on my scarce funds. So, when the train stopped at lunchtime we stayed on board while everyone else piled out. After a few minutes, a man came and gestured for us to get out. He herded us to the other passengers and into a big dining-room with a wonderful smell of food.

Joady and Brigid had long since finished Granny's food package and were very hungry. I was starving because I had been seasick and had not eaten since before rushing to Dublin. Dinner seemed to be compulsory so I took a plate. When they tried to hand me a second, I tried to indicate that Joady and Brigid were small, would not eat much, and could have some of mine. I secretly intended to feed the children and finish what they left.

The idea of one plate between three created a sensation. Everyone started talking and gesturing at once. They were, I think, trying to tell me I was too thin, that Joady was a growing boy and Brigid was blooming. They were shocked and insistent. Joady was lifted and passed around so they could check his weight – they seemed to be guessing his eventual size. Brigid was patted and pinched, and I was kindly but firmly scolded. I could see that I was not going to get away with one plate so I consented to two. They looked doubtfully at two-year-old Brigid and after some debate conceded. Joady was handed a plate overflowing with dinner. I ate hungrily dreading the moment at the end when I couldn't pay for this delicious and plentiful food.

We paid on the way out, it cost pennies and we were travelling again. Well fed, we slept. After dark, we arrived at a big train station. We opened the door blinking in the glare and there was Dec and Johnny Campbell. It was great to see them. They dropped us to the pension and hurried to the base to gig.

Joady and Brigid were up early so we went out to explore. There was a fruit market across the street. We wandered around the stalls and finally bought some fruit, the lady who served us was very helpful so I gestured and asked for the pillar. 'La Pilar', she said as she pointed to the side entrance.

There it was. It was unmistakable, a basilica towering and stretching opposite an enormous plaza. We crossed over and entered the church. It was unlike anything I had ever been in. It seemed like a row of churches under one roof with many side altars and several main altars. Darkened oil paintings lined the walls but were hard to make out in the dim light. We wandered until we got to the end – and there was the pillar, with its ancient Madonna and Child. The pillar itself was covered with an ornate cape.

The altar was being dressed for Mass so we sat down to wait. I had been asked to pray for many people. I got started, working my way through the list one by one: Miss Minahan's health, Teresa's leg, Dad's work – Megan. When I got to the end I prayed for us: Dec, Joady, Brigid and then for our new baby that he or she be 'happy and healthy'.

'This will not be.'

I turned to my right to see who had spoken. It had been a woman, but not the old Spanish widow bent over her beads a few pews away. I looked to my left but no one was there and besides the voice had come from my right. Then I looked forward to the ancient Madonna and understood. My baby was disabled. Coming to Saragossa had been a summons, an appointment.

'Alright, he won't be happy or healthy, but help me to take care of him.'

For some reason, at that moment, I also knew the baby was a boy.

We returned every morning before Dec woke. We fell into a routine, wandering about the courtyard and church. The children loved exploring. The church was very big with lots of dim dusty nooks. They always seemed to find something new.

As the time for Mass approached, we made our way towards the pillar. Joady had discovered that behind the altar, the pillar was exposed. Within an oval hatch, the marble was worn concave with the touches and kisses of pilgrims. We especially loved to come here because of the beautiful smell of roses and carnations.

During Mass, I thought about my son who was due in five months. A disability was not going to be easy to deal with but I had no fear of it. My close contact with disability had been very positive if very limited: my sister Megan and my father's cousin Arthur.

Megan was Down's syndrome and had a talent for affection. She was dearly loved and very loving.

My father's cousin Arthur had no legs. When I was a child, we often accompanied Dad on his house calls to Arthur. Arthur pulled himself up with a suspended triangle as we trooped in to stand at the foot of his big bed. Looking back, I'm sure we were a formidable line of staring eyes in freckled faces topped with blond or red hair. Cheerfully, he worked his audience like a master, telling jokes and talking with my brothers about baseball.

Once we were relaxed, he called his mother who was awaiting her queue in the next room.

'Have you something nice for John's children?'

Aunt Lizzy would give us doughnuts, and tell us stories of her childhood outside Newry or of my Dad's on Cicero Avenue in Chicago. My memories of Arthur are still so vivid that I can revisit them. Returning, I can now appreciate his pale face, the effort to sit up and the strain lines around his beautiful smile. He died while I was still young.

For the first few days, I speculated on the particular type of disability my baby would have. It would be more difficult if he were deaf because his father is a musician, blind would be better. I thought I might be a bit small to care for someone who needed a lot of lifting. But that stage soon passed. I knew he would be disabled, he would be loved and the form the disability took didn't matter.

But he wasn't disabled. At his birth, we stared at each other in welcome. He was strong, healthy and beautiful and I was grateful if confused. Saragossa was immediately relegated to the realm of things to be pondered later. I got busy with my new baby.

One winter evening, four months later, a group of us sat around the middle room like numbers on a clock, while Jamie, the clock's hand did a complete clockwise revolution on the carpet at our feet.

We cheered him and he seemed happy and excited with his new accomplishment. I knew from experience of the two older children that the next milestone would be to take his propelling foot, put it over the other, and roll. It was no longer safe to lay Jamie on the couch.

Over the next few days, I helped my parents and younger brothers and sisters pack for their return to Chicago. It was a sad time. They had come three years earlier hoping to stay but no medical vacancies had opened to my Dad. It seemed strange to us because Ireland had an unnecessarily high fatality rate for the very kind of cancer he treated so successfully in the USA. We were naive then.

I asked my father to vaccinate Jamie before leaving. He was four months and I wanted him to be safe.

The memory of my parents' departure and Jamie's screams will always be mingled. The scream was a high-pitched wail of pain. Jamie's clenched fists pushed at his head, which he could no longer lift.

Three months later, they returned. Jamie still screamed most of the day. He was at peace only at night. I had by now moved him to the foot of the bed. All my babies slept next to me, but Jamie was now only happy away, alone, untouched. He lay for hours in the dark staring at his little hand, which he slowly and rhythmically waved through the beam of light coming from the door. I remember those nights. I was so jealous of that faint light and so very very lonely for my baby.

My father seemed eager to hold Jamie. I was very relieved to hand him over. My father had a talent for calming fussy babies and even Jamie, who would challenge the best, succumbed and quieted.

One morning, I came into the sunny dining-room to find my father and mother looking down on Jamie lying quietly along my Dad's broad arm. Dad looked up.

'Kathy you know there is something wrong with Jamie.'

Up to that moment I didn't know, I had made excuses for Jamie's lack of development and had completely forgotten Saragossa. I now remembered.

'I know.'

Dad said, 'I think he may be blind or deaf.'

My James had already set out on that hard, long, lonely road. I had to hurry and catch up if I was to journey it with him.

# Meeting Luke

*Suzanne Power*

*(This story is based on David and Luke and their meeting which has changed both of their lives.)*

## Meeting Luke

There was a room. And Luke seemed to fill it. That was all there was.

In the school David had come to work in as a volunteer, Luke had long since been lost as a person. So was David. But Luke's loss was a problem for the school and David's was his own. Luke's angers, his running, measured as unmanageable.

David could get up in the morning and pretend. He was volunteering not for the children, but to be somewhere else. In his head all the art he wanted to make. In his hands no ability to. In his heart the grief of ended love and opportunity. No next. No plans. A sofa in a friend's place on a road called End Road.

Luke was to be moved from school to secure accommodation if his behaviour continued. So secure no one would see him who did not care to. No one in Luke's family could care. There were problems. His elder brother Martin, also autistic. At school everyone liked Martin. Luke broke a jaw because he could not see the sky. It had been taken by the ones who did not know how much he needed it.

David was given Luke's name and a character description, which amounted to how he did not fit. And then David saw what was evident. Luke was fine. A man. Head and shoulders above those who sought to contain him. Head and shoulders in a place that needed the air to be cleared for him. It was full of talk about him, as if he was not there.

And it all said: he should not be here.

Luke heard. His answer was to see open doors from squared-off rooms and manners and he could run like there was no floor to touch. David chased him like everyone else. And he brought Luke back to where he did not want to be. That first morning David apologised for those who should have known better than to speak in front of him.

David wanted to know Luke. And Luke allowed him to.

This was how it began.

## Luke does not like McDonalds

In Luke's house there were five children. His mother put food in a pot in the centre of the table and it was up to the children what they got from it. Martin was bigger than Luke. Luke starved.

In school Martin was not hungry. So he did not behave like a hungry animal. People liked Martin and hated Luke. Luke knew. He bit the dinner lady. He bit the child next to him because he wanted what was on the plate of the child who was not as hungry as him.

The teacher who had paid responsibility for Luke told David when David suggested Luke might be hungry: 'This child is the size of a man. How can he be starving? He should not be here. This child, what he does and does not do:

He does not read.

He does not use the toilet properly.

He could use the toilet properly, but he does not care to.

He does not swim.

He does not attend assembly with other children.

He does not go on outings.

He does use HMV records as a toilet and this is why he does not go on outings.

He does take off his clothes at every opportunity; this is why he does not go to assembly or on outings.

He does create havoc in the hydrotherapy pool. This is why he does not go swimming.

He tears up books. That is why he does not read.'

The teacher was overworked and was once kind. He did not want to have to tell David again. He did not want to have to go to hospital with a cracked rib again, because an idealist had decided to look at Luke with untrained eyes and thought it might be a good idea not to tie him to the chair when meals came around. Volunteers were more trouble than they were worth. But the teacher needed David to lift Luke, man-sized, on and off the toilet and on and off buses. Soon Luke would be gone. But removing a child from school took procedure. Procedure was slow. So Luke was still here and David was here and that was the part of what made the teacher wish he was not who he was.

Then Luke injured a driver and the teacher could not stop himself from being delighted. Luke was excluded from public transport. Excluded was not expelled. But it meant that. There were other children who could not be transported for this reason. They stayed at home where their parents watched them and the closed door with despairing eyes and let the hope of help slip away from them along with the hope of all else. Sometimes, when they needed the shops or time without a child who would never leave dependency, they would tie them up.

Luke was meek at home. He allowed the bonds to be slipped on. His mother would have cried if she had enough energy to see what she was doing. Luke was to be forgotten at fifteen years of age.

But there was David.

David had seen Luke. He had his own list and he tried to communicate this to the once kind, now worn teacher and then to the once kind, now ambitious head of department and then to the once ambitious, now knowledgeable head of the whole school, who had the government's ear and could make things happen.

His list said, first and foremost:

Luke does read. He can spell with facilitated communication. With David holding his index finger he moved to the letters on the alphabet board.

You. All. Hate. Me.

David tried to show the teacher, but Luke rubbed the end of his nose.

Luke Likes:

Rubbing the end of his nose.

Being naked.

Running.

David.


'Can you prove he can read?' The head asked David. The teacher and department head had decided David was trouble and were quiet around him so that he would not be encouraged to keep talking.

'No. I just know.'

'That,' the head said in a voice that was knowledgeable and had all the appearance of kindness, a learned thing, 'is unfortunate. There are curriculum standards. Luke must pass the development tests to be seen. Luke will stay at home, unless a way can be found otherwise.'

It had not been found. So David went to look for it.

He asked if he could drive Luke to school, to keep him from harming others. No, that is not a recognised way to transport Luke. What is? If you are willing to meet the driver at the depot and travel with him to all destinations, that would be meeting regulations.

David got up at 5:30 a.m. and went to the depot and then to Luke's house and sat with Luke while the driver collected all ten other pupils. Not him again, the driver spat. The driver complained about the inconvenience of having to go for tetanus shots after Luke's attack. Luke listened. David had the edge of the seat only, because Luke was rocking. He wondered what he was doing here.

In school David took Luke to the changing rooms and washed him. Part of the problem with the way people saw Luke was the way he smelled and his clothes. David took out some clothes that he had bought for Luke. Not cheap gear. Good stuff. For a fine man needs fine clothes.

The next day Luke came to school in old clothes. David bought more and they also disappeared. David cried when it was time to go home because he had to change Luke back into his old clothes and keep his new ones in a school locker. He took the bus home with Luke, then onto the depot, then back the thirty miles to his sofa on End Road. It was gone six every night when he got in. He was working at his art again in the evenings. And thinking of Luke.

David decides to take Luke out.

This causes consternation.

'Is it also against the rules?' David asks the knowledgeable Head.

'No, but it might not be wise, given Luke's record.'

'Don't interfere in what you may not want to follow through,' the worn out teacher snaps. David has already thought about this. He has decided.

If I get involved in this it is all or nothing.

Adam works in the school. He is a man with spaniel brown eyes and soft hands. His T-shirt says Nazi Punks Fuck Off. He listens to raw music and wears chains. He has been sectioned. Once he asked a man the time at the train station and the man took off his watch and handed it to him. Adam is not seen by anyone who has not the right eyes. The children love Adam because they sense all of him. David the same. David knows Adam to be the gentlest of men with the eyes and hands to do the work of opening up those who are closed. David asks Adam.

'Will you take Luke out with me?'

Adam knows this is dangerous, but if David is prepared to try then Adam is prepared to try with him. Adam is a teacher and has the knowledge. David is not a teacher but he has Luke in his sights and Luke's fineness will not be removed.

They take Luke to McDonalds in David's Lada. The car rocks with Luke's fear at this, what is new. Luke eats the seats and tears out lumps of upholstery and Adam prevents him from attacking David. In McDonalds Luke throws the food away and smashes a window and when he leaves, running, decides he would not like to wear his trousers or shoes.

They catch up with him in a park and David says, 'Oh dear' when Luke bites him hard enough to bring up welts.

The welts happen regularly. Concussion happens regularly. A fractured wrist. A broken jaw. To all of these David says, 'Oh dear.' He is not afraid of

Luke. He sees the spirit looking out of the ribcage of the man who is thwarted. He sees what is fighting in Luke and he knows that is why Luke survives.

He and Adam take Luke to the pub, to the café, to concerts. Luke likes Adam's raw music. David smiles to see them both rock to it in the same way. Luke likes Adam and he likes David. Luke begins to calm.

When David goes to sell his Lada he cannot because the seats are all no longer usable. In David's next car, a Renault, the seats are not eaten. Luke still throws the McDonalds on the floor. Luke, David and Adam realise, does not like McDonalds.

Luke likes good food:

Vegetables

Sandwiches

Yoghurt drinks

Falafels in pitta bread

Homemade pizza

Anything David is eating.


Luke also likes:

Adam's music

The Beatles

## How Martin died

When David was a boy he had a room, which he turned into a place of beauty and a world apart from what was happening outside. He had only what he was passionate about in this world. It was safe. It was small. Luke does not need small but he needs safe. This now is what David knows Luke needs. Adam has explained to him that Luke sees the world in straight lines. And David explains to Adam that as the crow flies is Luke's heaven. David must find it for him. But first a haircut. Luke can have his hair cut without sedation now.

Luke's good looks are apparent and are a sign of his fineness. He is calm because someone is looking at all of him and this keeps him calm, even given what he goes home to every night. Luke can endure. David breaks at the thought of that.

David is painting all the time, thinking of Luke all the time. His work is noticed and he is becoming successful. His work is taking him away from the school. Only Luke keeps him there. He has a pit of fear in his belly that when Luke leaves the school, in a year's time, the only place for him is council care and that will mean sedation. Council care is on Coventry Road. All are silent on it. To keep the peace those like Luke must be kept apart from their behaviour and so they are given pills and injections to take them to somewhere grey and quiet.

Luke is a risk. It is in the paperwork. There is nowhere else for those who are termed 'risk'.

Luke is not as violent in school. He still runs. David is not liked. He keeps asking why. Why can Luke not go swimming if I will be with him?

The teacher who has paid responsibility for Luke says the rule has been made about Luke swimming. It would be against the rules. To change a rule is slower even than to create one. Procedure.

So David looks for a way.

At lunchtime the school pool is closed. David decides to set up a swimming club.

If it is recreation and the carers all work voluntarily, then school rules do not apply.

But the rule, the fat lady in the office says, is the pool is closed.

We can open it, David says.

No. It is closed.

It is coming close to Christmas. David is to do the Friday assembly, which Luke now attends. He makes Christmas trees out of umbrellas and Luke, when he sees them, goes to sit under one. The teacher, the Deputy Head and the Head are all present. Everyone smiles. David is a bringer of colour and new eyes. They must give him that.

At lunchtime on Monday David is walking by the pool when he hears people inside. The door is unlocked. The fat lady is doing the breaststroke in a swimsuit that is the colour of all flowers. The colours are screaming at

David and he sees only one himself, blood red. The office staff scurries from the pool, where they take their lunchtime swim as part of a keep-fit regime.

They dress quickly and hurry back to administration where they imagine safety waits. But David follows them and the shouting continues.

'Why can't you people just learn to stay out of our way?'

The Head opens his office door and stands listening. When David has calmed down the fat woman is close to weeping. She feels shame and puts this to the Head as anger.

'What are you going to do about him?'

The Head says, 'What do you expect from a man who makes Christmas trees out of umbrellas?'

Two days later the swimming club starts with Adam and David taking Luke and another boy called Malcolm. Luke spends a long time in the water, watching the blue. He does not want to get out and when he does he sees Adam's leather jacket. He puts it on and runs. They catch up with him on a traffic island, barefoot, wet trunks and a biker jacket with skull and crossbones, pointing at the sky.

Later, on the alphabet board he points, with David's hand to steady him:

Under the sea.

In a garden.

In the shade.


The school breaks up. Regulations are over. David is invited to his father and his mother's houses and he does not go, because he does not know how Luke will be with two weeks at home. At home Luke is in danger from Martin. Luke will be hungry and his clothes will go and he will be bruised. So David calls to Luke's house and speaks to his mother and takes time to talk to her. She apologises a lot and laughs when there is nothing funny said.

'Sometimes,' she says, 'I don't know what will happen.' That makes her laugh.

There are no decorations in the house. No umbrellas. Nothing to keep out the rain.

David gets a phone call. There has been a fire. It is December twenty-third. Martin is dead and Luke's family have no home.

Luke smelt it first. The acrid black and the flame close behind, creeping up the stairwell and taking all they did not have in this shabby house. Martin and Luke share a room.

Luke runs, but Martin cannot. He has to stay for there are things he has to do. He must check his reflection in the mirror, open and close the wardrobe door three times. Check the four drawers of the chest of drawers are shut. The smoke is waiting on the landing and the flames after it and the explosion comes and takes the one thing Martin did have.

They find Luke, blackened and naked, walking a dawn road.

## Luke must have

Luke must have somewhere to stay or he will go to Coventry Road.

'If I do this,' David says to Adam, 'I have to do it all the way. This is all of Luke's life.' Adam comes back from Derbyshire to help. Other people come to help. So they become his family. David and Adam work all day and night with Luke.

The school gives them a spare classroom to sleep in. Adam learns to sleep in front of the door so that Luke cannot run. David cannot wake at night. The tiredness takes all of him in dark hours. Luke cannot sleep. All day and all night in school is no movement at all.

David has to move from End Road to a house. Luke comes to stay there. Every hour is phone calls, letters and pleas. Luke is losing it. There is too much new. His rituals, his security of the past months, are all slipping. There is no path through the day.

He runs to find a way back to what it all was, before the blackness. David has to paint now, because this is the work that gives him the time to spend making Luke's new life. Luke just knows David is too busy, and always talking, sometimes talking about Luke, in front of him. That is when David realises he is being what everyone has always been to Luke. Blind. Luke loses it when David gives some of his story to a woman in a room where they are all present. The story is a joke about Luke's behaviour, to alleviate what is a terrible pressure for them all.

Luke does not like:

The way things are now.

David's words about him.

The memory of black.

Gentle fine Luke. He points, points, points to the spelling board.

No.

David says, 'I am sorry Luke.'

And then it is the time when things get better. Money comes from the paintings and from the council to make a part of the family's new house into a suitable home for Luke. David sets up a foundation. Luke's Future. It helps others of Luke's age to be what they are. There is no silence. There is no Coventry Road.

The plans that no one had planned to make are coming together. Luke calms and those around who are not David or Luke or Adam discover what they have known a long time now. Luke likes people. Luke likes life.

## As the crow flies

David buys a chalet in heaven. Luke's heaven. It is on a shoreline with no sight of end from the window. On the beach Luke walks, being what made him. He is light and strong and the lithe make of him is unhindered by clothes. He takes a line along where waves meet sand and makes it his own. He walks, straight in all ways. At night he sleeps in a room which David has made knowing as much of Luke as he does, as much as Luke can let him know. It is a room of lights and colour and there is the sense when he lies in bed that there is no end to what is now. This is as a crow flies.

# Special Needs

### Brian Leyden

'Des has special needs,' the Director of Services said.

'He has the same needs as you and me,' said Vera.

Her husband, Frank arched one eyebrow as a sign Vera should keep quiet.

'Community living under the auspices of a dedicated team of carers will offer Des positive opportunities,' the Director said.

'It's for his own good,' Frank nodded.

The Director eased back in the armchair, a gold pen levelled between his fingers like a miniature hurdle to cross. 'Des will reside in this house under professional supervision during the week and return home at the weekends and during the holidays. On balance, I believe this move will be a respite for you and a benefit to your son.'

Vera understood they were lucky to have the offer of a place for Des in a community setting. He was eighteen and so physically powerful it was getting harder every day to manage his outbursts, even if the screaming and the stubborn tantrums were rare events. He had been a lovely baby and a sweet little boy, devoted to his father and mother. But they had to accept they could not look after him on their own much longer, as painful as it was to think of their son in the care of other people.

If they were younger things might be different. But Des was a late child. A surprise: more than a surprise. They had been told they could never have children. Then she got pregnant at the age of forty-five. The shock and delight of discovering she was carrying a child. The change that came over Frank was marvellous. Then the results of the amniocentesis revealed a genetic abnormality. Frank started to have second thoughts. It might be better to terminate, he said. But she couldn't give up her baby. And they both agreed in the end to wait and see.

When Des was born he was a beautiful baby. Only he had Down's syndrome and a moderate learning disability. That's what broke Frank's heart. If the disability had been more severe he might have been reconciled to his son's condition. But to come so close to being normal and yet be so dependent on both his parents for the rest of his life, he found that hard to take.

'I hope we're doing the right thing,' the corners of Vera's mouth turned down. 'Des loves my cooking. No disrespect,' she met the Director's eyes, 'but what's he going to make of the food there? And what if he's upset and all he wants is a hug from his mother?'

While the Director reassured Vera, Frank looked out the sitting-room window towards the footpath that led from the house to the roadway where a bus stood waiting. A stiff autumn gale blew across the green but the passengers for the bus seemed not to notice, pounding along the pavement with a tubby, unselfconscious gait, their heads thrust forward and the palms of their hands turned back with the fingers locked in unfathomable gestures. One or two appeared completely engrossed in the act of walking, and he could imagine them continuing straight onto the public road unaware of the danger. More dawdled until they were prompted to move along by a carer. People sometimes called a child with a learning disability a 'special' child, he thought, but there are times when it felt more like a kick in the teeth from God.

Des was being given an introductory tour and he spotted Des walking alongside a young woman with a ski-cap pulled down so far over her head she could barely see where she was going.

'At least her head is warm,' the Director smiled, following the direction of Frank's gaze.

'Sorry,' Frank said automatically, though it made him angry to have this man trying to second-guess his private thoughts. They were all the same, these healthcare professionals in positions of power: always pretending they knew more and knew better.

'We count ourselves exceptionally lucky to have you and your team looking after Des,' Frank said, smiling at the Director.

'We appreciate that every parent wants what's best for their child,' the Director said. 'And Des is a very charming and affectionate young man.'

'I love him,' Vera said. 'Loved him from the first.'

'I can see that, Vera. And we are all heroic when we feel wanted.'

'Have we got papers to sign?' Frank asked.

\* \* \*

Des had a tendency to overeat. During his first week in the new house he led a midnight raid on the pantry. Following his breach of house rules, his carers put him on a diet. But when he came home the following week, Vera relented and he got as much food as he wanted. For lunch on Sunday she coaxed Frank to take them to Ali's restaurant. Although the chef and owner were Lebanese they served Italian food and Des loved their pizzas and their ice-cream.

While he waited for Des to finish his ice-cream, Frank watched Ali, the restaurant owner, moving between the tables and greeting the regular customers. Ali had a word and a smile for everyone as he ferried plates between the kitchen and the tables packed in close together within the cramped dining area. With new arrivals, Ali recommended the specials and complimented their decision if they ordered something different. He treated regulars and people straight off the street alike, and Frank read this practiced inclusiveness as a ploy maintained strictly for business reasons. Ali had stiff competition from several fine restaurants in town, and Frank actually preferred the place up the street. There was more space between the tables. Here, everybody knew your business.

Looking at the clock on the wall Frank thought it had stopped. He checked the time on his watch. Both timepieces said five minutes past two.

'I should be going,' he said. 'I'm meeting people at three.'

Vera sat looking at her plate. He hated these wounded silences.

'What?' he said.

She clutched her handbag in her lap more tightly, refusing to speak. He knew the reason for her silence. But it wasn't his fault. He had a house to sell. The buyers asked if they could view the property on a Saturday; the only

F99,758

day they were free. He wanted to say this but spotted Ali gliding through the gap to reach their table.

'Everything okay with your meal?' Ali enquired, noticing the leftovers on Vera's plate. He seemed genuinely concerned, Frank had to admit, but it was good business to make certain his customers went away happy.

'Fine, thank you,' Vera said.

Frank thought she looked pale and distracted. Her appetite was failing and she hadn't been herself all week. He put it down to missing Des. She treated his absence not as a respite to gather her strength, but as a penalty for not being more able.

Ali gathered up their plates and looked at Des who sat bent over the table spooning ice-cream into his mouth.

'How are you, Des?'

'I am very good, Ali,' Des said in his flat, matter-of-fact voice. A run of ice-cream escaped down his chin.

'You like our ice-cream?' Ali smiled indulgently.

'Yes, Ali. It is very good?'

'Would you like some more?'

'We'll have the bill,' Frank said.

Ali looked at Vera and she nodded.

Bloody cheek, Frank thought, but he said nothing. He was the one paying the bill and he'd answer that kind of uppity behaviour by leaving the minimum tip. When Ali withdrew, Frank handed Vera a paper napkin.

'For God's sake, wipe his chin.'

She took the napkin without a word and passed it to Des.

'Thank you, Vera,' Des said and he dabbed the ice-cream spill with the napkin.

Frank got up and removed his coat from the back of his chair. It was another thing that annoyed him about the place: the way they were willing to squeeze in as many tables as possible but they couldn't be bothered to provide the customers with a coat rack.

'Frank, I have to go to the toilet,' Des said.

'You know where it is?' Vera said when Frank didn't answer.

'Yes, Vera.'

Des laid his spoon neatly at the edge of his plate and rose. When Frank moved aside to allow Des to squeeze by he bumped into the next table. But the people at the next table apologised to Frank, as if they were at fault. Then they smiled tolerantly and allowed Des to pass.

Frank could see the other diners watching the incident; see the patronising smiles on their faces making way for Des as he bustled towards the toilets. It was an attitude he'd encountered many times before. A polite reflex that masked suspicion and caution. And he remembered a remark made by the Director of Services while discussing a work placement for Des. The Director said in passing that people with a disability often suffer from the views of people around them. But Frank wanted to ask, what about the parents? Did no one realise how infuriating the bogus good will of other people could be? Since he recognised at a glance what the parents of normal children really thought when they met Des: how lucky they were to escape the same misfortune.

He put on his coat and stood looking around for Ali. There was no sign of the restaurant owner, which was typical of the man: hovering over your shoulder while you tried to eat and then you couldn't find him when you wanted to leave.

'Sit down, Frank,' Vera said. 'You're making me uncomfortable looking at you.'

* * *

Having Des home only at the weekends highlighted how many Saturdays Frank was out of the house. But it was a routine he couldn't quit at this stage in his career, especially while the property boom continued. And he defended the hours he worked saying the financial security allowed Des the full benefits of the care service.

The autumn tapered into winter and the evenings got short and cold. Frank liked to stay on at work, finishing paperwork while the evening rush hour dispersed. Most weeknights it was after eight o'clock by the time he got home.

On the last Friday in November a freezing fog made halos around the streetlights and by half-past eight that evening the frost glimmered on the roofs of the parked cars in the street. Walking up the garden path, Frank noticed every light on in the house. Des had a fear of the dark, and Vera kept the lights on throughout the house whenever he came home. The service had coaxed Des to accept a dim night-light only while he stayed with them, but Vera left the light on in his bedroom at all times. Frank told her it was wrong to undermine the work done by the service; she was doing more harm than good by giving in to his pleading. And of course he'd been fool enough to imagine that for once she'd listened to what he had to say.

He took a deep breath and turned the latchkey in the lock. As he removed his coat in the hallway the house seemed unusually quiet. When he was at home Des played loud music all the time. And whatever he happened to be doing, Des had a way of making noise; another reason Frank preferred to work late at the office where he had the quiet necessary to concentrate. No smell of cooking either, he noted.

Vera baked a lot when Des came home at the weekends. Des liked baking and she allowed him to mix the knead dough, to roll out and shape pastry and to keep an eye on the cakes and tarts and scones in the oven as they browned. Des and Vera sold cakes and scones at a charity stall on Saturday mornings. And Des took the surplus back to the community house on Sunday nights to share with his friends.

He resisted an impulse to call out for Des or Vera and instead poked his head around the jamb of the door to see if they were in the living-room. He found Vera on the sofa with her head thrown back and Des clutching her throat. Her face was scarlet and her eyes rolled back in their sockets.

'Get off her,' he screamed.

He shoved Des aside and put a hand on her cheek. She was alive but unnaturally cold. 'Christ, oh Christ!' he struggled to collect his thoughts. 'Vera say something. Tell me you're alright,' he repeated until her eyes began to flicker and she started to come round.

His first thought had been that Des attacked her but he quickly realised she was having a seizure of some sort. Epilepsy, perhaps. Though Vera never had any kind of attack before.

While Vera slowly came around, Des squatted on the carpet making a horrible moaning sound, rocking back and forth and banging his forehead against the armrest.

Useless, Frank though looking at him. Not even the wit to get help. 'Stupid, useless, useless ... '

When he got Vera to the hospital the doctors diagnosed a heart attack. Frank was relieved to hear it wasn't a stroke. And there was no trace of paralysis or brain damage. But as the hospital admitted her to a bed for the night he was unnerved by her shaky and exhausted condition. The nurses said this was to be expected after the trauma her body suffered.

Des was also in a distressed state, but the best place for him, Frank reasoned, was with the carers who would know how to calm him down. He had enough on his plate without Des to look after.

He dropped Des off, explaining to the night staff what happened. Afterwards, he collected a nightdress for Vera and other things she might need and he returned to the hospital. At the nursing station they told him Vera was sleeping and she needed her rest. He gave them her medical history. Then he went home to a house with every light on and the front garden rigid with frost.

The next morning he had to scrape the ice off the car and defrost the locks before he could collect Des and take him to the hospital. Des was very quiet. He might have forgotten everything that happened he was so placid and compliant. They drove in silence, collected a bunch of flowers from a filling station forecourt and found a space in the hospital car park.

The sight of the long polished corridors and the nurses bustling to and from their stations made Des frown and crease his face. From these anxious expressions, Frank could sense Des trying to demonstrate his appreciation of this difficult situation. But he simply wasn't equipped for the task.

A 'do not disturb' notice hung on the door of the private room where Vera was resting. He passed the flowers to Des and told him to wait. Des took a seat in the corridor, holding the cellophane wrapped bouquet upright in his lap.

Vera sat propped up in bed. She had no make-up on and her hair hung limp. He tried to hid his shock at how aged and shaken she appeared. Vera had always been such a robust woman with big, strong hands; he would pass her a jar or a bottle with a tight lid that she could open quicker than him. But the attack had drained that vitality. Her breathing sounded shallow and she had an air-tube fitted to her nose. That he noticed her fragile appearance must have been obvious from the look on his face and the jittery catch in his voice. But he mustered a smile and she smiled back weakly.

'How are you feeling?'

'Tired,' she said.

'You gave us a fright.'

'How is Des? Is he outside?'

He nodded.

'Ask him to come in.'

'In a minute,' he said.

She gave him an enquiring look.

'The nurses reckon this isn't your first attack.'

She hesitated, considering what to admit and what to deny.

'If you don't tell the truth, how do you expect the doctors to make you better?'

After persistent coaxing she admitted she suffered chest pains before and other dizzy spells. 'But nothing as severe as the last attack,' she said.

'Why didn't you say something sooner?'

'You had enough on your mind,' she lowered her eyes and plucked self-consciously at the bed covers.

'Were the chest pains the reason you allowed Des to move into community care?'

'What if something happened?' she lifted her face and looked him straight in the eye. 'How would you cope?'

'I can't believe you kept this from me.'

'Go easy on Des,' she said.

'It won't come to that,' he said, feeling a sharp tightness in his own chest.

But she would not lower her eyes until he gave her a direct answer and finally he said: 'I'll look after him, I promise.'

'Where is he?'

'Outside.'

'Ask him to come in.'

Frank opened the door and he beckoned Des forward. But Des stopped on the threshold and looked apprehensively at Frank when he spotted his mother lying in the hospital bed by the window.

'It's okay,' Vera coaxed.

He shuffled towards her, holding the bouquet by the stems with the petals facing the floor. 'We brought flowers for you, Vera,' he righted the bouquet and presented it to her bashfully.

She brought the blossoms up to her face and sniffed. 'I can't smell a thing with this tube in my nose.'

'They smell like petrol,' he said.

She smiled and Des began to laugh, rocking over and back on this feet.

* * *

On the morning of the funeral Frank kept looking over the heads of the mourners gathered around Vera's grave towards the black limousines of the other funerals taking place at the same time in the Municipal cemetery. Constant lines of traffic crawled along the cement driveways between the open graves. He couldn't get the thought out of his mind of the queue for the underground car park.

For his first visit to the cemetery since the funeral, Des wore his black coat and good trousers and his shoes were highly polished. He carried a bunch of lilies, but the flowers from the mourners that covered the grave after the commital the previous week were still fresh and there was no obvious place for his offering.

Frank had been taken aback by the enormous turnout for the funeral. Vera never made a career out of being the mother of a child with a disability. She concentrated her energies on caring for her son at home. And yet, the Director of Services and several of the carers came up to him to say what a marvellous fundraiser and campaigner she'd been. People from all walks of life approached him and Des to voice their admiration for Vera. Every handshake and short chat disclosed how she impacted on so many people in so many positive ways without being obvious in her kindness. Even Ali and his chef closed the restaurant to attend.

'We should say a prayer,' Frank said to Des as they stood over the grave. But he couldn't keep the hopelessness out of his voice.

They lingered in silence, Frank with his hands joined, shifting his weight uncertainly from one foot to the other. Des with his mouth slack, his shoulders hunched and his toes turned in.

Frank wanted to pray, if only for Vera's sake, but he found it impossible. Her death was too recent and too hard a blow to offer God a let-off for taking her from him so swiftly. Not the doctors nor the nurses nor all the medical machinery in that hospital had been enough to save her in the end. She died, they said, from a worn out heart.

Des stepped forward with the flowers and surprised him by suddenly dropping to his knees.

'Vera,' Des cried bitterly and began to claw at the grave. He swept the flowers aside and used his two bare hands to scrape up the newly-dug earth.

Frank watched in horror. But he remained upright, glancing around him at the people quietly tending to the other graves and walking the paths between the reserved plots and headstones.

'Get up Des,' he hissed between clenched teeth. 'Des, get up.'

* * *

Des shuffled up the garden path holding the cardboard box with the take-away pizza. Frank opened the front door and held it open for Des to go through. But Des wouldn't step inside the house until Frank went ahead and turned on the light in the hallway. He walked ahead of Des into the kitchen and switched on the ceiling light. Then he lit the gas oven and opened a can of cola from the fridge and handed the drink to Des.

When the pizza was good and hot he slid it off the tray onto a plate and passed the plate across to Des. Des sat on a kitchen stool at the breakfast counter with the pizza in front of him. His hand remained folded in his lap and he showed no sign of picking up his knife and fork to eat.

'I thought you liked pizza.'

'Yes, Frank.'

'And you can have the special ice-cream Ali made for us when you finish your pizza.'

'Thank you, Frank,' Des said without stirring.

Having to calm Des and find a place where he could wash his hands and clean up after the incident in the graveyard had tested Frank's patience enough for one day. But he knew Des was hungry. He had to keep his cool and figure out what was wrong.

They sat looking at each other with the pizza going cold.

There had to be a reason why Des was being so well behaved and looking at his pizza with such anticipation and yet he couldn't eat. What was he thinking? What was going on in his head? Why would he not eat even a single slice? And then it came to him. Vera always divided out his pizza in neat wedges. Des wanted it cut into slices before he'd eat.

He went into the kitchen unit nearest the sink. In the cutlery drawer he found a circular blade with a handle he'd seen Vera use to slice up the pizza. As he closed the drawer he knocked her apron from its usual spot where it was draped from the handle. It hadn't been moved since she had her attack. He lifted the apron off the floor, folded it up neatly and brought it to the counter.

When he had the pizza cut into segments the way Des wanted it he sat on kitchen stool on the opposite side of the breakfast counter. He stayed there with his two elbows on the counter holding her apron. He could smell the baked crust of the pizza and he picked up Vera's apron and crushed it to his face to gag the sobs.

His shoulders shook but the only noise in the house was the sound of Des eating. There was a pause and when he lowered the apron he found Des watching him.

'Would you like a slice of pizza, Frank?'

'Thank you, Des,' he reached out mechanically and took the smallest portion.

'Why are you crying, Frank?'

'I miss Vera.'

'Yes, Frank.'

He tried to chew the pizza he'd been offered, but the bolus of dough lodged in his mouth. He believed in self-possession at all times and as he resumed his dazed chewing his hand shot up to his face; a reflexive movement to hide his feelings from Des.

Des stopped eating and began to stare with his mouth open. He wriggled down from the kitchen stool and lumbered around the counter to Frank's side. Frank flinched when Des flung his arms around him. But Des held on tightly, with his glasses askew and his head resting on Frank's shoulder.

Not knowing how to respond to such a childish and needful embrace, he concentrated on his breathing. With every rise and fall of his chest he could feel the texture of the boy's hair against his chin and catch the smell of medicated shampoo from his scalp. He put his arm around the boy's shoulder and stroked the boy's head. The arms around him gripped him tighter and the pressure increased until he said, 'That's enough, son.'

# Parkinson's

*Micheal O'Siadhail*

## 1

Stealthily. One day that quiver in your ring
Finger. Or my impatience at your squiggling

Such illegible notes. Just your astonishment
Noticing the absence of an old lineament.

Once speedy genes, high-geared and fleet;
At twelve the school's swiftest athlete.

The oils of movement slower to lubricate.
Stiffness, a tremor, that off-balance gait.

A specialist confirms Parkinson's disease.
Failing dopamine. The brain's vagaries.

Then moments of denial. Again so strong
And confident: Those doctors got it wrong.

Your fright is pleading with me to agree.
I bat for time: Maybe, we'll have to see.

What can I do? These arms enfold you.
No matter what, I have and hold you.

And so you must travel painful spendthrift
Windings of acceptance. Giving turns gift.

Together. But is there a closer closeness?
Yet another shift in love's long process.

## 2

Flustered now by stress,
A need for time,
Days planned, a gentler pace;
Any breeze shivers in your limbs,
My aspen mistress.

Hardy, deep-rooted, light-loving
You learn to endure.
Pioneer tree in fallow or clearing.
A random sigh flutters in your leaves:
*O God, I'm tired of shaking.*

## 3

Often I wake early to taps on my pillow.
Last evening's tablet at the end of it's tether
Your forefinger begin its morning *tremolo*
As if counting in sleep hours lain together.
I think at first you'd pitied an over-eagerness,
My jittery hand that spilled half your coffee;
A headstrong giant-killer wobbly and nervous
That slowly over time you'd steadied in me.
Blurs and transfers between fellow travellers.
I couldn't but see your half-flirtatious sidelong
Glance at me that both asks and reassures:
*Even if I shake I think my spirit is young?*
Our years side by side tongued and grooved.
A face is beautiful once a face is loved.

# Blind Date

*Marisa Mackle*

*O*nly desperate people went on blind dates, didn't they? After all normal people didn't do it. No. Normal people met other people at parties and pubs. And at social events. And they met through work. By the photocopy machine. Or at office parties and conferences and things like that. Where there was a lot of free drink and therefore opportunity for romance.

That's just the way things happened. People were too busy to be spending nights out on the town looking for soul mates. So it was usually a case of fancying somebody who worked near your desk. Then you didn't have the bother of the whole 'dating a complete stranger' rigmarole.

Sadly though, it looked like nothing as convenient as this was going to happen to Deirdre. Ever. She didn't work at a desk alongside a bunch of eligible guys in suits. And most parties she went to were full of married people. Who talked about nothing but their children, the price of property and inflation.

The local pub wasn't much use either. Deirdre knew everyone who drank there. It wasn't exactly a trendy venue. And the faces never seemed to change. In fact, if you spotted a stranger in the local pub in Ballyknock, it was usually just someone off the street. Popping in to make a phone call.

Deirdre worked with two girls and a guy at the reception of the big hotel in the town. Her colleagues were lovely people all right. Very down to earth and always up for a laugh. And they knew a big gang of people in the town.

But nobody that you could realistically go out with.

Unfortunately.

Darren was the only male working on Reception.

And he was already taken.

So to speak.

He was a complete sweetheart. You could tell him anything in fact. He was like one of the girls. More girly than the girls themselves. He was getting married shortly. To Fritz. Fritz from Switzerland.

Deirdre and the girls were flying out to Zurich in July for the wedding. Deirdre was to be one of the bridesmaids. She couldn't wait for the trip. She had wonderful images of Switzerland, with its snow-capped mountains and beautiful lakes. But she was realistic about the weekend away too. Darren and Fritz's wedding was hardly going to be the ideal venue for meeting Mr. Right now, was it?

Sometimes she would read the personal ads in the *Evening Herald*. Just out of curiosity really. You know, the type of ads where people were looking to meet other people. And they wrote lots of good things about themselves in the hope that someone might contact them.

Some of the people sounded very attractive indeed. In print. Like they always said they were good looking. And a lot of them were homeowners with a good sense of humour. You couldn't ask for much more than that now, could you?

But in her heart, Deirdre knew she would never actually write to any of those PO Box numbers. You had to be careful. Especially nowadays. There were a lot of strange people out there and you'd never know whom you'd end up writing to. Imagine if it turned out to be someone from the town or one of the guests who recognised her from the hotel!

A friend of hers had met somebody on the internet. She said it was an ideal way to meet people. Because everyone in the chat room was looking for a mate. Not like in a pub where people might be there for all kinds of reasons. People in pubs sometimes were just looking for a drink. Or catching up with old friends. Or trying to clinch business deals. Not everyone you saw sitting in a pub was looking to meet a mate.

But Deirdre had clear reservations about meeting men on-line. These people were selling themselves after all. You hardly expected them to be completely honest, did you? Anyway, you heard such horror stories. People going missing and all that. It just wasn't the safest option at all. No. There had to be another way.

Mr. Cleary, the hotel manager, was worried about her. 'You need to get out more Deirdre, it isn't healthy always being on your own.' But Deirdre didn't agree. Mr. Cleary had got it wrong. So wrong. It wasn't as if she was *ever* on her own. Didn't she live with her parents still? And the neighbours were always in and out. God, her mother's house was like a train station sometimes! And sure, didn't she often babysit for her little nieces and nephews?

Often herself and one the girls or Darren would go for a pizza after work and then back to someone's house for a bottle of wine. So it wasn't like she was lonely or anything. No, no. It wasn't like that at all.

Sometimes she thought about leaving the hotel and doing something else. Something different. Like going up to Dublin to do a course. A course that would lead maybe to a job in an office where she could wear a suit and sit in important meetings with a laptop.

When she was younger she'd thought a job working in hotel reception would be very glamorous. You'd be meeting all kinds of people and maybe even spot the odd star checking in under a false name. But the reality had been quite different. The hotel catered mainly for families and the only famous person she'd dealt with had been a politician who'd asked for a free upgrade to one of the suites. And then quibbled like anything about his bill on departure.

Once a good-looking male guest of about forty asked her to go for a drink in his room. She'd been very flattered until she noticed his wedding ring and then very coolly declined his invitation.

Sometimes she felt life was passing her by. She was over thirty now. Not exactly a ripe young thing. No. Her best friend Geraldine had left the town eight years ago and always said she'd never return. Of course she came home every Christmas. And always turned up in the local pub on Christmas Eve looking spectacular. With her Toni & Guy highlights that she got done in London.

But many of her old schoolmates would avoid her. Even girls she'd been great friends with in school. Because they didn't want to hear stories about how well Geraldine was doing over in London. They didn't want to know about her recent promotion in the BBC. Success stories were never too welcome in the local pub in Ballyknock. It was much more interesting to hear about people who'd developed a drink problem. Or marriages that hadn't worked out. Or people who'd gone to Australia and had never been heard of again.

The girls Deirdre went to school with were always asking her questions. 'Are you still working up in the hotel?' they'd ask. She'd nod and wonder *why* they always asked. Sure didn't they see her there in Reception every time one of them attended a wedding or confirmation or christening? After all there was only one hotel in the town!

Of course the next question was always, 'Any men?' A question usually asked while they gleefully rubbed their own wedding rings. Deirdre didn't like it when people asked about her love life. It made her uncomfortable.

They didn't ask Geraldine about *her* love life though. No. Because everybody knew she was engaged to a successful Dublin lawyer called Charles. They had no interest in listening to Geraldine's romantic story about how Charles proposed in Monte Carlo. They'd no wish to try on Geraldine's massive diamond rock. Of course not. Sure, why would they? It would only make them feel inadequate. Instead, they much preferred to ask Deirdre about *her* love life.

Then one Friday night, out of the blue, Deirdre's Dad told her Geraldine had phoned. She was to ring back urgently. That was unusual, Deirdre thought looking at her watch. It was very late. She hoped everything was okay.

She rang her friend's mobile. Geraldine must have been in a noisy nightclub or something because the sound was terribly loud and she couldn't hear a word. But at least her friend hadn't sounded ill or in trouble or anything. It couldn't be too important, Deirdre decided. She'd call her again in the morning.

In the morning, Geraldine didn't seem to be too pleased to be woken by Deirdre's call.

'What time is it?' she croaked in a husky hungover voice.

'It's nearly ten,' Deirdre informed her. 'You rang last night – I thought something might have been wrong.'

'I rang you?' Geraldine sounded confused. 'Oh yeah,' she said suddenly remembering, 'I know what you're talking about now. I was ringing you about a man. I met this guy who works with Charles. I think he'd be ideal for you. I wanted you to talk to him on the phone last night. I dunno – it seemed a good idea after a couple of bottles of champagne. I must've been a bit tipsy. Still, I think you should meet him.'

Deirdre didn't think it was a good idea at all. She was *so* glad she hadn't managed to get through to Geraldine on the phone last night. She'd have only made a show of herself.

'We're meeting up with him again tonight,' Geraldine continued. 'Do you fancy coming up to Dublin and I could set you up?'

'I can't,' Deirdre said firmly. 'We've two big weddings in the hotel tonight.'

'You're never going to get any thanks for spending all your time in the hotel, you know.'

'It's my job,' Deirdre said defensively. 'And anyway I can't just be getting the bus up to Dublin at the drop of a hat.'

'He's very keen,' Geraldine continued. 'I was telling him all about you and he thought you sounded lovely.'

'Did he?' Deirdre didn't know whether to believe her friend. 'What's he like anyway?'

'Well he's handsome and quiet enough, very intelligent …'

' … so what's the catch?'

'God Deirdre, you've got to stop being so suspicious. Listen I've got to go now, but think about it, won't you?'

'I will,' Deirdre promised.

Geraldine put down the phone and awoke the sleeping Charles, 'Hey, can you give Robert a call?'

'Huh?'

'Come on, butter him up, make him curious. Tell him we've the perfect woman for him.'

'I'll try,' Charles mumbled unenthusiastically. 'But you know Rob, he just won't buy it. He's married to his bloody laptop.'

'It's worth a shot though,' Geraldine sat up in the bed and grinned.

On Thursday evening, Deirdre got the bus up to Dublin. She got off at Busaras and walked anxiously towards O'Connell Street. The sky was cursed with thick, threatening clouds. A brisk wind was playing havoc with her hair. Please God it wouldn't rain. Then she'd look a right mess altogether. She took a left at Temple Bar. She was nervous.

Very nervous.

She'd never done anything like this before.

Geraldine had given her the name of the restaurant and she'd written it down carefully. Hopefully it wouldn't be too hard to find. All those cobbled streets in Temple Bar were a bit confusing.

Suppose he didn't like her? Suppose he didn't think she was interesting enough? Or pretty enough? Oh God, this was head wrecking stuff! She was tempted just to run back to the bus station and grab the return bus home.

She got to the restaurant early and peered in through the window. The place was empty except for a middle-aged couple reading their menus in silence. Deirdre could feel the beads of sweat forming on her forehead. Whose idea was this anyway? This was madness. Complete madness. This guy was probably desperate. Sure if he was as great as Geraldine had made out, he'd have women hanging out of him! Well she was only going to wait five minutes and then she was out of there.

Five minutes later there was still no sign. The horror had become reality. So, he'd decided to stand her up. Oh God, the humiliation of it all! She should never have come. Never. What a fool she'd been. She was going to kill Geraldine for letting her walk into this, she really was.

Well there was no point going home now. Since she'd come all the way up to Dublin, she might as well make some use out of it. She decided to visit her cousin Lucy in Stillorgan. She hadn't seen her since last Christmas. Luckily there was a taxi rank across the road.

Robert reached the restaurant at exactly ten past seven. He hoped Deirdre hadn't gone already. He hadn't bargained on the taxi being late. And he hadn't wanted to drive. Not tonight. Not if he was planning on having a glass of wine or two.

He peered in the window to see if he could spot her. He didn't even know what she looked like. Geraldine had described her as attractive. Then again Geraldine would have said anything to get him to agree to this.

The restaurant was practically empty. Robert wondered if he'd got the wrong venue. He waited another ten minutes. The sky had clouded over and thick drops of rain were beginning to fall. This Deirdre girl, whoever she was, obviously hadn't bothered to turn up.

He made his way to the taxi rank across the way. Her no show was disappointing to say the least. What a waste of an evening. After all he was a busy man. With a mountain of paperwork still to get through before the weekend. He might as well head home.

He waited for ages.

She waited for ages.

He wondered why there weren't more taxis around.

She wondered how much longer she'd have to wait.

He wondered if the attractive dark-haired girl in front was going in the same direction.

She wondered if she'd meet Mr. Right.

Ever.

Eventually a taxi pulled up.

'Listen,' he asked her quickly, 'I don't suppose you're going Southside, are you?'

She looked at him. He was well dressed with a nice speaking voice, dark hair and handsome features.

'I'm going to Stillorgan,' she told him.

'I'm going to Blackrock,' he said, 'Would you mind if we shared?'

She didn't. She got into the front, he into the back.

The taxi driver ranted all the way to Stillorgan about roadworks and cyclists, pedestrians and politicians. He only stopped when they got to Stillorgan.

'How much do I owe you?' Deirdre asked the driver.

'Don't worry about it,' Robert insisted.

'No, please,' Deirdre said.

'Seriously,' he said with a twinkle in his eye. 'You probably saved me a half an hour standing in the rain.'

She smiled back, 'Thank you,' she said.

The taxi driver revved the engine impatiently. Robert looked out the window at Deirdre and watched her walk up to the house with the green door. God, that girl was a bit of a looker, he thought. Probably attached though. Girls like that always were. They were always spoken for. Not like that friend of Geraldine's who hadn't even bothered showing up. Who did *she* think she was?

'Ah Jesus,' the taxi man sighed. 'You're woman's gone and left her phone on the seat.'

'Do you want to go back with it?' Robert said suddenly. 'I don't mind.'

'Nah,' the driver shook his head, 'I'll just leave it in the office later.'

'I'll take it,' Robert offered. 'Hopefully she'll ring the number when she realises it's missing.'

'It's up to you.'

Deirdre sat in Lucy's kitchen catching up on the gossip.

Robert sat in his bachelor pad watching the telly.

Deirdre's phone lay on his lap.

Geraldine sat in her sitting-room wondering how the blind date was going. The suspense was killing her. Eventually she could bear it no longer. She dialled Deirdre's mobile.

'Hello?' Robert answered.

'Robert, is that you?'

'Who's this?' he asked, alarmed.

'Geraldine. Where's Deirdre? Put her onto me. How's the date going anyway?'

Robert was speechless. What was going on?

'Is everything okay?' Geraldine continued. 'I'm not interrupting anything, am I?' she giggled.

Robert opened his mouth to say something, then shut it again. He was stunned. Suddenly everything fell into place.

'Can I ring you back?' he said hurriedly, reaching for his jacket and car keys. He didn't have a minute to lose. He remembered the address, where the taxi driver had dropped Deirdre off. The house with the green door. Hopefully she'd still be there.

He ran downstairs and got into his car, the mobile still stuck to his ear. 'Are you still there Geraldine? Listen myself and Deirdre can't talk right now but we'll ring you tomorrow,' he added cheekily, 'and tell you everything.'

He switched off the phone.

Geraldine smiled to herself.

Wasn't she the right little matchmaker?

Robert and Deirdre were obviously getting on.

Exceptionally well.

Too busy to talk, eh?

Well, well, well …

# Two Little Clouds

### Joseph O'Connor

*I*t was twelve or fourteen years since I'd seen him. And here he was in the ample flesh, through the gleaming window of a real-estate agency on Fownes Street, a vision in shirtsleeves and Louis Copeland trousers. Three stone heavier and beginning to go bald, but it was him right enough. You'd never mistake him. Jesus Christ. So Ruth had been right that time. Eddie Virago, back home in Dublin, and hawking apartments for a living. He smiled and mouthed my name as he clocked me through the window. But he didn't look happy to see me.

'How's tricks?' I asked, when he came out and shook hands.

'Livin' *la vida loca*,' he grinned. 'Look at the bleedin' state of you. Victor Mature.'

Eddie was the kind of guy I used to try and latch onto, back in my early years in London. Cool, sceptical, dismissive of convention, he'd turn up last to all the parties and still manage to cop off with the finest thing in the room. Those were the dying days of the eighties; yuppiedom was still in; wild consumption was its badge; but Eddie had no need for flash suits or red braces. He'd slouch into the Bunch of Grapes in his tattered leather jacket, in his sprayed-on jeans and Sandinista T-shirt, his two-tone docs so utterly filthy it was impossible to imagine them having once been clean. Saturday night the place would be heaving with preppie Irish – I guess it was something of a home-away-from-home. Posters of Dublin doorways and Michael Collins. Pieces of farm machinery welded into barstools. Green condoms in the jacks, Shane Mc Gowan on the jukebox. An army of southside immigrants storming the bar. One look from Eddie and his pint would be put up. Not even a look. A raising of an eyebrow.

There was goss in my crowd that he was the singer in the band; that they'd signed to one of the majors and were about to record an album. I don't know if it was true, but he never discouraged the talk. He'd just smile this aw-shucks, studiedly modest grin – think Bill Clinton with cheekbones, you're not far away – and say he couldn't really go into the details. 'For contractual reasons,' he'd often explain. 'Nothin' personal, man. They just don't want the ins-and-outs leaked.'

The odd thing was that nobody I knew had seen his band play, though according to his mate, a yank called Dean, a ludicrously handsome bastard with a Maradonian coke habit, they'd gigged all the dives such bands played in those days. The Red Rose. The Roundhouse. The Dublin Castle in Camden. The Roxy. The Robey. St Martin's School of Art. It was said that they'd even opened a show for the Fine Young Cannibals, at the Town and Country, maybe, or The Fridge down in Brixton. ('They opened it the way dynamite opens a fuckin' safe,' Dean remarked.) But then one very drunken session – I think Paddy's Night of 1989 – Dean confessed that he had never actually caught them live himself. He had merely heard tell of their general excellence, their command of their genre, and Eddie's malevolent stage presence. 'But then, you look at the guy, you're lookin' at a star. The Lizard King of Finsbury Park.'

I don't know if I ever talked to Eddie for longer than a few minutes. He was just always *around*, yakking with some model; leaning against the brickwork like he was propping it up. He was like your man, Zelig, in the Woody Allen movie: it wouldn't have surprised you to see him anywhere. You'd notice all the girls giving him the hairy eyeball, but the more they gave it, the less he seemed to care. I suppose, to be honest, I thought myself too uncool for him to like me. (You're twenty-one in London, you want everyone to like you – even the twats and drooling gobshites. Not that our Eddie was either, of course. But he didn't mind helping them out if they were stuck.)

I'd spent two years after the Leaving Cert studying to be a Jesuit, and even after I'd made up my mind to jack it all in for a game of cowboys, I still had the idea that people somehow saw me as a priest. They'd watch their language – infuriating stuff like that. Or tell me their sins when they'd had a few jars. Eddie never confessed to anything much, and that was refreshing, I have to admit it. He'd kind of take you on your terms, I guess. And one night at some party – it was either for the release of Nelson Mandela, or the release of the *record* 'Free Nelson Mandela' – he got badly gargled on snakebite and ended up hurling into the breast pocket of my donkey-jacket. It's the type of thing makes you feel close to a person. Me and Eddie were bonded. And not just by love.

I'd see him at parties, concerts, clubs. He'd pitch up at the odd reading or literary night: some new Irish novelist flogging his Hibernian horse in Waterstones, some gaggle of intense poets at the Festival Hall. For a while, I was kicking around with this girl who did the London-end publicity for U2, and one time she got us tickets for a gig of theirs at Wembley Arena. At the backstage party afterwards, there was old Eddie – in the roped-off area for 'Absolute VIPs', one arm around the Edge, the other around Sean Hughes, his fag-ash being flicked into a polystyrene beaker held by a member of Bananarama. A face like an angel, someone once said of Eddie. And a neck like a jockey's bollocks.

It was whispered around the pubs that he had a serious on-off girlfriend – the girlfriend was serious, the relationship wasn't. She was said to be every bit as mulchie as myself, but that didn't seem likely, and I certainly never asked him. There never seemed time for intimate conversations, but that wasn't the reason. It's hard to explain. He was one of those Irish guys you don't ask questions, the sort with a weird kind of force-field or something. Often if you were jarred or a little bit stoned, you'd have the impression of him looking *out* at you from inside his head, through this swirling mist of just-don't-ask-me.

People say now that Maggie's London was a hole. I suppose it was, but it was better than Charlie's Dublin. All your gang were over there; you could have a few laughs; go and see a band; drink at the Grapes. Life felt fat: money was makeable. And back home in Ireland, life felt thin. Unemployment was high. The place felt defeated. You'd be far more likely to meet a smack dealer than a novelist in the wet, grey streets of 1980s Dublin. They may as well have given you a free plane ticket with the certificate you got for your Arts degree. (A graffito at Dublin airport remains in my mind: LAST ONE TO LEAVE, PLEASE TURN OUT THE LIGHTS.) Like most of my generation, I emigrated for a job – but also just to get out of my parents' house. London was simply the place you went. Yeah, the Tories were in, but then so was Ken Livingstone. Politics seemed more than aromatherapy and horseshite. Poll Tax riots and all the rest of it. Half a million people marching for CND. Positive action meets negative equity – you're going to get sparks, and London sparked in those days. Through it all strode Eddie, like a ghost on the battlefield, wearing his Mohican like a crown.

Now the Mohican was gone but his eyes were still bright. We stood gobsmacked on Fownes Street and he shook my hand like he was trying to break it. He hadn't even heard I was back in town; if he had, he would have belled me to see about hooking up for a scoop. Nah, he didn't see much of the old posse any more. Too busy with the job, man. Working his balls to the bone. Spinning the wheels of the prosperous new Dublin. Pulling the wire of the old C.T.

'Skinny bastard,' he chuckled, punching me lightly in the gut. 'What's your little secret, man? The old liposuction, is it?'

I was too busy thinking about what 'C.T.' might mean to give him the smart answer the situation required.

'Course I wouldn't mind havin' it all sucked out myself,' he cackled. 'Dependin' on who was doin' the suckin', right?'

It was almost five by now; he was about to finish work. So he invited me down to the Clarence for a bevvy. I said I was stuck for time – maybe we'd do it again. (I'd promised to be home by six to bath the baby, but for some weird reason I didn't tell him that.) 'Come on for one anyway,' he said, and he grinned. 'Let's chew the old fat. There's enough of it to chew, right?'

It was one of those summer evenings that smells of clean linen; that pale yellow light was shining in the streets and it seemed to make even the shop windows seem magical. There were couples strolling around; one or two stag parties. A punk with a guitar was singing 'Bittersweet Symphony'. Two happy-looking tourists were taking snaps of a pubfront. Helmut und Helga, getting down with the natives. You could fall in love with Dublin on an evening like that, but I wasn't in the mood for falling in love. One thing I've learned about old Anna Livia – you'd have a good night, but she wouldn't respect you in the morning.

'C.T.' I realised. Celtic bloody Tiger. Even Eddie Virago was talking the talk.

As we walked along the crowded street, he would sometimes nod a greeting to people we passed. ('How's the man?' 'Drop into me about that other thing?' 'What's the auld story?' 'How are they hangin', Holmes?') It wasn't at all how I remembered him talking. He was always very confident, but there was brashness there now. Like Ali G meets Young Fine Gael. Oh yeah, the old property bizz was treating him grand. Keeping the wolf from the front door anyway. Dublin was *lousy* with people wanting to get on the ladder. It was gone completely mad. It was *losing the plot.* Like London in the eighties, but even more of a head-wreck. But there was opportunity around, too; it wasn't all a hassle. Guy with a line in bullshit could pull in a few sovs. 'And you know me,' he said. 'I speak bullshit fluently.'

We turned down towards the river, to where his car was parked. He wanted to feed the meter before going for the drink. ('Wankers these wardens. They'd clamp the fuckin' popemobile.') And I suspected he also wanted me to see the car. It was an 02 Alfaromeo, dark metallic green, with a Winnie-the-Pooh sunguard on the back left-hand window. Yeah, he was a dad now, he quietly laughed. His mask seemed to slip, if just for a moment, and I glimpsed the innocent Eddie I once used to know, who would laugh at the weirdness of ordinary things. A boy and a child. 'Kurt and Courtney.'

He took a photo from his wallet and showed me the kids. They were happy-looking toddlers, pink and strong. Lucas and Emma were their actual names. A beautiful dark-eyed woman was dandling them on her knees. She was smooth and very cool, wearing sunglasses and sipping Evian. I knew her to see. Audrey Harrington was her name. She'd worked back in London on a women's magazine. The picture had been taken in some place like Glendalough – you could see a round tower and ancient gravestones.

He started showing me the sunroof and all the stuff on the car, but I was thinking about his kids: the strangeness of that. Eddie Virago was somebody's *father*. It was like being told the Queen Mother was actually a trannie. I said I hadn't even heard he was married, to be honest. 'Well, I'm not right now, to be honest,' he said. 'Didn't work out. We're still good friends.'

For the next few moments nothing much was said. He rummaged around scrupulously in the glove-box of the car, but I could tell he wasn't really looking for anything.

'Eddie ...' I said. But he shrugged and glanced away. 'I don't talk about it much, to be honest,' he said. 'Shit happens, that's all. It happened and it's over. It's probably for the best. I don't ever discuss it.' He stuffed the coins in the meter and pucked me a little too hard on the shoulder. 'So it's you and me tonight, babe. Just like London times. Young, free and single and out on the razz.' He locked up the car with one of those beeping remote controls and we headed off again in the direction of the Clarence.

'So anyways,' he goes. 'How's tricks with yourself? Ever see that mott – what's her name? – who worked for U2.'

I said no, I hadn't seen her for several years now, but I'd heard she was living in Limerick.

'Fuck me,' he said. 'I hadn't heard the tragic news.' It was a typical Eddie line. You suspected he might have used it before.

'What about baggage-arse? You know – Ruth Murphy? She was one of your old crew, wasn't she?'

'She was, yeah.'

'Awful looking minger. Mad as a snake. Bit of a slapper, they always said.'

'Actually, Eddie – '

'Went through more hands than a jazz-mag on a building site. Gave her the rub of the relic myself once or twice – when the beer goggles were on, of course.'

'I'm actually – married to Ruth,' I said.

He chuckled at the idea. 'Bloody sure you are. You'd need a license to keep that yoke in the house.'

'It's true,' I said. 'We're married six years now.'

He stopped walking. 'Shag off,' he said.

'Nearly seven,' I said.

'Shag *off*, you fuckin' mongrel. Before I bate you through that wall.' (I had forgotten how some Irishmen talk to each other.)

He was blushing so deeply, I was nearly going to lie. But you can't really lie about the person you're married to. I don't know why, exactly. It might be bad luck or something. So I confirmed it again – I was married to Ruth

– and by now he had the grace to at least look abashed. He started humming and hawing about some other Ruth. 'Ruth *Murray*, I meant. Used to hang around the Grapes. You know the one I mean. Tattoos and a crucifix.'

By now we were at the hotel, and we went in through the lobby. Some kind of party or event was going on. There were press photographers and cameramen wandering through the crowd. Chinese waiters in white jackets were distributing glasses of wine. Bono and Paul McGrath were standing near the reception desk, chatting very quietly with the Tánaiste, Mary Harney. 'How's the men?' smiled Eddie, as we passed them by. 'Fine, thank you,' Ms Harney said. The other two looked confused.

The bar was utterly jammers with beautiful people and students. He ordered two double Bushmills without asking me what I wanted, drained his glass in two swallows and ordered another. 'So what are you doing yourself?' he asked me, then; and when I told him journalism he rolled his eyes and laughed. 'Still at that crack. Will you never get sense? You want to make some sponds, man, and pretty bleedin' quick. You might hatch out a sprog one of these days, you know.'

'We already have three,' I said, and he nodded. 'See what I mean, man? My point exactly. Reproduction costs big-time. You'd want to suit up for it.'

I thought he might at least ask me about the kids, maybe enquire as to their ages or something. But instead he started into a lecture on the true cost of parenthood, which someone in *The Irish Times* with very little to do had recently calculated was half a million per child. 'You're not gonna pull in half-a-mill writin' shitehawkery for the papers. That's just irresponsible. I'm surprised at you, man.'

'I suppose you're right,' I found myself saying. Just for the sake of a quiet life.

'You want to get into the property crack. Money's obscene. Like shooting guppies in a barrel. Seriously, man – you're wasting your time. You should haul your arse back over here and get into the business. I could give you a few good contacts if you're ever interested. Brave new frontier just waitin' for you, pal. All it takes is a couple of testicles and a mobile phone.'

A house in southside Dublin could cost more than a million. Two per cent commission on every single sale. Selling a place in Dalkey could buy the estate agent a yacht. Even a decent apartment, you were talking three-fifty. 'Course, we all make our choices.' He tapped his large belly. 'I could have bought a mansion with what I spent getting that.'

He ordered more drinks, again without asking me. He was sinking the stuff fast; way too fast for my taste. I hadn't eaten since breakfast and I was feeling strange anyway. Being back in Dublin, it always makes me feel strange. Too many memories. Ghosts, I suppose. Another round was ordered; then another, and more. Soon we were on pints and things started feeling woozy. Friends were remembered; old enemies slagged; albums and bands were nostalgically recalled. He rarely went to a gig any more. All that sweat and beer on the walls. And he found standing up for two hours a bit of a strain. 'Worshipping some tosser, like Nazis at Nuremberg.'

He was sorry if he'd been brusque on the subject of his marriage; he just found it difficult to talk about now. I said there was no problem, I hadn't meant to pry. 'I dunno, but I find it better to let the shit go,' he explained. 'You talk and talk, it only brings it back up.'

'We won't say another word about it,' I said. 'I understand completely.'

'Everyone says that, but they don't,' he said. (I was getting the sinking feeling a confession-session loomed.) 'You don't understand it until it bites you in the arse. You're yakkin' and yakkin', but where does it get you? It happened. It's over. Get used to it, y'know?'

'Yes,' I said. 'I think I know what you mean. I felt that way when it ended with Anne.'

'With?'

'The U2 girl. – But anyway. Were you watching the World Cup?'

'Oh. Right. Exactly. You don't want to be carrying it around for the rest of your life. It isn't like it's the end of the world or anything.' He gave a bare laugh and looked into his glass. 'Mind you – the way I felt when she walked out with the kids, even the end of the world wouldn't have been the end of the world.'

A strained kind of silence descended over the table. It was as though an uninvited guest had sat down between us, but neither of us wanted to mention the fact. By now the drink had really begun to take hold on him. He wasn't slurring or anything – he just looked a bit dew-eyed. He undid his tie, loosened up his collar; and it occurred to me now that I had never seen him wear either.

'You look great,' he said. 'I'd ride you myself.'

'Thanks for the offer,' I said. He snuffled into his glass.

'So what do you reckon to the old town?' he asked. 'Dear auld durty Dubbalin, wha'?'

I said I was amazed by how quickly it had changed. Too bloody right, Eddie said. He leaned in close and began to speak furtively, checking over his shoulder to make sure nobody was earwigging. He wasn't a racist or anything. No bleedin' way. Hadn't he picketed the South African embassy in days gone by. (The only problem with the ANC was they weren't quite radical *enough* for Eddie.) And he'd do it again. Bloody sure he would. It was just – you know – these immigrant fellas. They were *different* somehow, not really like us paddies. There was just no sense in saying they weren't. Their *culture* was different; their view of the world. Their food, their music, their clothes and their customs. Moore Street now – it was gone like Timbuktu. Nothing *wrong* with that, of course. All very colourful. Arise ye starvlings from your slumber, et cetera. But these Nigerians, for example – what could you say?

'I don't know,' I said. 'What do you mean?'

'Well – loppin' off each other's goolies for havin' a ride outside of marriage? That's just not on, man; in all fairness. The Shariah law, they call it. Bag of shite, more like. You don't want that crack catchin' a grip over here, pal. Rastas in Carlow. Stuff like that.'

'Maybe Carlow needs Rastas,' I tried to say.

'So does my hole,' he bleakly replied.

A girl came in wearing a DROP THE DEBT sweatshirt. She was talking on a mobile and looking at her watch. I was beginning to regret coming to drink with him at all. Really, I was wishing I was some place else. You don't see someone for twelve or fourteen years, there's usually a good reason, if only you were honest.

'Here we are anyway,' he said, and he chinked my glass.

'Here we are,' I agreed. 'Old times and all that.'

'So where are you living?' he suddenly asked.

'Westbourne Grove,' I told him. 'Up near Notting Hill.'

He looked at me confusedly. 'I thought you said you were after moving back?'

'No, no. We're only over for a bit of a break. Ruth's mother isn't the Mae West. Since the Da died last year.'

He nodded once or twice and lit up a Bensons. 'Well, you're welcome to London. Armpit of a place anyway. Best thing I ever did was take the old boat home.'

'London's home for us now,' I found myself saying. 'It's been good to us both. The kids feel at home there.'

'Best thing I ever did, splittin' out of the kip. I dunno how you stick it. Fair balls to you, man.'

'Ruth likes the theatre there. I like the football.' I was trying as hard as I could to lighten things up. 'It's been good to us work-wise. She's lecturing now. She's a book coming out next year. On Boucicault.'

'Who?'

'Boucicault – you know. The Irish playwright.'

He pulled a jaded yawn and gave an amused little smirk. 'Whatever you're havin' yourself, I suppose.'

'We're fierce boring now. Real suburbanites I guess. I'm sure we'll be moving to Chiswick before long. Mowing the grass and complaining about the neighbours.'

'And buyin' the Sunday papers on a Saturday night, man.'

I laughed. 'That already happens, I'm sorry to say.'

'Wouldn't suit *me*, pal, I'll tell you that for real. Been there, done that; have a nice life, good luck. Out of it like a snot from a headbanger's nose. Once bitten, twice bite – that's young Edward's motto now. I've a good bit more of the range to ride before I jam the old nads in the mincer again.'

'You wouldn't want to be married again?'

'Yeah, right,' he witheringly said.

'You never get lonely?'

'Do in me shite. Out every night, and twice on Sunday.'

Matter of fact, he was heading to a party later. At Eddie Irvine's new gaff, out in Killiney. Several Corrs would be there; so would good old Van. Of course he knew the Corrs – he'd sold Jim a house. He'd sold a lot of houses to Irish celebrities – his firm specialised in the upper end of the market – but Jim Corr was probably the soundest he'd met. Great guy, Jim. Unsung hero, in many ways. He'd be dandering along to Irv-the-Swerve's later. Flatley was coming with a posse of hoofers. Samantha Mumba was flying in from the Apple. Keith Duffy from Boyzone. That lesbian nun off Big Brother. Even Lorraine Keane was rumoured to be showing up. I said it all sounded like a night to remember. He winked surreptitiously. 'You peeled the right banana there.'

More drinks were ordered before I could stop him. He was in flying form now, I couldn't even get away to go to the jacks, never mind tell him I was upping to head home. My head started reeling. I was starving hungry. The place felt kind of lurid, I don't know: like a nightclub. I was bursting for a leak but he was going off at full-steam – talking *at* me like I was interviewing him at some public event. It was the one thing he missed about London, he said: the diversity of social life in the big city. You got a bit sick of always seeing the same people over here. It was like there was a bus for Irish celebrities, lurrying them around to each other's gaffs. Back in London, you'd be saucing with a different crowd every night. You didn't have to deal with the same old faces. 'Man, that's a party town. I'll give you that much. London's all right for a rasher and a ride. But Jesus Christ, I couldn't stick living there.'

It was at one such London party that he had hooked up with Audrey – a piss-up in Soho for the launch of some movie. She had dropped the old *lámh* as they slowdanced in the tapas bar, asked him back to hers for coffee and oven-chips. On their first night together, they'd had sex five times. He'd been in entire relationships where that didn't happen.

'We really don't have to talk about it, Eddie,' I said.

He was in a mess when she'd met him first. Broke, overweight, with nowhere to live, several failed careers and an urgent need for many fillings. Evicted, dejected, fucking *rejected*, his beaten-up car had been repossessed ('by the devil'). His personal hygiene left a lot to be desired. He avoided showers like a blonde in a Bates motel. His overdraft was gargantuan, his self-esteem subterranean. Some people had baggage. 'Me, I had cargo.'

'I'm sure this must be hard for you talk about,' I said. 'Please don't feel you have to. Really I don't mind.'

'Call that waitress over, will you, man? I think we might have a couple of dry Martinis.'

They had moved back to Dublin, rented a flat in town. It was only a short hop from Temple Bar ('twinned with Sarajevo') but the cultural quarter was not all it was cracked up to be. They used to stroll there sometimes, if strolled was the word – rather skidded or slithered or, late at night, ran. The baby came along, another a year later. But Temple Bar was not the kind of place you would take a baby, unless the baby was a Caledonian inebriate or a Saxon thug. There had been talk back in London – beer-fuelled, brave talk – of the marvellous evenings they would spend in Temple Bar – a quiet cappuccino, an evening at the Project, a stroll around an exhibition of abstract photography. Ah, good evening, Madame President. Nice to see you again, Enya. Not now, Bertie, can't you see I'm busy *with the art.* After ten years in Sarf in London, Temple Bar would be magnificent. But the only real culture he ever discerned in the place was the kind requiring a hefty dose of penicillin. This glittered Hooligania seemed to him a symbol of why they should never have come home. London was a kip, but a very large kip, the kind where true happiness was probably not possible, but a much higher quality of misery was. Dublin was turning into Disneyland with superpubs, a Purgatory open till five in the morning. The maidens were no longer dancing at the crossroads, they were lapdancing their way onto TV3 . If he could have got his hands on the Celtic Tiger, he would have beaten it to death and turned it into a rug.

I tried my best to laugh, but it came out sounding dutiful. We were drifting, I felt, into the realm of the unwell. Like I said, I'd often listened to drunken fessing. But this was new. This was strange. It was like he was talking about himself in the *third-person* or something; spinning me lines that sounded as though he had written them down and learned them off by heart.

Eddie Virago and Audrey Harrington. It had started as the relationship for which he had always been waiting. It had ended as the cultural equivalent of a groinpull. Monday nights, they watched *Coronation Street* like a couple of zombies. Like on Tuesdays and Wednesdays and Saturdays and Sundays. On Thursdays she went to do Ashtangi Yoga at a class run by a feminist nun in a former seminary – 'Unleashing the Goddess Within: Beginners' Level' – leaving Eddie to do the dishes and scrub out her ashtrays and empty the nappy-bin and put the baby to bed. The nappy-bin terrified him. He had nightmares about it. How could such a tiny and adorable creature produce this appalling Croagh Patrick of shit? By the time he had done all his duties, she was usually back home – all Goddessed up like a Pagan in leggings, and ready to wedge herself into the minuscule bath with a bottle of tannin-free organic Beaujolais and the latest edition of Hello! He was invited to share neither bath nor wine. Sometimes they did a crossword. But most times they didn't. Every Friday night they sat down together to do internet shopping on the Tesco's website. And every Friday night, he forgot to remind her to buy razors. (Without them, she'd say, she had legs like Peter Clohessy's.) And every Friday night, she spread his balls on toast.

She was apparently not a Goddess when she argued with Eddie. The Dali Lama himself would have pissed his loincloth with horror at her language. Their arguments were furious, volcanic, *Vesuvian*. Thundering Wagnerian overtures of bile. She would say anything when she argued – nothing was sacred. He was cruel, unfeeling, emotionally unavailable. His mother should be pulling a fucking plough. His father was a weirdo. His sister was twisted. His granny had the kind of face you wouldn't want to wipe your feet on. He would try to answer back, but often it was difficult.

'You never say anything when we're making love,' he had said, once.

'I'm working,' she had answered. 'It takes concentration.'

And that was the kind of girl she was. The kind who could screw your head right *off* and hop it around the room like a basketball. Wonderful person in many ways. Fabulous mother, but as for unpredictable? It was like being married to Roy Keane in tights. He sometimes wondered if they called the feeling between them 'love' in order to save a lot of trouble. 'But as I say, I don't like to talk about it much. I'm trying my best to get closure on it all. Put it way behind me. I hope I'm not boring you.'

'No, no,' I said. 'But I have to go to the jacks.'

In the gents, I looked at the clock on the wall. Jesus Christ. It was *ten past eight*. And I'd promised Ruth I'd be home by six. I dunked my head in the sink a few times. There was a roaring noise in my ears; like a plane taking off.

When I got back to the bar, he was flirting with some girl who pronounced 'Phoenix Pork' as though it rhymed with 'New York'. Some mutual friend was being verbally eviscerated. His thinking, apparently, was '*so* two years ago'. It used to be kind of dotey but now it was just a drag. I grabbed my jacket and my bag of books.

'What's up with you, Horse?' he said. 'You're not *going*, are you?'

'I honestly have to.'

'But I thought we were gonna have a drink?'

'I'm really late.'

'Jaysus, these bigshot London bollixes,' he said to the girl. 'Going for a drink means going for *a* drink. Afraid of their shites they might have a good time.'

He walked me out to the lobby and embraced me warmly, as though the bar of the Clarence was his country retreat and I was a favourite cousin about to emigrate to India.

'Well – keep the old faith now. And say a decade for me, man.'

'I will.'

'One little thing.' He approached so suddenly I thought he was going to snog me. But instead he spoke quietly, his voice tinged with guilt. He was so close to me now, I could smell the beer on his breath. I could actually see his pupils dilating. 'What I said earlier – about Nigerians. I wouldn't want you paying any attention.'

'I wasn't.'

'Sound.'

'So look – I'm gonna run. I'll see you around, Eddie.'

'That was just bullshit. But you know yourself, man – if arseholes could fly, Dublin would be an airport.'

'Yeah.'

'So you won't – you know – mention that I said it? You promise?'

'No.'

'I wouldn't want Ruth knowing I said that.'

'*Absolvo te*,' I said; and he grinned and hugged me.

'You look terrific,' he said. 'It's great you're so thin. I'd happily screw your brains out. But I see somebody's beaten me to it.'

He clutched at my arse and started vigorously humping my leg. Mary Harney, passing by, gave us a disconcerted look.

'You should come home,' he said. 'It's a great town these days.' He gestured around himself with an expansive wave. 'Jaysus, just think, man – we could be doing this every night.'

I said I'd think it over, but I had to go now.

'Pram in the hall, huh?'

'That's it. Poor sap.'

'Well – better lep up on your Boucicault and pedal away, so. Wouldn't want to keep the old boss-lady waiting.'

'That's right,' I laughed. 'She has me on the leash.'

'Well – keep in touch, you skinny fuckin' freak.'

'I will,' I promised.

He gave me another bear-hug and a couple more slaps. And then suddenly his eyes lit up in a worrying way. 'You wouldn't – want to come with me, I suppose? Out to Eddie Irvo's party? Sure, come on for the crack. We'll just go for an hour. I'd love you to meet Jim. He's a laugh and a half.'

'I couldn't,' I said. 'I'd be murdered in the morning.'

He shot me a final smile. 'Smug bollocks,' he said.

I left by the back door and staggered over the cobblestones, up into Dame Street and down past the Olympia. It was still quite bright, the evening was hot. My head was pounding like The Chieftains on speed. I was thirsty; dry-mouthed; in need of a cool shower. That bloody awful feeling of being pissed by sunlight.

Down towards Trinity. No taxis on the rank. Up into Grafton Street. I was sweating like a pig. A fire-eater was performing by the Molly Malone statue, spitting out globes of fat orange flame. Nearby, two refugee women were begging with babies. Some geezer with a crew-cut was handing out coupons for a nightclub. An elegant Japanese bloke was playing a violin.

And that was when I bumped into her.

Almost literally.

She was looking magnificent, made up to the nines, in a stylish black jacket and a dark green dress. Jesus H. It was *Audrey Harrington.* But to see her like this, so soon after talking about her – it was an aspect of Dublin life I had kind of forgotten, and one I didn't miss: at least not very often.

She asked about Ruth, various friends in London; a couple of exhibitions she'd been meaning to get over and see. She missed London now; with the kids it was harder to head away. People often said children were little rays of sunlight, but there were times it seemed to Audrey that they were little clouds too. Sometimes on a Saturday she read my stuff in *The Guardian.* It was really fantastic that I was doing so well. Eddie was a keen reader of all my stuff, too. He loved finding a spelling mistake or a factual error. It made his Saturday. He'd be happy as a baby. 'But you know our Eddie. Loves to slag off his mates. It's kind of a sign of affection for him.'

'I was really very sorry to hear the bad news,' I said.

'What news is that?'

'Well, y'know – about you and the man himself.'

'How d'you mean?'

'About what happened. It's a shame. That it didn't work out.'

She looked at me quizzically.

'Your separation,' I said. That's a very hard thing.'

'Separation, my arse. I'm on my way in to meet him now.'

'You're – ?'

She laughed a bit uneasily. 'Yeah. We're going to a class.'

'A class?'

'A pregnancy class. For couples. You mean he didn't tell you? I'm having baby number three in six months' time. If that sod looks at me sideways I get pregnant again.'

A busker started into 'The Bucks of Oranmore'. A Garda who was watching him began to tap his foot. The roar in my head was louder; deeper. I had a sudden image of Eddie just laughing like a bastard – him and Samantha Mumba, howling with glee.

'Oh, that,' I managed. 'Yes, of course he told me that. I must have – got confused about the other thing. Sorry.'

'Confused? Jesus Christ. That's a hell of a confusion.'

'I'm just – not used to drinking any more. People don't so much in London.'

'Are you – *okay*?' she asked me seriously. 'You look a bit weird. Do you want to get a drink of water or something?'

'I'm grand,' I told her. 'But I really have to go.'

'Well – give us a call when you're over again,' she said, uncertainly. 'We're in the book. Virago in Ranelagh. Come out and have drinks. Look at the garden. Eddie's a dab hand in the garden these days. A regular Charlie Dimmock. He's even got the tits.'

My mobile started to ring as I walked away and towards the Green, but I didn't want to answer it, so I just switched it off.

The taxi-driver said the traffic was only bleedin wojus. Rush hour got longer and meaner every day. Longer in the mornings, longer in the night. What kind of country could stand for traffic like this? They were laughing at us in England. They were *breaking their shites* laughing. You wouldn't see it in *Africa*, traffic like this. Going over the northside was torture now. As for the southside – feck off and don't be talking. Luas, how are you? Port Tunnel, my hole. One of these days it would be rush hour all the time. And they said we were a civilised country.

# On the Market

### Kate Thompson

*Linette* O'Leary loved her house so much that she kissed the hall door any time she left home. The back of the hall door, of course, not the glossy front with its gleaming brass door furniture. She didn't want her neighbours thinking she was a looper. After she'd kissed the door and stroked its flawless surface, she'd whisper 'Bye bye, house'.

When she'd been first married her husband Gary used to find this little gesture endearingly idiosyncratic. Now she knew it irritated the hell out of him, so she refrained from indulging in the farewell ritual any time he was around. Which wasn't actually that much, these days. Since he'd been promoted in his job he was off travelling a lot in the UK and abroad. Linette didn't mind all the travelling. It meant that she had more time to be alone with her house.

She sometimes wondered if she didn't love the house more than she loved Gary. She certainly loved it more than the pet they'd once had. She'd fallen for a picture of an apricot-coloured cat being cradled by an actress in *Hello!* magazine, and she had boned up on this cat because it was exactly the same colour as the walls in her sitting-room. She had learned that it was of a breed known as 'Red Burmese', and because she thought that it would be pretty cool to have a pedigree cat that matched her décor, she had mentioned to Gary that a pet might be nice to keep her company while he was off on his travels. He'd agreed, but as it had turned out, the cat – which she'd christened Tarquin – had been a real pain. Instead of living up to its aristocratic name and looking elegant and refined like the one in *Hello!*, Tarquin would come in from the garden with filthy paws and climb all the way up to the top of her lovely cretonne curtains, where he'd cling on, glaring balefully down at her. He also had a habit of flinging himself upside down on the floor under her brocade *chaise longue*, and dragging himself along by his claws until the trim began to detach itself. She had been secretly quite relieved when Tarquin had come a cropper under the wheels of a Dynarod van, and had stoically refused to entertain any idea of a replacement. Even a fluffy Chinchilla that blinked at her bluely from the arms of another bimbo in *Hello!* – an accessory that she knew would look totally fabulous in her bedroom – failed to win her over. No, Linette, she told herself sternly. Think of the fluff that would be shed all over your alpaca throw!

Linette favoured throws and blankets in the bedroom. Duvets were *so* twentieth century! Even though it meant that bed-making was rather more of a chore for her, it was worth it for that classy look. A beautiful white robe in hand-embroidered lawn draped casually at the foot of the bed completed the effect. She never wore the robe, but it looked just fantastic on the bed. She'd toyed with the idea of hanging a mosquito net over the bed head, but had rejected it when she suddenly started seeing loads of them in soap opera actresses' bedrooms in *Hello!* Mosquito nets were obviously becoming a bit common.

More than anything when Gary was away on his travels, Linette loved to wander around her house, relishing it. She would pour herself coffee and sit at her beautiful granite kitchen island, sipping from her hand-painted Bridgewater china and admiring the way the light streamed in through the skylight in the extension they'd had built two years earlier. She loved the way light bounced off her beautiful glass brick walls and the way her streamlined worktops and steel blue units gleamed. In the evening, when the sun hit the front of the house, she would pour a little Chablis (it used to be Chardonnay until Chardonnay became so ubiquitous) into one of her elegant designer wine glasses, and go and sit on the antique prayer chair in her sitting-room, letting her gaze roam indulgently over the book shelves stacked with glossy coffee table books and classic novels. She couldn't bear the look of commercial fiction with its tacky jackets, and she shuddered any time she noticed one of Gary's John Grishams or Stephen Kings lurking amongst the Iris Murdochs and the Stephen Hawkings that she must get round to reading some day. The John Grishams and Stephen Kings flew off the shelves the moment Gary went travelling again, ending up in the second-hand book shop where Linette bought the paperback romances for which she had a secret, shameful passion. Once she had inadvertently left a Silhouette title indecently exposed on her coffee table, and she had blushed pinker than a Silhouette heroine when a visiting Green Party candidate had accepted her invitation to step inside for a cup of tea and had spotted the dog-eared book splayed face downward, looking as if it had been ravished.

Linette couldn't understand why some people moaned about political canvassers and Jehovah's witnesses and the like ringing your doorbell. She was always interested in what other people had to say, especially when they admired her sitting-room and asked her questions about her hand-embroidered cushions or her collection of sepia-tinted portraits in their antique frames. Of course the aristocratic-looking individuals in the photographs weren't really her ancestors, but there was no harm in allowing her visitors to think they were.

Linette was deeply ashamed of the fact that her father had worked in the elephant enclosure in Dublin zoo, and that her mother had worked as a seamstress, doing alterations for one of the more old-fashioned department stores. She was deeply ashamed of the name she'd been landed with (Linda Looney), and had vowed that she would change it as soon as it was in her power to do so. So she had studied hard at school and landed a good job with a top-class estate agency, where she had learned how important it was to present the correct image. She had blown her first wage packet on a stylish suit, and her second on two pairs of very good shoes. She kept her shoes polished, her suit immaculate, and she worked hard at perfecting her fingernails and her smile (she was exceptionally pretty) and pronouncing her 'th's as 'th', not 'd'. By the time she met gorgeous Gary, Linette was quite a catch – and when he told her three years after they'd married that he was now earning enough money for her to give up her job, they had cracked a bottle of champagne to celebrate. It was the first time the John Rocha flutes had ever been used.

Linette didn't miss her job at all. She'd been finding it more and more stressful, and at last she had all the time in the world to do the things to their Victorian semi-d that she'd always wanted. She had the floors and banisters and skirting boards sanded, she painted dado rails and executed stencils on the walls of the bedroom that was to be the nursery, she harried builders and plumbers when her pride and joy, the brand-new kitchen extension, wasn't as perfect as it needed to be. And finally, when it was all finished, she and Gary drank champagne from the flutes for the second time.

That had been two years ago, and still the nursery wasn't in use, but Linette didn't really mind because she knew that if they had a baby she'd have to have another (because no one ever chose to have just *one* baby, did they?). And she knew that if she had more than one baby she would have to leave the perfect home she had created, and move somewhere bigger, and it would break her heart to have to start all over again elsewhere. The other thing that put her off the idea of moving was that she had a sneaking feeling that she could never love another house the way she loved this one – she could never love another house so much that she'd want to kiss its front door.

The perfection of her house didn't, however, deter Linette from watching home improvement programmes on the television, or from buying home improvement magazines. She bought them all – *Homes and Gardens, Elle Decoration, Image Interiors, Country House Living.* She had bought *wallpaper\** magazine once, but she didn't think much of it. It was too radical for her tastes – she preferred her surroundings to be homey and the look propagated by that particular style bible was anything but. The only real concession to modernity in her house was her fabulous kitchen with its steel blue units and its glass brick wall.

Leafing through the pages of these glossies often filled Linette with a kind of anguish because she knew that her house could quite easily hold its own when compared with the ones in the magazines. What did you have to do, who did you have to know to get your house *in* there? She couldn't help but seethe when she read about the bloody lady novelists and fashion designers and freelance so-and-sos who had 'transformed' rooms and 'tamed' gardens and 'created' spaces. She wanted to scribble on their complacent faces when she saw photographs of these domestic goddesses 'working' in their studios or 'cooking' in their kitchens or 'relaxing' in their macramé hammocks.

These photographs Linette examined with the kind of scrutiny an art valuer might devote to a great painting, noting details that, magpie-like, she could appropriate and use in her own home – such as the miniature ferns displayed under glass cloches; or the wire trugs laden with gleaming aubergines; or the petals fallen from a display of peonies that had 'scattered themselves' artlessly over a pristine linen table cloth. And every time she opened one of these magazines and read about the miracles wrought by the denizens of the domiciles featured therein, she thought how unfair it was that her home wasn't included.

Because Gary was away so much, and because she had a lot of time on her hands now that the labour of love that was her home was finished, Linette took to viewing houses that were on the market. She scoured the pages of the property sections, seeking details of period houses that had been 'sensitively restored' or that 'oozed character', and she spent many happy afternoons wandering around other people's houses feeling smug when she saw that actually the restoration wasn't half as sensitive as hers, nor the character anywhere near as oozy. She listened to people admiring cornices and coving and oohing and ahhing over throne-like lavatories and pitch pine double-doors, and she looked at them gawping at state-of-the art kitchens and to-die-for bathrooms, and she wished that she could show them *her* house. And one day, when someone she knew from her estate agent days was overseeing the viewing and she was asked if she was putting her own house on the market, she heard herself saying 'yes'.

She said it because she knew it would appear more than a little odd if she told the truth and admitted that she simply got a kick out of comparing her house with other people's, but after she'd said it, while she was on her way to view the next property on her list, she thought: Why not? Why *not* put her house on the market? That would be a very clever way indeed of showing off her pride and joy to discerning members of the public. People did it all the time – put their houses on the market and then changed their minds again after a couple of weeks. It gave estate agents a lot of grief because there was no financial gain for them unless a sale actually went through, but there was nothing illegal about it. The only expense involved for her would be the production of the brochure and the placing of the classified ad – and really, wouldn't that be worth it for the pleasure she'd derive from witnessing people swoon over her house the way they swooned over residences far less desirable than hers?

Linette planned her strategy with the precision of a military campaigner. She phoned an estate agency (not the one she'd worked for), and told them that she would like her house valued and put on the market as soon as possible. 'We can send someone tomorrow,' she was told. 'We'll have photographs taken for the brochure and the board will be up before the end of the day.' Excellent! That meant that there would be two opportunities for viewing next week, when Gary would still be away. She would send the keys by courier, she informed the estate agent, because she was currently residing in her country residence in West Cork. This ploy ensured she remained incognito, which was important because she didn't want the estate agent recognising her when she turned up to view her own house on Thursday afternoon, and then again on Saturday. She would take the property off the market the following Monday, conjuring some useful family problem as an excuse. Next Thursday was her birthday, she noted with pleasure. What more enjoyable a way to spend her birthday than observing other people paying homage to the creative statement that was her home?

The next day she took herself off for a day of pampering at Powerscourt Springs, and when she returned home that evening she was delighted to see the estate agent's board on display outside her front door. She had no worries about word getting back to Gary about this – he was away so much that he didn't know any of their neighbours, and Linette herself was only on nodding terms with them. She could always deny it, anyway – say that the dozy neighbour had made a mistake, and that the sign had actually been up outside the house next door.

Linette spent an entire week cleaning and polishing and effecting minor repairs. She even got the mini-maids in, even though she didn't trust them to give her home the kind of TLC it deserved. And when the first viewing Thursday came around, she kissed the front door, and popped into town for a spot of indulgent shopping and a birthday cappuccino in Brown Thomas, returning at around half-past two to a house that was gratifyingly, spectacularly full of total strangers.

'Hello!' she breezed to the man who was overseeing the viewing.

'Good afternoon, madam,' he returned, handing her a brochure. 'The auction details are all there. May I take your name and telephone number in the event of our having another property that you might be interested in viewing?'

'That won't be necessary,' beamed Linette. 'It's this property or nothing for me! It's not often such a desirable house comes on the market in such a prime location.'

The estate agent treated her to an urbane smile. 'A lady who knows what she wants. Feel free to look around – and I'm here to answer any questions you may have.' Then he scrutinised her more closely. 'Have I met you somewhere before?' he asked.

'I don't think so.'

'Strange. Maybe I just saw you somewhere recently? At another viewing, maybe?'

'Impossible!' sang Linette. 'This is the only house I've been interested in viewing for years!' And not a word of a lie!

'Well. I hope you enjoy it.'

'Thank-you! I will!' She moved down the hallway towards her kitchen, pretending to consult the brochure that had already been sent to her in the post.

'Oh! Isn't it gorgeous!' A woman's awed voice made Linette's ears flatten against her skull the way Tarquin the cat's had when he'd heard sudden birdsong. 'Oh! Look at those units, Toby! And the floor! Is it Amtico, I wonder? Or a laminate?'

'Neither,' said Linette, veering towards the couple like a heat-seeking missile. 'It's solid Scandinavian pine.'

The woman acknowledged Linette's observation with an 'Oh, really?' and a polite smile, before returning her attention to the kitchen. 'Fabulous cooker, Toby! You'd have fun with that.'

'Neff,' remarked Linette.

'I beg your pardon?' said the woman, giving her an uncertain look.

'State-of-the art Neff. That's the make. It has an ergonomic rotating handle, a single control knob and a highly-effective Hydro-Clean.'

'Oh. I see.' Looking even more uncertain, the woman took hold of Toby's hand and led him away from this peculiar person in the direction of the sliding glass panels that opened on to the garden. Here the delights of

Linette's immaculate flower beds, her elegant Teakhouse patio furniture and her impressive Hartley Botanic glass house awaited them.

Looking round for more victims, Linette noticed someone opening the door of her store cupboard. Thank goodness she knew from experience how outrageously nosy people could be on views! She'd made sure that all her bottles and jars of homemade preserves and Balsamic vinegar and extra-virgin Tuscan olive oil had been carefully positioned to conceal the more commonplace items. She allowed herself a little smile when she contemplated how clever she'd been. Her house was a veritable dream home!

She spotted a woman admiring her granite kitchen island, and she was just about to move across and engage her in conversation with some opening gambit such as 'Beautiful, isn't it? I wonder how much it cost?' when a younger woman joined her targeted quarry.

'Fantastic house, isn't it, mum?' she said, and Linette prinked. 'Everything's so perfect! Down to the last detail! Did you clock the porcelain door handles? And the embroidered cushions? And the fantastic collection of photograph frames in the drawing room?'

Linette knew that people would be tempted to inspect her photograph collection. They always were. Oh, God. They always were…

A flash of panic hit her, and she bolted in an ungainly fashion towards her drawing-room, attracting curious looks from fellow viewers as she went. The room was crammed with people oohing and ahhing obligingly at the beautiful furniture and the *dernier cri* curtains and all the tastefully whimsical *objets* and artefacts, but, surprisingly, Linette didn't pause to eavesdrop. Subtle as a serpent, she insinuated her way through the crowd to where her photograph collection was displayed on top of the highly-french-polished piano that nobody ever played. There, in pride of place in its ornate ormolu frame was the striking portrait of Mrs Gary O'Leary that her husband had commissioned from a top Dublin photographer around a year ago, for her birthday.

Linette checked out the couple standing directly to her left. Their heads were together, absorbed in their brochure. The pair on her immediate right were gaping upward, admiring her ceiling rose. With the legerdemain of a conjurer, Linette slid the incriminating evidence of her identity off the piano and into her Brown Thomas carrier bag.

As she sidled from the room she overheard a woman saying 'I wonder what kind of fabric those curtains are? They look incredibly expensive.'

'Cretonne,' said Linette automatically, adding 'And yes, it is incredibly expensive,' over her shoulder before heading for the stairs.

She spent a delightful half hour wandering from bedroom to bathroom to bedroom, listening to people saying all the right things and occasionally volunteering nuggets of information herself – such as the make of the power shower, or the provenance of the lit bateau, or the estimated date of an antique. She hugged herself inwardly when she heard someone say that her house was the most beautiful they'd viewed yet, and she wanted to jump for joy when she heard someone else say that it was worthy of *Irish Homes and Gardens*. She couldn't have given herself a better birthday present!

The smile she wore as she glided back down the stairs was beatific. The estate agent was still at his greeting post in the hall, in consultation with a man whose face was obscured by a bouquet of red roses and a bunch of helium balloons. The man was gesticulating so animatedly that a couple of the balloons detached themselves from his grasp and started floating towards her up the stairs. One had the word 'Surprise!' printed on it in swirly yellow letters, and the other bore the legend 'Happy Birthday!' in swirly red ones. And the beatific smile froze on her face and she wanted to turn and flee back upstairs as the man turned, his eyes automatically following the direction of the balloons to where she stood mid-staircase.

'I came home to give you a surprise. It seems the surprise is on me. I suspect you may have some explaining to do, Linette,' said Gary.

# The Bee Box

### Kevin McDermott

*It* came this afternoon. The box you ordered at the meeting of bee-keepers. A month ago. Before all this. Before you left.

The bees were always your idea. I'd play Bathsheba to your Troy, Sylvia to your Ted. You fantasised about taking me in your arms, in my leather gloves, straw hat and veil, in the hollow amid the ferns. A wild thought, you called it.

Four weeks. A lifetime ago. We were still living our idyll then, or so I thought. All it wanted, you said, was bees to make it complete. And, poor eejit that I was, I believed it.

There was no talk of bees before the notice appeared in the window of our grocery-cum-post office. Our neighbours were in collecting their dole. You liked Thursdays in the village, didn't you? Liked to chat with the men, in the sun. Liked to talk of hurling, EU grants and the old ways. Sitting on the wall, your backs to the sea. And then, later, in the pub.

Ever since I've known you, you've liked the company of old men. Never minded the dirt of their nails; the shine on their trousers; the stains on their jackets; the stale smell of tobacco, beer, urine. The smellier the better. I picture you in a café-bar in Arles, sharing a beer with the local lunatic, with his one ear and his bloodied bandage. Not a bother on you.

Ever since I've known you!

That's a laugh! Did I ever know you? For that matter, did you ever know me?

I know that Thursdays had become a bit of a ritual.

'I'm just popping into the village to PJ. I'll settle up with him. And I might look into O' Donoghue's, on the way back.'

'Might look,' indeed. You never arrived home before midnight. Ah, not that I minded.

I liked being in the house on my own. Liked the space. It gave me a chance to think. I developed my own Thursday ritual. After I'd tidied around, I'd load the range with turf, build up a big blaze and then slack it down for the day. Then I'd sit at the kitchen table, reading or writing. Or sketching. Sometimes just sitting, catching up with myself. I liked the silence of those Thursdays. The way the fire made me drowsy.

Anyway, it was PJ who pointed out the notice to you.

'You'd like that kind of craic,' you told me he said, 'bee-keeping. That would suit youse now. You and the little woman.' He was half right. The idea took your fancy.

You came home, comfortably drunk, excited, quoting Yeats, 'The bee-loud glade'. How corny. But I was carried along, as usual, on the tide of your excitement.

You marked the date on the calendar. You counted down the days and then off we went. Winding down our little road, around the headland, up the coast. In the Morris Minor. Our Morris fucking Minor. I cringe now to think of us.

We were early enough to have a drink. You were full of the business possibilities of what you called 'home-enterprise' – our own honey, my sculpture, your writing. My arse!

'The internet's the key.'

That was your mantra.

'You can live anywhere and still reach your market. We could access Japan from here, for God's sake.' All that global village stuff that you went on with.

There were a good few people there, all the same. Mostly blow-ins, like ourselves. There was a hive with a window. I couldn't stand to look at it for long. All those bodies crawling over each other. That black mass of tangled life appalled me. You, of course, were fascinated. Pointing at this and that. You picked up the lingo in no time, and stood conversing with 'the aul lad', the local expert in bee lore.

You were in your element. And, as people drifted away, you were still there, buying drink for your new friend.

You loved him, his stories, his way of laughing. He couldn't look me in the eye. It was all sideway glances, like an old dog who's been beaten once too often and won't meet his master's stare. He looked at me, like lots of those old fellows, with a sly hunger that unnerved me. I retreated into myself, sat lost and shapeless within my zipped jacket.

'Good-bye now, Ma'am,' he said, as we parted, at closing time, his breath all beery.

'You were very quiet.' It sounded like an accusation.

Two days later, he arrived with an old hive he'd promised you. You weren't here, so he put it around the back of the house. I wanted to bend over and take a good look at it, but I couldn't do it with him there, his eyes greedy for a sight of my flesh.

When he was gone, I took a shower, soaping myself all over. That's how he left me feeling, your friend, the bee-keeper, the story-teller. You didn't understand or try to understand or want to understand.

'For fuck's sake,' you said, 'stop being neurotic.' 'Neurotic', that was one of your favourite put-down words. Wasn't it?

Later you were sorry. And then to make it up to me, you came and hugged me, reached into my blouse and fondled my breast. I felt you hard against me. When I pushed you away, you looked at me with … with what? Distaste? Not hatred, no. But something. Something cold and unloving. Or am I being unfair?

'I'm going to PJ's.' You pulled the door angrily behind you.

I stood for a while. The clock tick, tick, ticking. I knew then.

So what did I do? I baked. It was therapy for my neurosis. Scones and soda bread. An apple tart. Things you like. I wanted to be a good housewife, someone who could make you happy. I even thought of babies. Our babies. The baking did that to me. All that yeast and dough. The fecundity of the hot oven. Dangerous bloody thing, baking.

Later I searched out some drawings I had made of a Sheela-na-gig. The round head, the smile, the open legs. What about it as a water feature in our garden? Our shameless joy. I sketched it out for you. I could make a mould and produce it for garden centres, advertise it on our home page. Sell in Japan. I was sure you'd be pleased, amused. Marvel at my cleverality.

It was after dark when you arrived home. You were silent and unrelenting. You declined the bread, the scones, the apple tart. You didn't smile when I showed you the sketches. I refused to become the nag you wanted me to be. You wouldn't become the soft lover I wanted you to be. A nil-all draw.

I went to bed alone. You came when you thought I was sleeping. Slipped between the covers, turned your back to me. Fuck you.

After that I stopped going down to the pub in the evening.

And then your mother, with her impeccable timing, arrived, for a 'little visit'. You hadn't the gumption to put her off. There was no agreement, but we put on a show of sorts. I think we did it for our benefit as much as for hers. You called me 'love', quite naturally. You had fancied yourself as an actor ever since that one-act festival in Scariff. Your one and only venture on stage.

Though I don't think we fooled your mother. She knew there was something wrong and it put her on her best behaviour. The house surprised her – its cosiness, its warmth, the range. She sat and sipped Baileys and reminisced. I nearly warmed to her.

Funny how the range does that to people – softens them, makes them expansive. All the ferret watchfulness, the ferret fierceness left her face when she spoke of her mother, cooking on a range 'just like this one. You've never tasted soda bread like hers.' I'd never seen her like that before.

'Everyone loved her,' she said, 'she should never have died that young. Never.'

We brought her to Hylands for Sunday lunch. It was a great success. Your mother thought the roast beef was 'just lovely'.

'You can't beat honest-to-god, plain cooking.'

I'd served lasagne the previous night, with a salad. No spuds, no mayonnaise. She declined the yoghurt dressing.

'Sure yoghurt's for dessert.'

She pronounced 'yoghurt' so that it sounded indecent.

She showed us her invitation to your cousin's wedding.

'You'll give us the next big day out,' she said, all smiles. 'Father Eamonn is coming home in spring. He could say the Mass for you. And your Nana Quinn has me tormented to know have you set the date.'

'For Christ's sake, Ma, give your mouth a break.'

She left a day earlier than she'd planned.

'I don't like to leave Daddy to fend for himself,' she explained, giving me a hug. 'You're a great girl, living out here, with that fellow.'

You drove her to the station. I don't know what time it was when you got back. You slept in the spare room, in the bed that your mother had vacated.

Very Freudian. You bastard.

That was it really. A couple of cold meals, some sharp words. It would have been easier if there had been someone else. I pretended for a while that there was. That young Italian who'd camped with her boyfriend in our field, for a few days. Her. She of the brown eyes and full lips. She was the one.

And the taste of blue cheese I kissed from your fingers was really the traces of her sex on your hands. I tried to work myself into a fury over her. Tried to imagine you making love with her. But it was always me in the pictures. Always me. That wasn't much of a help, was it?

You sneaked around for a few days, gathering your belongings, hoping I wouldn't notice.

And then, finally, 'If you want, I'll leave the car.'

'Go, fuck yourself.'

'The rent's paid for six months.'

I wouldn't answer.

'I'm sorry.'

'Huh!'

* * *

I suppose it took some courage to leave.

In fairness.

* * *

I walked down to the lighthouse. I stood for a long time on the rocks, looking across the bay, watching the sea. Watching the gulls. My mind was numb. It was all I could do to drag myself home and go to bed. Sleep embraced me and I surrendered to it. For days. And then I woke and didn't want to fall back asleep. Grey light filled the room. A dream was just out of reach, but the feeling, the good feeling of the dream stayed with me. I worked all that day.

* * *

Your shaving brush appeared this morning, in the bathroom. A pair of underpants and socks in the wash basket. If I walk by the shore, will the sea wash up bits of you too?

Already, I've lost hold of your face, its form, the colour of your eyes. I cannot conjure you. I cannot abjure you. And I no longer want you.

* * *

Mrs Mc thinks I'm mad to stay. 'Stark raving mad.' Thinks hanging wouldn't be good enough for you.

'You can't stay here on your own, love, without a car.'

'I've my bicycle. And the phone, and the internet.'

'Fat lot of good they'll do you when it's teeming rain and it's five miles to the village and you've no milk.'

'Then I'll come over to you.'

'It's not right, pet, a lovely girl like you on her own in the middle of nowhere. Not with the fellows that's going around nowadays. Jesus Mercy, what kind of man is he at all? I'd love to wring his bloody neck. Or give him a good slap for himself.'

* * *

I don't feel anger. I'm too spent for that.

What I did feel was that I'd failed you. It's ridiculous isn't it? Guilt! I don't think a man would've felt like that – 'If there wasn't someone else, it had to be my fault.'

'Bless me, father, for I have sinned.'

'Go on, my child.'

'My husband's left me, father.'

'Examine your conscience, woman, and see what you did to drive him away.'

'I will, Father, I will.'

That kind of rubbish.

But I couldn't throw off the feeling that there had to be something wrong with me, some fault, some lack. I looked at myself in the mirror, trying to find the blemish. I couldn't see anything.

* * *

I know that I can make my life. I know this for certain. And the omens are good. The sky is clear, and for the first time in days I can see the mountain. (I was going to say 'our' mountain.) There've been other signs. Last night there was a hedgehog outside the back door lapping the milk I'd left for Tilly. And this morning a baby hare ran round the field. I sat on the bed and watched him. So, you see I am not falling apart.

I've made plans.

I'm going to convert the outhouse into a studio.

I am going to make contact with the Artists' Co-operative.

I am going to start marketing my work.

I am going to be successful.

Do you hear me?

I've read the leaflet on bees. The box is standing in the kitchen, humming and thrumming. I'm not afraid of it. Not now. Very soon, I'm going to put on my moon suit and transfer the bees into the hive. I'm going to set them to work for me. I don't fear their stings.

Very soon.

That's your gift to me.

These bees.

This immunity from pain.

# Flood Warning

*Martina Devlin*

'Your turn, Clare,' they chorus. 'It's the middle of the night, the flood waters are rising and you have only seconds to escape. No time to think. What would you save?'

'She doesn't need to think about it,' objects Tim. He's already had his go and is still smarting after his teasing as a pumped-up pedal pusher, addicted to skintight Lycra, and most wounding of all, predictable. Just because he opted for his racing bike. 'It's a foregone conclusion in Clare's case, everybody knows that.'

'She has to decide for herself,' insists Nicola, who is orchestrating the game. She always takes charge in these situations.

Clare envies Nicola her demeanor of serene command. She sits there, pearl-pink manicured nails glinting against the bulbous body of her wine glass, looking as though she has life on a plate. A Wedgewood one with eleven other matching place settings. Furtively, Clare examines her own nails, always splintering no matter how often she paints strengthening products on them.

Nicola is watching Ross out of the corner of eyes enhanced with three blended eye-shadows and finished off with liquid liner. Which she never smudges. He pretends to be unconscious of her scrutiny, although she knows him well enough after four years of marriage to realise his air of only marginal attention to the proceedings is a façade. Nothing escapes his notice, despite his apparent sloth. Ross is sprawled in an armchair, eyelids at half-mast and bare feet crossed at the ankle on the coffee table, but a few moments ago he noticed Jo coughing and fetched her a tumbler of water.

Nicola has engineered this game for the sole purpose of hearing what Ross would rescue from a flood. Which memento from their life together would he count irreplaceable? She's hoping he'll plump for their silver-framed wedding photograph, which catches him forever frozen in an attitude of worship. As though Sarah Lynch could never supplant her.

Nicola allows her gaze to drift over the group of friends gathered in the sitting-room of the home she shares with Ross, its tasteful elegance glimmering through the morass of cups and glasses. She unleashes her cosmetically whitened smile on Clare. 'Take your time,' she encourages her.

But Clare needs none. 'I'd grab a rug and scoop my collection of teapots into it.'

'You'd never fit all of them, you must have sixty or seventy by now.' Ross smiles his secretive grin, activated by some internal source of amusement.

They all find Clare's devotion to her teapots endearing – and a little pathetic. She chatters away to them as though they're human and uses each teapot in strict rotation. Transferral of affections, classic sign of spinsterhood, they agree. When she's out of earshot.

Clare savages her lip, fingering wispy black shoulder-length hair which never manages to either curl or hang straight. 'Maybe I could persuade a fireman to go back inside for the rest – I can explain how important my teapots are, I've been collecting them since my ninth birthday when my aunt gave me the ballerina one.'

'You can only save as much as you're able to carry.' Nicola is crisp now, impatient to move on to the next candidate. Moving closer along the chain to Ross. 'Anyway it's a fire officer, not a fireman.'

'Sorry.' Clare lowers her button eyes, outwardly meek, although she bridles at Nicola's correction. She's always so precise. You daren't say euros instead of euro, or even attempt to pronounce a French word in front of her. Nicola always makes her feel as though she's a failure, just because she's a gift shop manager. But she doesn't want to be a high flier like Nicola; high fliers can singe their wings.

Tim nudges Clare. 'You could always start a new collection with the insurance money,' he teases. 'Toby jugs, maybe, or snuff boxes.'

Aghast, Clare is beyond answering; her teapots are irreplaceable. Straight after breakfast tomorrow she'll store her most precious ones in watertight metal boxes in the attic, safe from rising flood waters.

Good-natured Jo intervenes, to spare Clare's feelings. 'I'll go next, Nicola. Since my nearest and dearest' – she pulls a face at Tim, with whom she's been living for eight years – 'was so romantic as to grab his racing bike, presumably leaving me behind to sink or swim, I won't rescue him either. I'll save my teddy bear.'

The others regard her with uniform consternation. Sensible maths teacher Jo, with her low maintenance cropped hairstyle and her livery of canvas jeans and desert boots, isn't the cuddly toy sort. She's interested in tennis, science fiction and chess – they didn't even know she had a teddy bear. Only Tim is unmoved.

'He's called Bear,' she continues, enjoying her friends' flabbergasted reaction.

'You never even mentioned him before,' complains Nicola.

'Why don't you keep him somewhere visible if he means so much to you?' queries Clare.

Jo shakes her head. 'Not at all, I couldn't take the risk of something happening to my Bear. He's precious – priceless, in fact.'

Even Ross is curious now, no longer peeling the label from a wine bottle on the pretext of disassociating himself from this after-dinner game Nicola is bent on playing. Her determination needles him: she applies it to every aspect of life instead of using it selectively.

Jo obliges her audience with further information. 'I've had Bear since the day I was born. My father brought him to the hospital when he came to see my mother and I. Mum says he lifted my dimpled wee arm and slid the bear in alongside me, then he kissed the tip of his fingers and touched me on the forehead.' Tim stretches out a hand and strokes hers. 'Aye, he did, he kissed his fingers to me,' she adds softly.

Everyone falls silent. Each of them is familiar with the story of how Jo's father was killed by a bomb returning home from hospital on the day of her birth. No warning was given and the security forces didn't have a chance to seal off the area. He was unlucky enough to be driving past the pub just as it was detonated – his dental records helped identify him. Jo has no memories of him and only a couple of photographs. Her mother's second husband adopted Jo and is an affectionate parent; she calls him Dad and loves him in return.

Jo threads fingers through her sandy hair, spiking it. 'I have a keepsake box under the bed with some of my father's belongings. Bear lives there, in a nest made from an old scarf. He's a bit battered, his eyes had to be sewn back in and there's a patch over one of his paws where the stuffing fell out. So I slapped a conservation order on him. I take him out sometimes and hug him – he's all I have that my father gave directly to me.' She laughs, to defuse the sombre mood. 'Unless you count his genes, of course. My mother says he loved chess and science fiction too. But not tennis, that comes from her.'

Three sets of eyes swivel towards Tim.

'Did you know about Bear?' Nicola interrogates him.

'Of course,' he shrugs, 'I sleep above him every night. He's been in the wars but he's a distinguished old fellow. Am I allowed to change my mind about what I rescue from the flood?'

'No,' snaps Nicola, setting her jet earrings dancing. They were an anniversary present from Ross and she's wearing them as a reminder of the bond between them. 'First choices only. The beauty of this game is it's supposed to be kneejerk and therefore more illuminating.' She realises her tone sounds arbitrary and adopts a more conciliatory approach. 'Don't you want your ninety-six-gear racing bike with go faster mirrors any more?'

Tim drains his glass of water. He's in training and switched to non-sparkling Ballygowan after two glasses of red wine. 'I'd prefer my Ulster Road Race trophy instead.'

'Hearing my teddy bear story has turned Tim all sentimental,' Jo interprets. She plants an indulgent kiss on the bony bridge of his nose.

Tim scratches it, in the damp aftermath. 'Actually, I've just remembered the bike's on the insurance so I could always buy another and they've modified the pedals on the latest version – I'm sure I could shave a couple of seconds off my time. The thing is I'm not getting any younger, I might never win another trophy.'

He's thirty-one and convinced his physical powers are on the wane, although he goes for punishing fifteen km cycle rides – with the stopwatch ticking – before and after work every day.

Jo polishes Tim's trophy once a week. 'Excellent choice,' she smiles at him. 'It'll be an heirloom one day.'

'Sarah's late,' remarks Clare. 'Wasn't she supposed to join us after work for dessert and coffee?'

Nicola's slate blue eyes graze Ross and just as swiftly dart away. 'I reminded her this morning we were all meeting up. She promised faithfully she'd be here – it's been almost a year since the six of us were together under one roof. And yet we lived in each other's pockets at Queen's, it seems a lifetime ago now. I told her she couldn't be the only renegade not to show up. "We'll gossip about you in your absence," I warned her. That did the trick. She said she was going to grab a sandwich at her desk and work on but she'd be with us later. I've saved her some dinner, just in case she didn't bother eating. You know Sarah, skinny as a rake, she forgets to eat. She'd forget to breathe if her lungs didn't do it for her.'

'I wouldn't call Sarah skinny.' Ross's low voice strikes an indolent note after Nicola's helter-skelter chatter.

'What would you call her?' Nicola challenges him.

'Fragile.' Ross tilts his head to one side, an appealing gesture that's his trademark. 'A piece of porcelain. But she's strong – not easily broken.'

Nicola is a tall, handsome blonde with a rangy build and clearly-defined bone structure. However, she's hyper-conscious of her size and Ross's words jibe; her hands ball into fists and her breath pants in shallow gasps.

The others are agape as the tension mounts. Surely Nicola and Ross aren't about to have a row in front of them? Their marriage is flawless, as perfect as the life they've constructed for themselves. The others envy them their Victorian house on the Malone Road, their partnerships in a law firm, their matching blue-eyed blond perfection, their aura of having everything sorted. Right down to which neighbour's daughter they'll employ as a babysitter when the time is right for them to start a family. Together they are one plus one equals six of the best. Gilded coupledom stooping to conquer.

'Nicola, you haven't had your turn.' It's Jo again, defusing the atmosphere.

Everyone glares at her. Tim and Clare because they want to see what might happen, Nicola and Ross because it interferes with their personal vendetta.

'What would you save if the flood waters were lapping at your door?' Jo continues, affecting not to notice how she's become the focus of general resentment. She lifts one of the Butler's chocolates Nicola has arranged in a bonbon dish by the coffee pot and bites in. She'll give it ten minutes after Sarah's arrival and then she's signalling home time to Tim. Tonight definitely isn't the easygoing catch-up session Nicola flagged.

'Strictly speaking they belong to Ross, he keeps them in his half of the study.' Nicola is contemplative. 'But I'd choose the wooden giraffe book-ends I brought him back as a souvenir from Kenya. It was our first separation – I missed him every minute of every day.' Her gaze pinions her husband and her tone shifts. 'Do you remember how one of the giraffes lost an ear, sweetheart?' She masticates the endearment. 'It happened after you collected me from Aldergrove Airport and drove me back to my apartment.'

Tim winks at Clare; in the early days the rest of them lived in bedsits, flats if they were lucky, but Nicola always rented an apartment. Or at least referred to her rooms as such.

Nicola twirls her glass by the stem. 'I was hardly in the door with my suitcases before you pulled me onto the floor and we sent the book-ends tumbling. Later I scrabbled around to find the broken ear and you said, 'Let's not glue it back on, let's keep it as a reminder of how love and passion can fuse.' I knew you were the man for me when I heard that, I thought it only happened once in a lifetime – if you were lucky. Little did I know that love and passion can fuse at the drop of a hat for Ross Davies.'

'You're embarrassing our guests, Nicola.' Ross's tone is mild; if it weren't for the trapped nerve twitching in his cheek there'd be no visible sign of uneasiness.

'Really? I thought I was riveting them.' Nicola scatters a disdainful glance around the room. 'And now, Ross, I'd like to hear what you'd play saviour to as the monsoon pelted down.'

The doorbell rings but nobody moves. It sounds again. The shrilling seems pre-determined, as though woven by design through this tense exchange, an integral facet of the drama. Someone taps a key against one of the stained glass door panels and it demands a response.

'I'll go.' Clare's offer is reluctant. Nobody breathe a word in my absence, is the implicit admonition. She patters down the mosaic-tiled hallway, a dumpy figure in an angora jumper that has already shed onto everyone else's clothes. As the front door opens, cold air gusts towards the sitting-room and a candle splutters.

Sarah Lynch has arrived.

Sarah is smiling as she enters the sitting-room, but almost instantly the smile withers as she senses a disturbance in the atmosphere.

Nicola rises, towering over Sarah by seven inches. 'Angel,' she purrs, 'you look frozen. See how pinched and pink her wee nose is, everybody. I want you to sit here beside Clare while I heat you some goulash. You're not nervous about eating meat, are you, Sarah? Of course not, a feisty criminal barrister like yourself. I hear all the rapists in town want you to represent them. Sweetheart' – this is directed at Ross and oozes from her in twin elongated syllables – 'pour Sarah a drink while I take care of the food. Would anyone like some more tarte citron while I'm in the kitchen? I'm sure you could manage another slice Tim, you simply burn energy on that bike of yours.'

In Nicola's absence, the group shifts warily and sends covert glances in one another's direction. Jo towards Tim in case he's distressed – she knows how sensitive he is, even if the others think him a cycling-obsessed bore; Tim towards his former flatmate Ross, who is coming in for a pummelling – although he's holding his own, not betraying any agitation; Clare towards Jo, for one of those eyebrows raised dialogues; Sarah towards each of them in turn, hoping for some clue about the turbulence detected by her antennae.

Ross alone appears at ease as he hands Sarah a brimming glass. 'You might need this,' he cautions.

Nicola bustles back in with tart for Tim, cutlery and another bottle of wine. Sarah is still wearing her barrister's tailored black suit and she shrinks inside it as Nicola clatters everything onto the coffee table, making more noise than seems strictly necessary.

'We're playing such an amusing game, Sarah.' Nicola's voice is louder than usual too. 'Everybody has to choose one object to save if a flood was threatening their home. We're still waiting to hear Ross's answer and of course you must have a turn too. I can't begin to imagine what you'd take, although it's always more fun taking what doesn't belong to you, isn't it?' She wheels around and returns to the kitchen, kitten heels punishing the floorboards where the rug doesn't stretch.

'Party games.' Sarah is subdued. 'It's been a long day, I don't know if I have the energy for them.'

'It's only a bit of fun,' Tim consoles her. He tests a palm against his ergonomically shaven scalp. 'It was Nicola's idea, you know what she's like, you may as well try to stop water running downhill. Sure just make it up, a book of poetry or anything.'

'I knew there was something missing, something odd about our choices,' interjects Jo. 'Nobody rescued any books and yet we all claim to love reading. Especially you, Tim, you're supposed to be a librarian.'

'I'm a cybrarian, I do it on the web,' he corrects her, lifting his third helping of pudding. 'Anyway I don't have any first edition books worth saving, they're all paperbacks.'

Ross hefts Sarah's briefcase, a battered leather bag so heavy it amazes the others she can hold it let alone carry it everywhere, and smiles into her eyes. She relaxes visibly. 'You look a little tired Sarah, I'm afraid of you tripping over this. I'll just move it out to the hall.'

There's an intimacy about the exchange that does not go undetected by their onlookers.

'You work too hard, you should have a lie-in tomorrow Sarah,' advises Jo. 'I love Saturday mornings. Tim goes for a mammoth cycle ride and I loll in bed with the newspapers and a pot of coffee. Then he arrives back, a whirlwind of ravenous energy, and we amble out for brunch.'

Sarah sips her wine, a furrow indenting on her forehead.

Nicola is back with enough food on a tray to give everyone in the room a portion.

'I really only wanted a snack,' protests Sarah.

Nicola slices across her. 'Nonsense, you eat like a bird, you'll end up with brittle bones in your old age. Ross loves to see a woman with a hearty appetite, don't you Ross? I remember when we first started courting he was always cooking me steaks to build me up. Steak and salad followed by crème brûlée and chocolate-sprinkled cappuccinos, that was your seduction speciality, wasn't it Ross? I wonder if he's changed it to keep pace with the times. Do you have any insights you could share with us Sarah?'

'I have absolutely no idea.' Sarah pushes away the tray of food. Her narrow face with its cap of auburn curls radiates defiance. 'You obviously have an axe to grind Nicola, but I don't appreciate your using me as a whetstone. I came here tonight at your invitation, your insistent invitation, to meet some old friends. If you're determined to be tiresome I'm going home.'

'Don't go.' Ross crosses the room in a few strides and hunkers beside her. 'This is all my fault. Here,' he lifts a forkful of goulash and coaxes it to her lips, 'try eating a little. Nicola is a superb cook – she excels at everything she sets her mind to do. And you know, you do live on ham sandwiches and packets of Maltesers. I bet there's a half-eaten packet in that briefcase I left out in the hall.'

Against her will, Sarah smiles. 'There might be,' she confesses, then she parts her lips for the food.

Nicola's face is an obelisk as she watches them, the candlelight haloed around her neck-length blonde bob. Jo decides she's had enough of intruding on another couple's death throes and drags a mesmerised Tim to his feet. 'We have to be going, everyone, the week is catching up on me. I can't … '

Nicola disregards Jo. 'Ready to play our flood game Sarah? Clare's rescuing an apron full of teapots, Jo's bringing her teddy bear, Tim wants the only trophy he's ever won and I'm taking some broken book-ends. What would you clutch to your breast as you waded from your doll's house of a home?'

Sarah looks at Ross who nods, fringe flopping into his eyes. He brushes it away, tilting his head as he returns Sarah's gaze; humour her, he appears to urge.

She sighs and trails the cool glass of wine she's holding across an aching temple. 'Granny's watch,' murmurs Sarah. 'It doesn't keep accurate time but

I love it for her sake. She's been dead almost a decade but she taught me something I'll never forget – that love must be unconditional or it's not worth having.' She closes her eyelids, the lashes casting shadows on her cheeks.

'Well said Sarah.' Ross lays a hand on her head, in benediction it strikes the others, then stands to face his wife. 'Nicola, this charade has lasted long enough. I'm leaving now and I'm taking what I choose to salvage from the deluge with me.' He extends his hand towards Sarah. 'Are you sure you want to do this? It means giving up a lot.'

Sarah bites her lip and nods. She slips her hand into her pocket and pulls out a dog leash, reaching it to Ross. 'I'm positive,' she says. 'It's selfish of me to keep Elliot, I can't spare him enough time. He'll have a better quality of life with you.'

Ross is almost at the front door before Nicola springs to life. 'You're leaving me for a dog,' she wails at his retreating back, her complexion blooming crimson. 'I'll be a laughing stock.'

'Call it puppy love,' Ross advises. Then he's gone.

In the aftershock, the friends wrestle with their reactions. Tim reflects that he'd never walk out on a looker like Nicola – although she can be a bit of a madam, no two ways about it. Jo withdraws her gaze from Nicola's stricken face and plans to take off a few days from work and spend them with her devastated friend. Clare alternates between feeling sorry for Nicola and relishing the novelty of the emotion. As for Sarah, she cracks her knuckles and wonders how everyone could have been so blind. It was obvious Nicola and Ross's relationship was shipwrecked, it was only a matter of time before it sank without a trace. Of course, she did have inside information.

'I was convinced he was seeing you,' Nicola mumbles at Sarah. 'He was always singing your praises.' Her poise has deserted her, she seems almost human as she slumps there. Even her linen dress is creased, a condition that affects others' clothes but never Nicola's.

Sarah is brisk. 'The hours I work don't allow me time to take a holiday, let alone find the energy for an affair.' She lays a tentative hand on Nicola's shoulder. 'But it's true I had the odd coffee with Ross, he was unhappy and confided in me. Then he started taking my dog Elliot for walks, sure the poor old boy was cooped up at home and getting no exercise at all.' She turns to the others. 'Ross told me about wanting a dog, he always had one as a boy. He said he pleaded with Nicola but she shuddered at the thought of hairs on the furniture and half-chewed bones in the garden. So he used to borrow mine.' Sarah folds her arms around her thin body and sighs. 'We shared Elliot for a time until finally I realised it was wrong of me to have a pet and give him virtually none of my attention – my free time is all gobbled up by work. I told Ross I was trying to find Elliot another home and he lit up like a child on Christmas morning. "I'll take him, please let me have him," he insisted. You see, he found he wanted to be with Elliot more than with you Nicola. I'm sorry, but that's the truth.'

'I suppose that explains the hairs on his jacket – I thought they were yours,' admits Nicola. She pours herself a glass of wine and drinks it in a single gulp. A dribble glistens on her chin.

In the car on the way home, Clare leans forward from the back seat towards Jo. 'It could have been worse, Ross could have gone off with Sarah. There'd have been outright war and Nicola would have forced us all to take sides.'

'Yes, it could have been a lot more unpleasant,' agrees Jo. But after dropping off their friend, Jo purses her lips. 'I know Ross went off with Sarah's Red Setter and not Sarah but I wouldn't be surprised if they end up together.'

Tim scrapes his thumbnail against the steering wheel, baffled. 'Can't imagine how you arrived at that conclusion Jo.'

'Haven't you ever wondered why she called her dog Elliot? It hit me like a ton of bricks the first time she mentioned it. Surely that's all the proof you could ever need.'

Tim's jaw opens slackly. 'I'm still not following you Jo.'

'Ross's initials are R E D. You must remember how we used to tease him at college that it meant his parents had latent Communist sympathies. He'd turn all defensive and say his father was a capitalist factory owner.'

Tim shifts in his seat, memory struggling to surface. 'Ross,' he mumbles. 'Ross Edward?'

Jo hits him playfully on the knee. 'Eejit,' she remonstrates. 'His middle name is Elliot.'

# A Day in April

### John McKenna

The countryside had been swollen with fog for three days. The clothes on the washing-line, at the end of the orchard, were no more than suggestions, looming and fading in the numb morning light. John Hardy threw an armful of turf sods and two buckets of slack into the mouth of the kitchen range and opened the damper before banging a kettle onto the hot-plate and pulling his still-damp working trousers and coat from the rack above the range.

As he dressed he sang quietly: *'April come she will, when streams are ripe and filled with rain.'*

It was a few minutes off seven on what should have been a clear, bright, April morning. Instead, the small windows of Hardy's cottage were grey with mist. Twenty minutes later, when he opened the half-door, the fog swept in around him. Swinging onto his bicycle, he glanced quickly across the yard and up Barn Hill and knew that the sky was set for another dreary, drooping day. At the top of the lane, he turned for Prumplestown and work.

As if the winter hadn't been bad enough, hanging on until the middle of March, the spring wasn't turning out any better. The fields were still hefty with floods. After four weeks of lying snow, from the week after Christmas, there'd been another month of torrential rain.

Everything was behind time and there was nothing anyone could do. Twice that week, he'd had to take a team of horses down to drag a tractor out of the muck. And there'd be no ploughing done this week or next. What they needed were clear skies and a sore east wind to suck the wetness out of the land. This weather was unnatural, the seasons were turning on their heads. Most of all he felt sorry for the children. He'd seen them walking to school in the winter mornings, the rain slapping their bare legs. And he saw them, these days, trudging home in the half-light, their clothes damp and raw against their skin. This wasn't how the spring was meant to be for children. They should be out and running, enjoying the warmth of the April afternoons, getting a taste of what the summer days would be about.

He tried the song words again, surrendering to them, ignoring the curl of the fog banking in his face. He was damned if weather was going to get him down. Weather was nothing. And so he sang out loud, careering into the farmyard with his song echoing ahead of him.

His arrival drew a shout from one of the stables.

'Hardy, have you nothing better to be doing than annoying me with your singing on a miserable, bastard of a morning like this?'

Hardy laughed, freewheeling through the open door.

Inside, Paddy Lawrence, the farm foreman, was brushing down a mare.

'No sun, no wind, no drying today.'

'I could go into Doyle's, have a few hot whiskies! I might even be persuaded to sing a song by dinner-time.'

'Aye, but could you be persuaded not to?'

Lawrence stepped away from the horse.

'I think you could take this one into the village and have her shoes done. There's not much else to be at the morning.'

'That'll be grand. Is there anything you want, while I'm there?'

'Ten Woodbine.'

'Ten Woodbine it is.'

When he arrived at the forge, the blacksmith was already shoeing a horse.

'Nowhere better to go in this weather,' the waiting ploughman said as Hardy poked his head around the corner, into the warmth of the forge.

He knew the ploughman but not well.

'What've you brought me?' the blacksmith asked.

'Dogger.'

'Fair enough, I could do with a quiet one. This whore'd kick you into kingdom come if you didn't watch her. And she's jink-backed.'

'But her drills are straight,' the ploughman said.

'That'll be a consolation when I'm prising her shoes out of my forehead.'

Hardy eased himself onto the worn, wooden bench that ran the length of one wall of the forge. It was, indeed, a good place to be on a cold, damp day. Through the open doorway, he could just make out the School Lane.

'Have youse got a start at all?' the ploughman asked.

'Not a sod. They brought the tractors down last week but this one ended up pulling them out of the field. It'll be late.'

'If we ever get there.'

A figure passed on the lane, a woman bent low, the mist smoking around her and settling again when she'd gone.

Hardy began to sing, not too loudly but loud enough for the blacksmith to hear him.

*'A blacksmith courted me, I loved him dearly,*
*He played upon his pipes both neat and trimly.*
*With his hammer in his hand he strikes so steady;*
*He makes the sparks to fly around the smithy.'*

The blacksmith grunted and the ploughman laughed.

*'I love to watch my love with his hammer swinging.*
*I love to hear it fall on the anvil ringing…'*

'That's what she said last night, the very words,' the blacksmith smirked.

'Rumour has it, rumour has it.'

They were silent for a while, the only sound was the hammering on the anvil and the swoosh of a hot shoe dipped in water. The horses stirred and then the smothered sound of children's voices came from somewhere beyond the lane. Dogger snorted and Hardy walked out to pat her head and whisper a few sounds to her.

'Have you the word?' the ploughman asked.

Hardy shook his head.

'Never in our family. You?'

'No.'

The blacksmith looked up from his work, the firelight catching one side of his face.

---

'There's a lot that says they have but devil the one I ever met in here that convinced me,' he grumbled. 'Mind you, I could be doing with it myself, save me a few kicks in sore places.'

The voices from the schoolyard came and went, dampened for a time and then, suddenly, clear again. One moment there was nothing, the next individual voices were sharp and certain, words carried the length of the lane-way, before silence flooded back. Hardy had never been to the sea but he imagined this might be how it was, the waves breaking and creeping away, sound and then hardly any sound at all.

'Did you ever go to the sea?' he asked, walking back into the warmth of the forge.

The ploughman shook his head.

'A few times,' the blacksmith said. 'Not a place to be of a day like this.'

And that was it. Hardy wanted to ask him about the sound of the waves, whether the water was loud when it turned to go back out, what kind of noise it made when it fell on stones and rattled them around, how it smelt and tasted. Things like that. But he knew he'd be wasting his time. Not that the blacksmith would laugh at him, just that he wouldn't have answers because he wouldn't have the interest.

'I'm just going over to Kinsella's for fags,' Hardy said. 'The horse'll be alright there. I'll be back to hold her.'

The forge yard, the lane and the village street were soundless. The schoolyard had emptied of children and crows swooped for crusts, scowling out at him from across the wall.

'And feck you, too,' he muttered.

Suddenly, he wanted the fog to lift, wanted to catch sight of the sun, wanted to know there was a blue sky up there, to be reassured that life was going on and would go on.

Clattering in the door of Kinsella's shop he said, loudly: 'Ten Woodbine, Bill, and I want you to be the first to know that I'm going to go and look at the sea before the summer is out.'

'Jaysus, good man yourself,' the shopkeeper said, already counting out the cigarettes. 'Give it my regards, when you get there.'

'I will because I'm going to do it. I decided coming up the street. There's going to be sun and warm days and dry land and weather that'll make people want to get out and enjoy themselves and, when it comes, I'm going to be on the bus and going to the seaside. The summer of nineteen and forty-seven is the summer John Hardy goes to the sea.'

'Would you say this weather's getting you down?'

Hardy laughed.

'It is but I'm serious about the sea. It's something I'm going to do. It's madness living to forty-seven years of age and never catching sight of it and we surrounded by it. So, it's done and decided, and there's the money for the fags.'

Cycling back to the farm, the mare trotting beside him, Hardy ignored the wet fog and imagined the sea. He allowed its resonance to build around him. Listened to the sound of water on the pebbles. A sound, he imagined, like mugs swinging and clinking gently on a dresser. Inhaled the smell of the seaweed, something sharp like nettles. Tasted salt on the air. Considered how the little runner waves might quiver at his feet.

He forgot the clock-clocking of the horse at his shoulder. Missed the outlines of the new houses down through Abbeyland and out the Mill Road. He would visit the sea, it was something he would definitely do. He had harboured notions, once, of singing with a dance-band, but they had faded. And, for years, there had been the possibility of marriage but that hope had sunk now and the woman was living in Birmingham. The last time she came home she had a husband on her arm and, when he met her on the Square, alone, all she'd said was: 'I couldn't wait forever.' So, dance-band or not, Mary Liddle or not, the sea would be his.

It was only the rise of Prumplestown Mill, among the fog-tattered trees, that brought him back, to or from his senses. Hupping the horse, he turned at the bridge and picked up speed on the last hundred yards, before angling in the gateway of the farm.

As he led the horse into the yard, Lawrence roared at him from the doorway of a shed the farm labourers used as a canteen of sorts.

'You must've smelled the tea. It's a good man gets back for the tea. And, I bet you, you forgot the fags.'

'God, I'm sorry, Paddy, clean forgot,' Hardy apologised but his grin gave him away.

When the men came out of the shed, twenty minutes later, the mist had thickened.

'Jaysus sake,' Lawrence said, 'this is enough to make a man go and stand in the canal.'

He looked up and down the yard. Hardy waited, wondering if he'd be sent home, knowing it would cost him half a day's wages.

'I'll tell you what, John. Take the horse and cart and throw a crowbar in the back and go up to the quarter field and pull out the three granite pillars along the primrose bank. The boss wants that fenced off with wood posts and wire, so we might as well get the pillars out of the ground and bring them back here. Do whatever you can.'

'Grand.'

'And take it nice and handy. There's another day's work in it. But, sure, who am I telling?'

'Thanks,' Hardy laughed.

When Dogger was in the shafts, Hardy threw a crowbar, a length of chain, two ropes, a shovel, a pick and a spade into the cart and covered them with a tarpaulin. Climbing into the seat, he jigged the mare out of the yard and onto the track that ran along the headlands of the fields. It was difficult to make out the gates until he was on them. He could see the outline of the hedges but not the wooden-barred gates.

'If we get lost in this, horse, we won't be found for a week,' Hardy said as he climbed down to open the first of four gates that would lead them up the back of Barn Hill.

The headland tracks were firm, despite the rain and snow of the previous months. Here and there, the wheels gave him trouble but, all in all, it was an easy journey.

Going up the last field, where the three granite pillars staggered crookedly on the headland, Dogger slowed and pulled to the side. Muffling his coat around him, Hardy sang to the horse, to calm her.

*'One night as I lay on my bed, a lying fast asleep,*
*by chance there came a pretty young girl, so bitterly she did weep.*

*She wept, she moaned, she tore her hair, crying: 'Alas what shall I do,*
*I must come into bed along with you in fear of the foggy, foggy dew.'*

Two fields away, through a break in the mist, Hardy could see the back wall of his own house. He got down from the cart and spoke to the mare.

'You stay here now, girl. Not a meg out of you till I run over and check the fire.'

Crossing the field, Hardy stopped at the ditch to check, but the mare was standing her ground. Pushing his way through the white thorns, he moved into the field that backed onto his garden. From there, it was only fifty yards to the orchard.

Going up the yard, he took two buckets from the coal shed and carried them into the house. Riddling down the ashes from the range, he threw in the slack and opened the damper slightly.

'That'll be a fire by the time I get home,' he said out loud.

Turning to go back out, he caught sight of an envelope on the mat inside the door. What was seldom was wonderful. And the stamp was English. Nine chances out of ten it was from his brother but then again, you never knew. His heart leapt. He put the envelope on the mantle. He'd save it, like a promise, and read it over his dinner. If it were from his brother there'd be plenty of news, enquiries about local characters, the pledge of a visit in the summer. Then again, it might be from someone else, from Mary Liddle. His name and address were carefully printed, the writing might be anyone's. You never knew!

And then he was out, cutting down through the orchard, over the ditch, across the field and through the second ditch. The mare was standing where he'd left her.

'Good girl, horse,' Hardy said loudly. 'Maybe we have the word between us.'

Taking the tools from the back of the cart, he set about his work. The granite posts, used as fence carriers, with the wire run through them, stood at the edges of fields all over the farm. In the previous two years, the boss had begun to replace them with wooden fencing. There was a shed in the low yard, filled with granite posts that had been taken out of the ground, hundreds of them in neat stacks. There was no doubting that the wooden fences were easier to wire but there was something about these pillars that was stout and reliable. And there was a tradition to them. They might be a hundred years in the ground, maybe longer. He had no real idea, but he did know local people had erected them, men like himself, farm labourers who were out in all kinds of weather. And there was a lot to be said for that, for the reminder that he was one in a line. The wooden posts might be there for fifteen years and then something else would replace them. They had no custom about them. You couldn't look along a fence of stakes and barbed wire and wonder about the men who put them there. You'd know who had done the work and when and how. You might, even, be replacing them in your own lifetime, three or four times in your own working days. There was no mystery about cutting and carting them. The wire and the posts came from Cope's. But these pillars were hacked out of the face of some granite cliff up in Wicklow, loaded onto sturdy carts and lugged down into Kildare. Slow days on the road before they were dropped off around the fields, buried feet deep in the sandy soil, chiselled and wired. There was work and sweat and history in them, something to be thinking about.

He spat on his palms, grabbed the pickaxe and started on the first pillar, peeling back the strips of sod and then driving the head of the tool well into the sand, cutting around the stone. To look at it, you'd expect the pillar to keel over but Hardy knew, from experience, that it was well buried, its root jammed hard with rocks and shale. He picked away at the ground, loosening the soil and the small stones. Then he took the shovel and cleared a dyke before picking deeper again.

Sweat bubbled on his face and he could feel it dropping from his armpits, streaming down his back and sides.

'Summer weather, horse,' he grunted over his shoulder.

He was digging deeper now, shovelling out fists of stone, the shovel catching on awkward corners of rock, levering them with the head of the pick, painstakingly rooting them out until, finally, the first pillar swayed slightly in the ground.

'Now, horse,' Hardy said. 'Your turn to do a bit.'

Putting one end of the chain around the pillar, he tied the other to the back of the cart and slowly urged the mare onward.

'Easy now, easy now, easy. Easy.'

His tone was low but firm.

He kept his eye on the pillar, watching its progress. Inch by inch it grated out of the rocky ground before falling quietly among the wet primroses.

'Good, horse. Good,' he said, patting the animal's head.

The second of the pillars, resting between two boulders, was going to be much more difficult. Again, Hardy dug a shallow trench. He'd have to move at least one of the boulders, if he were to loosen enough earth to pull out the pillar. Nothing for it but to dig the clay and gravel from around the boulder and then try to shift it with a crowbar and chain.

Methodically, he picked away at the sods, the clay, the sand and loam, opening a wound around the squat, mossy boulder. As he dug, the mare stirred uneasily, her harness creaking and brasses jingling dully.

'Easy, horse, easy now, good horse,' Hardy said, without looking up from his work.

But the horse didn't quieten. Instead, she backed away further, pushing the cart awkwardly behind her, the wheels catching and scraping on brambles. Hardy looked up from his work and into the animal's startled eyes. If she kept backing like this, she'd end up with the cart in the dyke. Dropping his shovel Hardy took the head collar, running his fingers inside it, soothing the animal, leading her gently away from the ditch and down along the headland.

'Easy there, horse. Easy on.'

He walked the horse twenty yards down the field, calming her as he went.

'What's at you, hah? What's at you? Now, take it easy there.'

He knew there was no point in trying to rush things and, anyway, he still had an hour's work ahead of him before he could even think of trying to chain and shift the boulder. No point in aggravating the animal in the meantime.

'Now, you stay there. Stay there, girl.'

Going back to his work, Hardy began to dig again. There was no telling how deep or wide the base of the boulder was. Better to dig now and clear away the shale and see the damage. The longest way round and all that.

He drove the spade into the ground. It sank cleanly and he lifted the sand and threw it to one side. And down, again, the face of the shovel shining after the wash of gravel. Each time he dug, the shovel face came up cleaner, catching whatever light there was in the dull afternoon. And then, the shovel jagged on something. Hardy propped it against the boulder and took up the pickaxe, angling the sharp head under the obstruction, prising it out of the ground. It came away easily enough and he bent to lift what appeared to be a soft rock from the ground. But it wasn't a rock. Turning the light shell in his hand he found himself staring into the empty eye-sockets of a yellow skull.

By the time Hardy and Paddy Lawrence had uncovered the rest of the skeleton it was getting on for dusk. The boss had gone off in his car to find Sergeant Kavanagh and Doctor Bates. In the meantime, the two men dug carefully around the remains of the body.

Hardy told his foreman about the mare's behaviour.

'And they'll tell you horses have no sense! What do people know? They know nothing.'

'How long do you reckon this fellow is here?' Hardy asked.

'Jaysus knows. Though he has the look of a Carlow man about him, the thin jaw and the sunk eyes'.

The two men laughed quietly.

'That's if it is a fellow.'

For some reason, the possibility that the skeleton they were exhuming was that of a woman seemed to subdue them. They worked on silently, brushing away the sand with their hands, the remains taking shape before their eyes. Finally they knelt beside the grave they had dug. Around and above them the birds sang in the early evening. And then, Hardy saw the metal piece, dull beside the finger bones.

'Paddy, look at this.'

'Take it out, give us a look.'

Hardy eased the metal band from beneath the bone and held it up in the light. It appeared to be a ring but it had turned green and rough from its time in the ground.

'The Lord have mercy on them,' he said.

When, finally, the boss arrived with the sergeant and the doctor, the skeleton had been fully uncovered. Hardy had put the skull back, more or less, where it belonged.

'A while there?' asked the sergeant.

The doctor knelt over the bones.

'Can't say, for certain, but he might be a hundred years. We'll find out.'

'It's a man, then?'

The doctor nodded

'This was under one of the hands,' Hardy said, handing the ring to the sergeant.

'Now,' the doctor said, finishing his examination. 'We'd better get him out of here. I'll get Carver to send out a hearse and a coffin, take him to Naas, put a date on him. Can we take him somewhere, in the meantime?'

'Put him in the cart, bring him down to the yard,' the boss suggested.

'I don't know that the mare'll take him. We can try but I doubt she'll do it,' Hardy said.

'She was always like that,' Lawrence said. 'She'd never pull a dead heifer out of the fields.'

'Right,' the doctor sighed. 'We'll just have to carry him.'

'There's a tarpaulin in the cart,' Hardy said, quietly. 'If you want, and I'm just saying, my house is only over the next field. We could take him there till Carver comes.'

'That'd be handy,' the sergeant said. 'If that's game ball with you, doctor.'

'Fine,' the doctor said and Hardy went to get the tarpaulin from the cart.

While Paddy Lawrence and the boss took the horse and cart back to the farm and the doctor went to get his car, the sergeant and Hardy carried the skeleton carefully in the tarpaulin, manoeuvring it through the gaps in the ditches.

'Reminds me of a murder I was on in Kilkenny one time,' the sergeant said. 'It was a day like this, thick fog, only November. We had to carry a body down through the woods to the road. It was in the mid-twenties, I was only a rookie, first time I'd ever seen a murdered body. There was blood dripping out of the blankets we were carrying the chap in. Put the heart crossways in me. At least this fellow is dry bones.'

When they reached Hardy's yard they left the tarpaulin in the shed and went inside the house.

The fire was blazing in the range, the kettle humming softly.

'A cup of tea, sergeant?'

'I wouldn't say no.'

The two men sat at the kitchen table and the policeman took the ring from his pocket and held it up to the light. It looked more black than green in the electric glow.

It was almost eight o'clock before the hearse arrived and the skeleton was taken away. Hardy had gone out with the sergeant, the doctor and the undertaker and held a lamp for them while they lifted the tarpaulin into a plain coffin and slid it into the back of the hearse. Sometime after nine, he sat down to his evening meal. The sergeant's words came back to him.

'Mark my word, John, once someone sees the hearse coming out your lane, they'll have it all over the town that you're dead.'

He smiled at the thought, it appealed to his sense of humour. He decided against going into Doyle's for a drink. If the word was out, it might as well take wings.

Only after he'd finished the meal and the dishes had been washed did he open the letter that had come that afternoon. It wasn't from Mary Liddle. Instead, he mulled over the news his brother had sent from England, smiled at the comments about men they'd grown up with, read that his niece was getting married in August and they'd love him to come over. His brother's letters came every three months or so – Christmas, spring, late summer and Hallowe'en, more or less – and they were always worth waiting for, packed with bits and pieces of gossip, sharp comments about the locals.

When he'd finished the letter he found a pen and a copybook and sat at the table to write back. He was glad to hear they were well. It was great news about Eileen. Yes, of course, he would come to the wedding, why wouldn't he?

He thought of the sea, again. Of sailing across it, seeing both shores. And he thought of Mary Liddle. The Castledermot community in Birmingham was closely knit. There was every chance she'd be at the wedding. It'd be nice to see her again. But he didn't say as much in the letter, just that he'd love to be there to share Eileen's day and it'd be great to see them all and to catch up with some of the old crowd.

And he had a bit of news himself, he'd found the remains of a body that very afternoon.

His letter ran to four pages and he read it over with satisfaction before putting it in an envelope and leaving it on the table for posting.

Lying in bed he pictured the scene when he'd walk into Doyle's the following night, half the village assuming he was dead, and he laughed out loud. And then he thought of Mary Liddle, ten years younger than himself, thirty-seven and still beautiful, so young looking, still so like the young girl he'd fallen in love with. He remembered singing for her, to her, on evenings when they were walking back to her house. She listened, took in the words, knew what they meant to him and why he was singing them to her.

And then he drifted off to sleep and woke around midnight to hear the wind blowing outside his window, rising with every gust, and knew the fog would be gone by morning. And he thought, again, of Mary, of singing for her, and he sang out loud in the dark, solid echo of his bedroom. Sang for her, for the first time in fifteen years.

*'There is a flower that bloometh, when autumn leaves are shed,*
*with the silent moon it weepeth, the spring and summer fled,*
*the early frost of winter, scarce its breath over cast.*
*Oh pluck it and it withers, tis the memory of the past*
*Oh pluck it and it withers, tis the memory of the past.'*

He lay in the darkness and sang, using the raging wind as a level, his voice rising above the gusts that roared through the trees around the house. He sang, he thought, like he had never sung before, his tenor coming back from the bare walls of the room, ringing around him, each line being swallowed by the echo of the one that had gone before.

*'It wafts its perfume on us, which few can e'er forget,*
*all the bright scenes gone before us, of sweet though sad regret.*
*Let no heart break its power, by guilty thoughts o'ercast,*
*for then a poisoned flower is the memory of the past,*
*for then a poisoned flower is the memory of the past.'*

# A Moment Beyond Paralysis

## PJ Cunningham

'Answer it, answer it,' she pleaded into the mouthpiece as the beep-beep sound continued for what seemed like an eternity.

She rechecked the number she had written down on a torn off piece of newspaper and wondered if perhaps in her state of near panic, she had dialled the digits incorrectly.

To calm herself, she went through the procedure again, this time more slowly.

One year into her search for her natural mother, Joan Palmer was at that moment suffused with a sense of failure on her mission.

As she stood in the booth the thoughts of twelve months graft flicked through her mind, particularly the obstinacy of the nuns, who had arranged her adoption? It was as if they enjoyed seeing her suffer. Then the coldness of the red tape from local civil servants, who had to finally hand over information on registration and birth.

Now, after all the leg work to get a number, it rang without being answered.

'I shouldn't have bothered,' she muttered to herself as her thoughts travelled backwards on her trail via London to the hotel kiosk in which she now stood.

Armed only with her mother's maiden name – Maria Walsh – and a vague description of her address – the Irish midlands – she arrived in Dublin to trawl through convent orders, adoption files and council records.

When she finally unearthed the number, the prospect carried a huge rush of elation but also a chill factor. And when the cold hand of fear touched her, she lay on the bed in her hotel room in a state of paralysis for a day before eventually summoning up the courage to ring.

Even then, she felt that if she did it from a booth in the hotel foyer, it would somehow make the first conversation with her mother easier than if she was in the wide expanse of a room.

She took a drag on her Rothmans cigarette and lifted her eyes to heaven as if in prayer.

'Please, please answer,' she entreated.

She was about to hang up when the phone was lifted at the other end.

'Hello,' said an unsure voice. 'Sorry for the delay but we were out in the garden. Who do you want to speak to, Bob is it?'

Joan dropped the cigarette out of her mouth with the shock – it burnt the back of her left hand as it fell. She gave an involuntary shriek with the pain.

'Oh, sorry, is that Maria?' she asked trying to suppress the rising excitement she felt.

'Who is this?' asked the voice suspiciously.

'Am I speaking to Maria?'

'Yes,' she said hesitantly. 'Who are you?'

'I'm Joan. Your daughter,' she said meekly.

There was no response at the other end. Joan tried to imagine what the voice looked like. One of the old nuns had finally broken ranks with others in the convent to tell her she remembered her mother: 'she had stunning high cheekbones just like you, dear, but she had dark raven hair.'

Further investigation revealed she had got in trouble as a student in Dublin, but her father, a doctor, had arranged for her to have the baby without the word ever filtering back to the community in the midlands.

Such a stigma would have ruined her prospects in life, the nun explained, especially of a good marriage.

Joan had often done a mental reconstruction of those months when her mother was pregnant and stashed away in a safe house. How had she felt?

How had she coped knowing that the baby growing inside her would be whisked away as soon as it was delivered?

Was there a relief to get rid of the baby or a huge wrench at seeing her own flesh and blood being given away?

Now though, she could sense panic at the other end of the line. She fancied she saw a grey-haired woman in her sixties, tall and thin, like herself, wondering what to do or say next.

'Are you there?' Joan asked kindly.

'Yes,' said the voice in a whisper.

'I need to see you,' she said, deciding that she would have to take the plunge by putting the hard question on the table.

'Never,' the voice said firmly. 'Never. Do you hear me?'

Joan whispered 'yes' into the mouthpiece with an unmistakable quiver in her voice.

'I don't ... I won't ... I can't ... please understand ... my husband, I could never ... didn't. He doesn't know. It would shatter him.'

She was all over the place as she tried to make a sentence to explain, but her conviction on the issue sounded so absolute that it didn't brook further discussion.

The tone told Joan she would bring that secret to the grave.

Now almost forty-seven, it was the death of her adoptive parents two years before which had triggered Joan's mind to trace her real mother. Her husband, Tim, was working as a computer programmer in Poland on contract for three months, and her daughter, Sally, was in her final year at medical college in Cambridge. As an out-of-work part-time actress, Joan felt she owed it to herself to find out where she came from.

But the journey was now at an end unless she could think of something very quickly.

'Can I call you then?' she asked longingly, as she begged to keep the line open.

'Please. Please don't. Let the past be in the past and God bless you. God bless you,' her mother said, a forlorn sob ending the sentence.

Then the phone went dead.

A pain welled up inside Joan like she had never known before. The pain of rejection. It hurt so much that she put her hands to her chest as she gasped for breath.

It felt like the time she nearly drowned on Brighton beach; the gasping for air, the fear before the strong hand of the lifeguard pulled her to safety.

But there was no one now to save her from this drowning. Like a deluge, the pain burst through her banks of resistance and she wept helplessly like a little girl in the hotel kiosk.

A man waited outside walking up and down briskly as if he wanted to use the phone. She turned her back on him. She was so weak she could not move. Several times, she tried to make a bolt for the sanctity of the bedroom. But her legs had turned into jelly and she felt totally incapable of walking across the foyer to the lift.

She thought she had come to terms with the darker age and Catholic Ireland and all it could and did throw at her. But this first-hand rejection totally unravelled her. It had knocked her senseless. Like a fighter in the ring who was taking a count after a knock down, she waited for her head to clear and the strength to re-enter her body.

It was the anger which worked as smelling salts to help her retrieve her senses. The anger of loss, not just for her, but for Sally, who would never now know her real grandmother.

As she began fidgeting with her cigarette box, she thought the best thing that could happen her world was if somehow the word 'adopted' could be dropped from the English vocabulary.

It was responsible for giving her the first numbing pain of her life – the day her mum and dad told her she was not biologically theirs, but adopted.

That led to long weeks of withdrawal from her parents and incarceration in her own mind.

But she came through this collision of two worlds – her own and a parallel one she knew nothing about – but it took time and, more importantly, it took the support of her parents for that to happen.

Alone now in the hotel foyer kiosk, she felt sorry she had started this quest.

Where was Tim? She wanted him there to hold her, to soothe away the numbing ache like her adoptive parents had done all those years ago.

How could that woman be so cruel? How could she herself hang up if it had been Sally at the other end of a line trying to trace her mother in similar circumstances?

She was about to immerse herself in the syrupy warmth of self-pity when she remembered her mum's dictum: 'Self-pity is pitiable.'

Mom was right. She took two deep breaths and opened the kiosk door, her head lowered to hide her reddened eyes, and crossed swiftly to the lift.

As she pressed the 'up' button, she recoiled at the face which looked back from the mirror. She pulled down a notice pinned beside the steel shutters of the lift and pretended to read it with interest.

She kept the printed notice up high, swung into the lift when it opened and was glad no one joined her in the ascent to the second floor.

In the few seconds it took going up, her eye caught the wording, which forced her to re-read it.

It said there was a seminar the following day for 'Blue Rinse Assurance', in the Redwood Suite.

It was as if a light had come on inside her head. Instantly, she felt the blood course through her veins, her heart pump stronger. When the lift doors parted, she strode with purpose towards her room.

The notice was fate's hand intervening. Instinctively, she was back on the trail and ready to go for it.

As an actress she would play the most meaningful role she had ever taken on. She would take on the bearing of an insurance rep; she would find some material at the seminar which would help authenticate her appearance for her day on the midland's beat, and she would see her mother in the flesh by hook or by crook.

Then and only then could she go back to Tim and Sally knowing she could rest easy about this unread chapter in her life?

*   *   *

She half-slept the night in the company of a tapestry of imagined conversations, rejections, hugs and kisses.

Before she woke up she had a dream where a little girl was playing with her doll. When she put the little doll in the pram, it rolled away from her.

The more she tried to run after it, the further away the pram appeared to be. She woke determined not to be the doll in the pram.

*   *   *

It rained incessantly on the taxi ride from Jury's Hotel in Ballsbridge to Heuston Station and continued all the way on her journey down to the midlands.

She thought of Shakespeare and of countless directors telling her classes of the importance of pathetic fallacy. She chuckled to herself as she watched the unremarkable flat plains whisk by quicker and quicker as the diesel train gathered momentum on the straight tracks now that it was out of the city.

After a short while, she recognised the Curragh. Tim, a keen fan of the turf, flew over to Ireland every year for the Derby. She always tuned in without interest because she thought she might see him in the crowd.

Then the landscape changed to the beauty and intricacy of the Monasterevan viaduct. This fascinated her, but before she could take it in, she was back into the poor rush-strewn land. The bogs around Portarlington reminded her of the moors she visited as a child in England. They were dark and unwelcoming and appeared totally lifeless in the evening downpour.

Subconsciously, she had begun lifting her feet ever so slightly off the floor each time the train passed a telegraph pole.

She was regressing into the little girl who played this game with her mother when they went down to Gran's house in Brighton. It was silly she knew, but she continued to do it.

She was, after all, living out her pathetic fallacy part.

*   *   *

It was, she was told, quite a walk from the station to where her real mother lived.

She passed a council housing estate and a TV repair man pointed the way from there up to the house. He estimated she would have to walk a mile and a half.

He had a moustache and a lecherous look and gave Joan the once over as he pointed animatedly with his right hand. 'Of course, seeing as it is raining I could always drive you up,' he ventured.

'No thanks,' Joan replied curtly. 'I prefer to walk.'

She preferred the walk indeed because in her mind, she knew that even if her cock-and-bull story about Blue Rinse Assurance didn't hold up, they might take pity on a poor wet waif and invite her inside out of the rain.

The TV man had said the house she was looking for had redbrick pillars, so she couldn't miss it.

As she walked up over the Railway Bridge and the rising road to the edge of the bog, her mind ran ahead of her. She was a little girl in her mother's town going up and down to the shops. She would have done so happily until someone asked her about her dad. And then her mother would have told her she had no father. And then she would have lived with a big black mark in the community until she was old enough to go away and live in England, or some other place where birth outside of wedlock was not a damning verdict on an innocent head, for the rest of her life.

She wept softly as she explored the parallel universe her life could have experienced. As she approached the house in the distance, she was happy to have made her mind up on one thing – what her mother had done was the greatest act of altruism that one human being could do for another.

She was shivering as she opened the ornate gate – partly from the wet and partly with nerves and expectation.

God, she was tired – tired from the walk and the train journey and of what now lay before her. Like in the hotel phone booth, she knew she must push herself beyond the paralysis of the moment.

She felt weak as she passed in through the most wonderfully manicured lawns, overhanging bushes and aisles of busty rhododendrons, which led up to a dark blue doorway. The rain had lightened off a little, changing from continuous heavy drops into a web of moisture dampening her face.

She took out her Blue Rinse material from her carrier bag and rang the doorbell.

A dog barked immediately and ran to the inside of the door. She heard an internal door opening and a voice – that of a woman – talk in soft tones to the animal.

'Okay, Shelly, quiet girl, quiet.'

The door half-opened before getting stuck. For a few seconds, the person grappled with the door before forcing it over the blood red mat. A finely-built woman with soft blue eyes and high cheekbones squinted as she tried to focus on Joan's face.

It was like looking into the mirror at the lift back in the hotel. She felt her own face – with the addition of a few wrinkles and a greying of the hair – would end up very like the woman in front of her.

She composed herself and put on as winsome a smile as she could muster.

'Hi, sorry for disturbing you, but I was wondering if I could take your time for a few minutes,' she asked using the best Irish accent from her acting repertoire.

'Step in love, sure you're drenched,' said the slightly hesitant voice she thought she recognised from the telephone conversation from two days before.

The woman led Joan into the sitting-room where everything was showhouse clean and neat. 'This is Bob, my husband.'

Bob looked up from his newspaper, took his pipe out of his mouth, stood up and shook her hand warmly.

'Would you like a cup of tea, a ghrá?'

'Yes, I'd love one,' she said.

'And you'll have one, Maria?'

His wife nodded.

They watched him walk from the room into the back kitchen.

'Have a seat,' offered Maria as she pointed to the burgundy coloured *chaise longue*, which was placed at an angle alongside the glowing fireplace.

Now for the hard part, thought Joan. 'Please excuse me,' she said. 'My name is Joan and I'm from Royal Liver. We're starting this new policy for people who are ... have ... are looking for late life assurance. I just wondered if you need any?

That was pretty pathetic, thought Joan, but at least she had engaged the conversation, however phoney or unlikely she had come over.

'Oh, I leave all that to Bob, dear. We'll ask him when he comes back in.'

Joan wanted to look more than talk but she knew she would have to keep the conversation going to get a chance to scrutinise the face of the woman that begot her.

She would love to have hugged her mother at that final confirmation but she couldn't. She wanted to cry, to scream, to allow the best part of half a century of untapped emotion to flow into this chamber of her mother's doll's house.

Instead she exaggeratedly gestured towards her bag and flicked at papers in her free handout file. She took out a load of different assurance options and put them on the *chaise longue* beside her.

Bob brought in a tray with tea, scones, milk and butter. 'I hope you don't take sugar, we haven't for years and we don't buy it anymore, isn't that right love?'

Maria nodded as she began to pour the tea.

'No, I don't take it in tea, only in coffee,' Joan replied.

Maria gave the assurance papers to Bob, but he just laughed. 'I hope you won't feel offended,' he chuckled, 'but we're over endowed on these types of things. You see there's only two of us and we even have our funerals paid for.'

Their chuckles turned into a laugh. Joan thought it polite to join in.

'I sure know how to pick good clients then,' she ventured. They all laughed again.

She ate the currant scone, accepted Maria's invitation of another and told her they were the nicest she had ever tasted.

Maria glowed at the compliment. She lifted her toes up and down off the ground in a ritual, as if she too was making a train journey.

Joan complimented them on the warmth of the open fire. Maria told her that Bob had cut all the ash logs himself from the wood and the turf from behind the house.

'Look, you have the steam rising in me,' laughed Joan as the moisture from her walk begun to evaporate in front of the fireplace.

This time the old couple watched the grey steam on its journey from Joan's trousers and chuckled politely. Nervously, Joan laughed louder as she watched their reaction. Then, their ripples of laughter turned into fission – as if they had been waiting to explode for a long, long time.

The flames lapped their tongues longer and longer around the logs which, spent of sap, succumbed to the fire's growing intensity.

Joan watched in an almost hypnotic state as the fire danced from core to flame in a variety of sunflower colours. She had found a sacred moment of communion in the presence of her mother and she wanted it to last. The thought released a calm inside that her she had never previously known.

She would drink of this wondrous hemlock, savour every nuance of its flavour here in the sitting-room of the doll's house and then bring it with her. This sacred moment would sustain her for the rest of her life.

She would close her eyes so that every little intimacy would be remembered as if they were on celluloid.

Bob tip-toed quietly as he collected up the cups, plates and teapot and put them back on the tray. He went out to the kitchen where he washed up the delph quietly and quickly.

Coming back into the room, he saw the fire was still gathering strength and did not need stoking.

From behind the sofa, he watched his wife of forty-five years gently stroking the visitor's cheek. She smiled at the sleeping person before her with a look of happiness he had not seen before.

Bob turned around and stole quietly out to the kitchen again.

'Poor Maria,' he thought to himself with a sadness of heart.

'She would have loved a daughter like that.'

# Help!

*Dermot Healy*

He came to town with a kitbag on his back
a tourist from France
and went off with a map to see
The sights of Sligo.

He did not come back that night
Nor the next, nor after
and the B and B,
Rang the police.

The search began. A treck
Through Hazelwood. A boat to
Inishfree. Maybe out to Glencar.
And perhaps Yeats's Grave.

Then someone thought of
Diarmuid and Gráinne's Grave.
A climb was made
And at the entrance

They found him dead
Of a broken leg
Shouting Help!
Like all travellers do

In a different language.
Help! to the tourists below
Who might have thought
He was telling them

Keep off his land.
Help! to the shepherd
The circling rook, The RTÉ mast
To all in his guide book.

But I doubt anyone heard
Him. I never really heard him myself
Till this morning. His bone-pain
And thirst and cold

Suddenly imploded inside my head
And after years of telling the story
I heard him yell
At my kitchen table

As he lay there
Miserable, broken-legged,
Alone
At the high dark entrance

To the Lover's Cave
Eating the last
Of what he'd brought
With him as he waited

To be saved.
And what a terror to die
Overlooking the view
Of the Horsehoe

Glen, that steep fall
Into beauty,
The quarry, the plantation,
With the bone gnawing

Away at his brain
As the heavens opened
One last time.
His cry of pain

Echoing through
The Valley of Jealousy,
Till at last it reached me
Here, years later,

Broken-shouldered
Too late to help,
Painkillers to hand,
Crying for all who make

The lovers' climb
And reach the top
Enter, fall, and call to no one
On the dark beautiful incline.

*Dermot Healy,*
*Sligo, June 2002.*

# A Letter to Olive
## (Who died June 25, 2001)

*John Quinn*

*My* darling,

They say it's good to write, so here goes. It's entirely appropriate anyway. Thirty-five years ago I courted by letter. We were patients in a TB sanatorium and the day I saw this vision in a black leather coat I was smitten!

It was March 1st 1966 and that evening I put pen to paper. Tentative first step! As for the postal system within the sanatorium – we were dependent on a friendly nurse or porter to smuggle letters from one unit to another. Just like boarding school! What a way to treat twenty-somethings – but it worked.

And then the waiting. And then … the reply! We were up and running! The letters continued. Wonderful, wonderful letters that brightened up long boring days, weeks, months … Wonderful, wonderful letters where we gradually unfolded our personalities and slowly learned about each other. And then we actually met, six weeks later at Mass on Easter Sunday morning (how appropriate), it only confirmed what I was already feeling. This was no pen-pal exercise.

Do you remember the Bank Holiday Monday when we went for a walk, slipped away through the woods and walked around the sanatorium boiler-house seventeen times? Exotic or what? It was the most wonderful day of my life up to then. I was in love.

What you saw in me then I do not know, but thank you for all seventeen laps. And thank you for replying to that first letter. It was meant to be. Little did either of us think on entering the sanatorium that we would meet our life-partner. Two-and-a-half years later we married. It was meant to be. Thank you, my love.

A few weeks after your death I came across those first letters again. I had kept yours in a biscuit tin for thirty-five years and never looked at them. I suppose I knew there would be a day … I was delighted to find that you had kept some of my letters too. I read them in tears, and just fell in love with you all over again. It was a beautiful feeling. I walked on air just as I had all those years ago. Everything was possible. Nothing was a problem, except for one thing. You were no longer physically present … But the wonderful innocence of those letters, the gentle unfolding of those personalities, the gradual realisation of love. Thank you. Again.

It hasn't been all joy of course. Far from it. The emptiness, the loneliness. And the regrets. If only I had done this, hadn't done that, had said this, hadn't said that … I KNOW it's wrong to be like that. All the textbooks, all the counsellors tell you not to think like that. I know. But I'm human …

And I know they weren't thirty-years of unending bliss … (far from it, I hear you sigh!) Arguments, disagreements, rows. Irritation. Exasperation. All the 'stuff' that got in the way. Money problems, health problems. Worries over children. LIFE! We stuck at it. The foundations were solid. It was meant to be.

That's why I tell couples now to cherish the arguments and rows. They are part of the warp and woof of married life. I know it's hard to see it at the time, but believe me, the scales have been lifted from my eyes. I can see clearly now. For putting up with my stubborness, selfishness, stupidity, thank you, my love.

And of course it wasn't all black! We had wonderful times, memorable days, deeply-cherished moments. Just look at the photographs (how I cherish them now). The laughter, the smiles, the memories. And not always the BIG occasions. Very often it's the little things that warm me now …

## TRIVIA

Let us talk of trivia ...
Inconsequential
Insignificant
Half-remembered things.
What the children did.
And said;
Characters we met,
The antics of
A much-loved pet;
Our secret language –
'The K is B, (kettle is boiling!)
I'd love a tup of tea' –
Nothing events
Like the note I left
'I leaned against
The washing machine
And set it going ...'
You laughed so much
Like I said
Silly, inconsequential
Trivial things.
Things that bound us
Together
Impenetrably ...

For all the trivia, thank you, my darling ...

John O'Donoghue has put it beautifully: 'The kingdom of memory is full of the ruins of presence.' His writings have been a great consolation to me over the past few months (or is it centuries?). He also quotes Meister Ekchart in maintaining that the souls of the dead don't 'go' anywhere. They are here with us all the time. 'You can sense the presence of those you love who have died. With the refinement of your soul, you can sense them. You feel that they are near.' *(Anam Chara)*

I'll second that. I believe in your 'presence'. That's why I talk to all the time ('Much more than you did when I was here,' I hear you sigh!). That's why I write to you every night (You see I'm still courting you!). The damnburst in my heart has released the most intimate outpourings …

That's why I recognised you in St Stephen's Green, four weeks after you died. There I was, sitting on a bench remembering a lovely evening a year ago when we sat on a bench in the Green, just enjoying the loveliness and contentment of it all. There I was with my memories when I was accosted by a down-and-out who proceeded to tell me his life story. A former jockey who fell foul of the racing law, hit the bottle, lost his home, marriage broke up, now living rough. A most engaging fellow, not in any way obnoxious.

I thought to myself: Olive would love this guy, knowing her feeling for the downtrodden. I gave him a few bob and stood up to go. For some reason I told him how I had lost you suddenly a month earlier. He put his arms around me, whispered in my ear '*the seed in your heart shall blossom*' and walked away.

I was totally stunned. When I looked back he waved to me and mimed that sentence again. Weird! Wonderful! We talk of drink, gambling, broken marriages, etc. and then he comes out with this poetry.

Only then did I realise that it was you or your angel. Had to be. I'm totally convinced of that. And of course you (he) were right. The seed in my heart has blossomed, wonderfully, beautifully – and continues to blossom. Thank you, my darling.

Let nobody think it's easy though. It's a hard and lonely road and ultimately it's a road you walk alone. I MISS YOU! Terribly. Frighteningly. You were so much part of the fabric of my life, the warp and woof of my existence.

Only now do I realise that you were truly and literally my 'other half' and that with your going a great part of me has gone too. And I owe you so much … and never told you how much! Well I'm telling you now. You made me the person I am. My real date of birth was March 1st 1966. Do I make myself clear? I NEED YOU. Now more than ever. So stay very close to me, please. Or else I shall fall apart …

## AS I MOWED THE LAWN AT SUNSET

As I mowed the lawn at sunset
Did I see you
Give a little wave
On returning from your walk?
Did I see you
Move about the kitchen
Making your 'tup of tea'?
Did I watch you
watch the sun set
From your conservatory chair?
Did I smile as you gesticulated
To a friend on the phone?
Did I notice you
Glide past the window
With a little glass of Muscadet?
And when the dark descended
And I came in
Exhausted
Did I hear you call out
'If you're making
A tup of tea
I wouldn't mind another one ...?'
Of course I did
But when I went to make it
The dark was all around ...

*Love you. Miss you. Thank you.*
*John xx 29 October 2001*

# Treasure Island

*Anthony Glavin*

$\mathcal{T}he$ summer Mam got sick, Pops put Brian and me on a plane to Ireland. It sounds straightforward now, but travelling from downtown Boston to Donegal in 1964 was like journeying to another planet. Both Brian and I were wide awake when we landed at Shannon, the sky above unlike any sky we'd ever seen. Giant clouds scudding past as the sun broke through, highlighting trees and fields greener than I ever imagined. We stood inside the small terminal, myself clinging to my brother, until a woman who looked like a slightly younger version of Mam detached herself from the crowd behind the red braided rope. 'You must be Brian?' said Aunt Chrissie whom we'd never met. 'And this is Maeve,' shaking both our hands before taking our baggage checks.

I clearly remember that journey from Shannon up to Donegal. Crammed into the back seat of a neighbour's Morris Minor which seemed as foreign as everything else – the narrow roads or the acrid turf smoke in the small villages at which our driver periodically stopped. Twice we followed him into tiny shops – shops with a dark room attached, where our driver knocked back what looked like a massive glass of creamy root beer. Just as foreign was the way everybody said 'Cheerio', which Brian and I knew as a breakfast cereal. Or the cup of tea and tomato sandwich we got in the second shop-cum-pub, both of us exchanging a quick glance at the bizarre idea of tomato on its own, but both too mannerly and too scared to ask for a peanut butter and jelly sandwich instead.

The rest of the journey was a blur, the excitement which had us wide awake at Shannon giving way to utter exhaustion. All I recall is being jolted awake on the bumpy roads, marvelling momentarily at the sunlit hedgerows, then nodding off again. Or later waking to marvel at our driver, steering with his head stuck out the window into a fine mist, which I assumed was to afford a better view of the road ahead, but suspect now was more a stratagem designed to keep himself awake after an extended pit stop in what must have been Bundoran, where Brian and I were allowed down onto what we'd have called a beach, not a strand. To throw stones into the breakers, while I tried not to cry at being the breadth of that same Atlantic from Mam and Pops.

Two hours later we reached Glenmore, fifteen miles west of Killybegs. Chrissie's cottage, which had been Mam's home too, sat up a long lane just outside the village. Uncle Hughdy came out from the small byre just as we pulled up. Stockier than his sisters, he spoke sharply to the black and white dog that had chased our car up the lane, then shook our hands as Aunt Chrissie had done. After that he just stood there, dressed in a tweed cap, old suit jacket, and dirty dark trousers tucked into muddy black rubber boots. Looking like any man his age and station in the West of Ireland, he looked unlike anyone Brian or I had ever seen.

Inside the cottage was as strange – the wooden table and chairs, the open fire, the hearth brush fashioned from chicken feathers. Or the chicken itself which kept jumping onto the window ledge and peering in. We had our first fry that evening, eggs which Chrissie had gathered from a nest in the byre, to my amazement. Plus a pink plump sausage that was nothing like the shrivelled brown specimens we ate in Boston. We were put to bed immediately following, exhausted by jet lag, and the weirdness of it all. Chrissie and Granny slept in the upper bedroom, while Brian and I had cots in the lower bedroom, where Uncle Hughdy also slept. 'Are youse still awake?' Hughdy asked when he came in. When both Brian and I answered yes, Hughdy led us in a prayer: *'And if I die before I wake, I pray the Lord my soul to take.'* Moments later I pulled the bedclothes up to muffle my sobs, terrified the Lord might think I was ready to die at age ten.

I found Brian outside the cottage that next morning, holding his baseball glove and ball, and looking for a wall against which to play 'outs'. The day was cool, and the ground muddy underfoot from heavy showers the night before that began just as I was finally falling asleep. So we played that morning instead with a pair of untamed cats that raced around the byre. Or tried to play, for they never let us near all summer. Lolly the sheepdog also ignored us outdoors, but he'd let us scratch him behind the ears in the kitchen, the closest thing to a pet we ever had.

All of it remained alien at first, but children adapt quickly, and after a few weeks we had fairly settled in. We had chores; mine included helping Chrissie with the washing up, while Brian went out a few times a day with a bucket to the turf stack beside the byre, bringing in sods enough to keep the fire going. Chrissie also showed me how to tease the wool which she spun into yarn that Hughdy would weave into tweed winters in the loom shed down the lane. I know that sounds like Bord Fáilte's Ireland – tiny thatched cottages beside salmon-lepping streams – but Chrissie had an actual spinning wheel which she kept behind her chair when she wasn't using it. There was also a butter churn which Chrissie and I cranked for what seemed forever, whenever she had enough cream set by. I thought the homemade butter tasted a bit off, however, which meant I ate my bread, both home-bake and shop-loaf, dry.

Brian and I had plenty of time to play too, there being no TV in the house, just an old radio that Chrissie called a wireless. We weren't allowed down the road to the sea, but we were let roam the hill behind the house. It's hard to imagine a landscape – or an experience – so different to what we knew from Boston, but that's exactly what we had that summer. And there are moments I can recall so clearly yet – and probably always will. Rainbows like coloured brushstrokes on the mountain opposite, or sunlight breaking through clouds to highlight swathes of heather and bracken like a spotlamp. Or pausing one afternoon on the hill just to listen to the sound of the wind in the grass. Of course I didn't know to call things by their proper names yet – bracken was 'ferns' to me – but I was slowly getting to know the things themselves.

We even gradually grew accustomed to our relations. Chrissie was often cross but she seldom went 'missing' like Mam often would – lost in a fog of her own making. Plus she asked countless questions about Boston, our apartment, Mam's job in Filene's Basement, and so forth. Of course I wanted to ask as many questions back, only I hadn't the nerve. Like why had Chrissie never visited us in Boston, or how come she wore a scarf in the house?

Even more remarkable is how we grew used to Uncle Hughdy, even though I was initially terrified of him. Not just his prayers about dying, but his large nicotine-stained hands, or the fact that he always kept his cap on indoors. By our third week, however, Brian and I were following him and Lolly up the hill after sheep. Or up to the bog on the mountain opposite, where we helped turn the turf he'd already cut and thrown along the bank. It was a hot, dry week early in July, which pleased Hughdy no end. 'Sure, they're turning up like sausages,' he enthused, pouring out tea from an old lemonade bottle and handing us each a hard-boiled egg. It was lovely up there on the bog, skylarks singing themselves silly overhead, the sea all shimmery and turquoise in the distance. And warm enough to make you drowsy, only I was terrified of falling asleep, in case the sun on the glasses I'd got that spring made me burst into flames!

It was on the bog that week we three became friends, even if we didn't talk much. Hughdy loved the tiny transistor radio Mam had sent over for him, bringing it along every day and carefully propping it on a few lumps of turf. Brenda Lee had a big hit that summer, and Hughdy loved her voice so much he cut her name into the turf bank, so as to remember it. And you could still make out the lettering weeks later, when we returned to load the turf onto the trailer behind a neighbour's teensy tractor.

One August evening Brian and I saw a small brown animal darting along the turf stack by the byre. It was about half the size of a grey squirrel on the Boston Common – which was the only wildlife we knew. Only it was even quicker, threading its way into the stack like it had no backbone at all.

'A weasel,' Hughdy said when he came home from the bog. That night he spoke more about them. How as a youngster he'd once seen weasels swarming over a tossed ditch. 'Thousands,' he said, sounding like he meant that many, not just a lot. 'Running in and out, like the one youse saw today. It must've been a funeral I saw, for if one dies they all gather round.'

'Will you stop frightening the child!' Chrissie said, seeing me shudder. But Hughdy paid her no mind, going on to say a purse made from their skin was extremely lucky.

Possibly because neither Brian nor I laughed at the weasels, Hughdy began to tell us other stories too. About the fairy shilling a strange woman once gave to a neighbour. Or a story about another neighbour farther up the glen, who Hughdy said could bring the sea into your kitchen, and have you up on the table for fear of the waves. I loved the stories, which invariably featured some corner of Glenmore, an actual rock or bend in the road, making them seem realer than real. But I still went to bed most nights half-terrified, fearful I'd meet my double or a pooka in my dreams. And I still got homesick, usually at bedtime.

But most of the time I was content. Chrissie was teaching me how to knit and while she was often quiet like Mam, she didn't seem as abstracted – as if she were always elsewhere – and I was learning to relax within her silences. But it was Hughdy who truly made that summer, once he got used to the idea of us. Certainly I struggled to understand him a lot of the time. 'Stupid as mud is, there's a trade to it,' he might declare, clearing a drain in the field below the cottage. A field which he insisted on calling a *park*, though it looked nothing like the Boston Common or Public Gardens. Just rushes and ragwort in lieu of the lovely flowerbeds I waited on every spring to bloom.

A few nights before we left, Hughdy told us one last story. 'Did youse ever hear about the O'Byrnes and the evil fairies?' he began. Never before had he given names to a story, but I was too keen for him to continue to notice. Anyhow, he went on to tell of this treasure trove buried in a Donegal hill. Only a family of O'Brynes knew where it was hidden, yet to this day it lay unclaimed.

'How come?' interrupted Brian.

'I'm coming to that part now,' said Hughdy. 'There was a kind of a curse, you see, attached to the treasure by these evil fairies. Three O'Byrnes have to die, digging it, before it can be unearthed.'

Suddenly I remembered helping Mam address her few Christmas cards last November, printing THE O'BYRNE FAMILY, GLENMORE, CO DONEGAL, IRELAND on an envelope.

'Are you, Mam, and Chrissie those O'Byrnes?' I blurted.

'Aye, now you have it,' Hughdy said, giving me a queer stare. I glanced at Chrissie who usually paid no attention to Hughdy's yarns. But this time

Chrissie stared straight back, shaking her head a little, like a raven in the know.

If I was spooked, Brian was nearly jumping out of his skin. 'Have you dug it up yet, Hughdy?' he shouted.

'I'm after telling you three O'Byrnes have to die digging it,' Hughdy fixed him with the same strange stare. 'Only two have died so far.'

That shut Brian up good. Nor did Hughdy say anything for a time.

'Do you know where it's buried, Hughdy?' I finally asked.

'Oh, aye,' said Hughdy. 'I do, surely.'

'Will you show us?' Brian asked, almost whispering now.

'Oh, aye, some day maybe. If you come back another summer.'

* * *

Mam seemed better when Brian and I came home that September. Less anxious and distracted. What's more, I came home in a small way more able for life myself. Not consciously so, for what are you conscious of at age ten? But I do believe I was more able for my differences. Donegal was already like a dream – the cottage, Chrissie, Hughdy, the bog, mountains and sheep. So different to shiny, up-to-date Boston, far too different to explain to the few friends I had. But my Donegal summer wasn't a troubling *difference* – unlike my parents' Irish accents, or my mother's odd ways. Or how we lived in a downtown building where Pops was the Super, instead of a proper neighbourhood like everybody else.

'What did you do last summer?' somebody'd ask at school.

'My brother and I went to Ireland.'

'What was that like?'

'Okay,' I'd say. Or 'Cool.'

But that was all. I didn't have to say anything more – nor could I have. Instead Glenmore remained a secret, like buried treasure, to which only I had the map.

# Snow House

## Meeghan Piemonte

*The* entrance has been smoothed to a clean curve of ice. The sun throws a thin line of colour along its wet surface before I lean forward and make a shadow with my shoulders. I fold at the knees and waist and push my head cautiously in. The snow walls are glowing; the light is caught in sharp geometric spaces too small to see, like morning wound in fragile ice-sliver fingers.

Matthew is just there, playing at the rough surface of the glowing wall. He's dropped his borrowed mittens and is putting his bare fingertips to the cold snow.

Lunch.

'You'll go call him in, won't you?' My sister had arrived without a proper coat. She had stepped off the airplane with just an olive-coloured raincoat thrown over her arm.

'Oh, I have the lining in my bag.'

'We have over a foot of snow,' I told her and wondered how she could grow up in New England and still show up for a visit in January wearing sling-back shoes. I brought the car around and when we arrived home, I pulled out extra sweaters from their cedar-scented boxes. She took two and angled the armchair so that she could leave her feet propped on the hissing radiator, which was how she was set when I announced lunch. She told me to go and collect her son from the snow igloo at the corner of the yard.

Matthew has been out here for more than an hour already. Without the mittens I'm afraid he may have let the cold burn his skin. I was afraid to leave him out here in the first place, alone, while I prepared lunch and my sister surrounded herself with wool. Matthew is seven and this is his first visit here.

This is the first snow he will remember. I would have imagined myself teaching him to pack a good hard snowball, hunting the refrigerator for a carrot and the front-hall closet for an old hat and scarf, and rolling long strips of snow into three misformed spheres. I would have imagined grabbing him around his soft snow-suited middle and lifting him up to choose the spot for the carrot nose. As it is, I'm afraid to reach across this snow dome to tap his shoulder. Last time I saw him, he was five and crouched in the corner of his own living room, waving a piece of paper furiously in front of his face.

The snowplough wakes me in the mornings. First the scrape of its metal edge moving forward and back on the tar, then the strain of its motor lifting the rusted metal cup, then the soft thump of snow against snow, and finally the light tin clang as the blade hits the newly-bare road. Three days ago the snow mound at the corner of the street and the corner of our yard was only as high as my waist. This morning, when I sat up and looked out, its peak was touching the edge of the green street sign. The boys from the yellow house were out with shovels and their father, hollowing it out.

They've gone in to steam their crisp socks and mittens on their own hissing radiators and they've left the igloo silent and glowing for Matthew to explore alone. I turn my shoulders and edge myself in. At the center I can almost stand. Matthew will hear me and turn. I'll say 'lunch', and wave him back out with me to the house. His mother will unzip his jacket and pull off his rubber boots and socks. I'll hang them to dry. Unless he turns and, seeing me, screams and begins to wave his hands fast, to flutter them like two butterflies accidentally caught in this frozen globe that lets only the wrong kind of light bounce off their wings. I reach back for the smooth ice edge of the door. He has not turned yet. I'll go back and say I couldn't catch his attention. His mother can stick her feet in my boots, I've warmed them now, and run out and call him in.

With my fingers along the edge of the door, I can feel the wind rush over the curved exterior. I realise that I cannot hear the wind or the cars passing through the brown slush on the main road.

My brother built an igloo like this when I was small. He waited for the plough to push the snow up in a mound to reach the street sign, then he went out with an empty coffee-can and hollowed out the mountain. The snow must have been dirty and the surface of my brother's igloo must have been, like this one, marbled with the watering lines of mud and speckled with gravel. But I remember it white, white and silent.

The door was slight and short. My brother could pass through only by sitting down, angling his shoulders in and then dragging his long legs behind him. My mother, curvy and plump, couldn't pass through at all. The igloo lasted for weeks in the still winter air. I spent hours in its silent interior, believing I had found the dead centre of the earth.

We kept stores of ammunition by the door, snowballs to keep the neighbours, and sometimes my sister, out. We used hot water and spoons to make carvings in the ice walls. Those walls, too, glowed underneath our fingers.

I move in from the door again and reach along the wall. I draw closer to Matthew and try to scratch a design in the packed snow. He watches me awhile and then I notice that his thin fingers have already gone whiter than the glowing walls. Lunch, I think to say, but don't. This silence that expands and contracts with our breathing has grown familiar again. I shift my head towards the door and Matthew comes close and wraps his arms around my neck. He wants a piggy-back, and I remember that this is how my brother coaxed him from the corner that day in the living-room when I backed away from the paper which he was fluttering and beginning to tear.

I crouch and let him onto my back. His body is like a sweater someone has just taken off and wrapped around my shoulders. I think that we will not fit through the door like this but it is wide, wide enough.

# Roadkill

## Peter Woods

*I never* knew why I took up with him that time. I had a week before the job in Cologne started and I already had a gang. Mick Coen and Ready-Mix were going south with me. A trip to Amsterdam must have seemed like a diversion – two days there and back. I was to meet Roadkill in the banhof in Hanover on Wednesday.

He was late. A group of Turks had already boarded the train before an apocalyptic voice boomed out over the tannoy listing stops and destination. They had been alerted by the barely perceptible increase in the noise its engines made. They were well used to trains, the Turks. I saw him coming through the crowd towards me, rather I saw his top hat over everyone else's heads.

'Where the fuck were you?' I asked.

Within minutes he was asleep in the carriage. The last thing he said, the only thing he said that made any sense was, 'Look, whatever you do don't call me Roadkill until we're off this train.'

'Why?'

'Just don't. You'll see.'

I should have known then that it'd all go wrong. I should have got off the train at the next stop and left him sleeping. Sure didn't I know well enough that it wasn't the Van Gogh Museum we were going to see. I was thinking of him the night before in the bar near the station in Hanover. It was no different than the bars he'd favoured in Bremerhaven. Places down on the docks, lost to geography. Neither in nor out of the red light districts. Dingy, crepuscular places stuffed with narrow booths and battered furnishings, the bar scuffed and gouged, the walls and floors splattered with people's blood and sweat and another type of person – those that just don't have a clue – would describe it all as 'character'.

It was in such a place in Bremerhaven that he'd taken up with two Argentine sailors. Their boat had lisped into port, an old-style tramp steamer that had been involved in every dodgy enterprise since Joseph Conrad had hove to within sight of the mouth of the River Thames. The Argentinians were intent on off-loading some undefined contraband and Roadkill was willing to act as a conduit. Their English was perfunctory, his Spanish non-existent. It did stretch to calling them *amigos* though. They were saturnine and taciturn, but then they didn't need to speak, didn't get a chance. Roadkill greeted them like revolutionary confrères, high fiving and back slapping and rattling on about Franco, Zapata and Pancho Villa. I became accessory to this.

'You speak Spanish don't you?' he said.

My Spanish was like my German, or my French indeed – I could find an ill-lit bodega, bôite or kniepe in any town.

I went along out of curiosity and dragged Ready-Mix with me – on a last minute whim – as security. 'Muscle,' Roadkill called us. Not that we made much impression on the Argentinians. They were exasperated to see us. Conferred amongst themselves. We left our drinks untouched, there were lipstick traces on my glass and the beer lay flat and dank, placid as a greasy puddle.

'See that shape in your man's trousers?' Ready-Mix said. 'Well he's either hung like a donkey or carrying a machete.'

The Argentinians were reluctant to do business in front of witnesses. 'The merchandise,' Roadkill said. 'We need to see the merchandise.'

One of them said something about women.

'Women,' Roadkill said, 'we'll come across later. We can have all the women we want – but this is later. Later understandee? Later?'

Ready-Mix said he was under the impression that women was what they were selling.

There was more conferring and the same man said jiggy-jiggy? He formed an O shape with his thump and forefinger and thrust his other forefinger through it rapidly. His hips were buckling on the chair.

The other one turned to me and machine gunned me with Spanish. The only words I picked up were 'mujeres' – women – and 'sex'. He was either deeply frustrated or Ready-Mix had got the drift of what they were after. They left – giving us to understand they would be back in thirty minutes. We bailed out, dragging Roadkill reluctantly with us. He was accusing us of blowing his big chance. We could see their boat at anchor, listing slightly to one side, as we left the bar. There were no lights on board. It lay low in the water as if it could submerge at will back into the subterranean world it had come from. We heard later that it had sailed leaving one of the Argentinians behind. The Argentinian, a German told me, was looking for someone. He gave, he said, a very good description of Roadkill.

The incident in Hanover was relaxing compared to that experience. Two drinks, Roadkill said, that's all. I just have to check something out.

'How do you find these places?' I asked. I was even more puzzled at how he found his way back to them. You might stumble into a place like that unawares. Your natural reaction would be to leave as quickly as possible and your memory – perhaps employing some atavistic survival technique – would forget where the place was. As if you would be doomed to lumber through backstreets for an eternity otherwise.

Roadkill made no response.

He said he had to meet some associates and left me at a table on my own, being eyed up as prey by a coven of wrung-out whores. The associates blended in with the décor. I could see them sitting alone in a corner, where the least amount of light might get to them – like twin cultures of some deadly virus being nurtured in the dark. It wasn't for nothing that the Germans sent Lenin on a sealed train through their own lines to the Finland Station. Anarchy ferments in the dark. I tried in vain to overhear their conversation, catching odd words of it. One of them put money in the Jukebox and signalled for the barkeeper to turn it up. Roy Orbison's 'Pretty Woman' throbbed through the place. I saw a fat envelope cross the table. Roadkill stuffed it into his crotch awkwardly. He bought them two beers. The drinks were never touched. One of them sat back in the shadows, his voice seemed to quaver hoarsely in time with the song. It looked like he might be singing along, except for he wasn't. Roadkill nodded eagerly. The other one got up with Roadkill and approached where I was sitting. He blocked out the light for an instant and then he bent over, offering his gnarled hand. The veins stood out on the back of it like a river delta on a school map. He crushed my hand.

'You know Abie for a long time?' he asked.

'What?' I said, 'Abie?'

'You know Abie for a long time?' he exaggerated every word.

I nodded.

'He is crazy – no?'

I nodded again and he went back to the table. Roadkill gestured at his retreating back. 'Ex-Legionnaire,' he said as if I was to draw what inference I wanted from that. The problem with Roadkill was all his conversations had come to sound like something heard, coming crackling over the radio in the back of a police car.

He awoke in the carriage, apparently refreshed, before I could fasten on any resolve to get off the train. He was feeling nostalgic and described for me his route through Europe, years before. France, Spain, Marakeesh. He told me about how the hippy trail had ended for him when he'd had to cut his hair to get into Morocco. 'Standing there at the Moroccan border with a pair of shears in my hand thinking of nothing but dope,' he said.

I pushed him on his Limerick background but he seemed reluctant to talk about it. He mentioned his old man and said the best present he ever bought him was a scanner. The old man sat up in his room monitoring the police airwaves. It was, in its way, a telling image. Then he turned to London and the years he'd spent there. The train was by now trundling through the monotonous Dutch countryside. I felt we'd been somehow lucky – there had been no passport check.

'I hate the cloggies,' he said and he told me he'd lived with a Dutchwoman in a houseboat down on the Thames. When the tide receded the flotsam and jetsam of city life encroached, the stench of old mattresses, dead fish and rotting vegetation awash on the mud flats. They were living like bilge rats.

The boat needed caulking. She'd been beautiful, he said, that woman. Beautiful in that Dutch way, high cheekbones, healthy looking and all. The boat stank in the winter of dampness and mildew and its planks secreted the same stink, concentrated, during the hot summer months. He was rarely there, always ducking and diving, on the scam. He bought her a Wurlitzer jukebox to mollify her. Everyone has a dream, he said. She dreamt of flashing lights. But the jukebox was too big to fit down the stairs into the cabin. It was worth some money that jukebox. It sat amidst the clutter on the deck through the rains that fell incessantly from autumn through winter and into spring. The Dutchwoman turned yellow, unhealthily jaundiced looking. She left and returned to her family. They were some strange religious sect, some cankerous offgrowth of Protestantism. Not that it mattered, he said, they had no time for me.

He fell asleep again, Holland stretched like purgatory about us.

When we arrived in Amsterdam he disappeared once we'd booked into the hotel. The receptionist asked for our passports as collateral against the bill. I argued when Roadkill paid for both of us in advance. A man needs to be able to get out quick, he said. There were two American women in the reception area. We overheard them giggling and commenting that one of the newcomers was a weirdo.

'That's you,' Roadkill said.

I stretched out on the bed, mumbling something about going out to eat later and fell into a deep sleep. When I woke up he was gone. Passing traffic moved as shadows across the ceiling of the room. I went down to the bar. The receptionist was behind it. I tried my hand with her. She took it in good part but it was obvious that all she was going to do was flirt. Then the two Americans came in. I could hear them talking and bent to stifle my laughter. One of them was going on about being up a grapefruit tree when her diaphragm slipped.

'Straight up, Rach,' she said, 'I nearly fell outa that tree.'

I bought them a drink. The receptionist winked and made some comment about rich virgins. But when they joined me they told me they were broke. I was going to say I never saw any of nature's poor with Sony Walkmen and what were they doing staying in a hotel if they were broke?

But I forebore and bought them more drink. I ended up spending the better part of the night futilely groping one of them. The receptionist was obviously a better judge of character than I was.

The following morning I woke up, muzzy headed, in my own bed. For a few minutes the contours of the room appeared indistinct. Then it all wavered into view and I could hear Roadkill – who was obviously back – ranting somewhere. I thought, hardly for the first time, that the man was inexorable.

'I did it man,' he said.

'You did what?'

'I fulfilled the fantasy of a lifetime. Do you know what it's like to fulfil the fantasy of a lifetime? To have all your dreams come true?'

'*Hey Mrs Dolan, you're son he isn't working,*' he sang.

'What do you mean the fantasy of a lifetime? What are you going on about now? Jaysus,' I said, 'will you give it a break?'

'Did you ride the Yank?' he said. Then he laughed. 'No you didn't ride the Yank. If you rode the Yank at least you'd be in good form.'

'What are you on about?'

'I'll tell you what I did. I spent two hours with a whore in a taxi. Two whole hours ... nothing on her but suspenders and a fur coat ... not a stitch on under it ... can you believe it? And I never laid a hand on her. Is that kinky or what?'

'Jesus,' I said, 'you're for the birds. How much did that set you back?'

He laughed. 'Look,' he says, 'I only came back to grab the bag. I still have business.'

'What business? For fuck's sake will you tell me what you're at.'

'I'll see you at the train,' he said. 'Don't be late.' With those words he disappeared through the door.

He only showed up for the train at the last minute. The same crowd of Turks were there. I was breathing deeply reminding myself that he wasn't my responsibility, watching the Turks; how they knew when the train was about to move off, how close they stood to their cases: they said that when the Turks came to Germany first they were taken through reception centres where they were treated like livestock and the only time they protested was when their cases were taken away. I remembered how a character called Lonesome Tom had told me to watch the way men stood close to their suitcases. It was a particular type of man he said, a working man and you should never take away his case: it held the notion of home, even if that man was going round in circles like a pilgrim on a relentless pilgrimage to a shrine that didn't even exist – the bag was all.

Maybe that was why Roadkill slept, arms wrapped about his bag, in the carriage. He was completely deflated. I was in no mood to talk to him in any case. Still, I was wondering what he had in the bag and whether it could land us in trouble. But I drifted off and I too was asleep when the German Border Guards entered the carriage. I woke with a start and moved towards the bag. Roadkill was still flat out.

'Pass,' the German demanded, his hand already outstretched. I handed him my passport. He looked at it and handed it back. The other Guard had pulled the bag from Roadkill's grasp. I could hear my heart vaulting. He shook it out, upside down. A shirt and a British passport fell out on the floor. He nudged the shirt aside with his boot and bent to retrieve the passport. He looked at it and blinked and bent over towards Roadkill.

'Ah so …Weintraub,' he said, 'Weintraub.'

Roadkill stirred groggily. The guard bent forward and tilted his chin upwards. A skein of spew dribbled from Roadkill's mouth onto the cuff of the Guard's uniform. The Guard let go his grip with alacrity.

'Scheishund,' he said and he flung the passport onto the seat. Both of them left the carriage. I waited a few seconds and chanced a look into the corridor of the train. They were giving the Turks a hard time. They'd taken them out of the carriage. I hurriedly retook my seat and reached for the British passport. Roadkill was fully awake.

'Jesus,' I said, 'what are you at?'

'I thought that was a great touch with the sick,' he said.

'You were awake the whole time?'

He nodded.

'But Weintraub?' I said, 'Weintraub? You don't even look Jewish.'

He laughed. 'That's what's wrong with you your eminence,' he said, 'no fucking sense of humour, no fucking imagination. All that matters is the picture. They don't ask to see down your trousers you know. Anyhow, you have to admit it's not a bad likeness?'

I looked at the passport again. He was right. It was just about imaginable – if it was at all possible to picture Roadkill as a more baroque figure, with ringlets – an Hassidic Jew even. I didn't know what to say. Finally I said, 'Do you know what the worst of it was? I thought all the time you were smuggling drugs. I thought the bag was full of them. I wanted to get hold of the bag but I fell asleep.' I knew that saying it I sounded relieved.

He moved across the carriage and sat beside me.

'Do you want to hear the truth?'

I nodded.

'I am smuggling drugs.'

He leant over me, took a paper bag from his pocket and tipped out the ashtray into it. He fished a small, tin-foil wrapped package from the bag and held it up for me to see.

'There's four ashtrays, on average, to a carriage. The train's twenty-one-and-a-half carriages long. That's eighty-two ashtrays. As soon as the bastards leave we'll start. Sure you might as well help me now. I can't wait to see the faces on some of the auld ones on this train.'

Though I never saw Roadkill again I didn't fully escape him. Four years later I got a phonecall in London. It was the middle of the night. I was living in Finsbury Park. There was a payphone at the far end of the house. I didn't give out the number and usually ignored its intermittent ring. It was the province of the dole scammers in the bottom flat. They gathered about in convocation at all hours of the day or night, sparsely-bearded anarchists and neo-punks – why didn't somebody point out to them that all that ended back in '77? From what I knew of them they were orchestrating a vast fraud, signing on in different names all over the town. The phone was vital to their purpose and – from my perspective – was probably tapped. I knew enough not to invite the police to kick my door in. There didn't seem any great current of intelligence amongst the lot of them.

The phone rang at two o'clock in the morning. I cursed it knowing that I had to be up at half five for work and would be unable to get back to sleep. It rang off and then took up again, growing increasingly strident in the quiet house. Just as I got to it, it stopped again. I cursed it again and turned to lumber, half-asleep still, back up the stairs. It jumped on the hook once more and I felt I caught it in mid-air.

'Yes,' I snapped.

No matter how I tried afterwards I never found out how she got my number. I'd lost contact with almost everyone I'd known in Germany and my progress, over the past four years in London, had been labyrinthine – Finsbury park was my fourth change of address. She said her name was Gundula and that I didn't know her. She was the friend of a friend and he had asked her to contact me if anything went wrong. I had been a difficult man to find, she said. I felt she was on the other end of the phone wondering if I would prove worth the trouble.

The details she gave me were sketchy but I had them confirmed over the next couple of days. Roadkill had moved to Karlsruhe in Germany, he had returned to his previous career as a tree surgeon. He had ended up in the university there, as a mature student. He was living the good life. He even had a long-term relationship with this woman and then he had fallen off a balcony. She told me she'd seen it happen. He'd stepped backwards, the rail on the balcony was lower than it should have been, some modernist design, and he'd got caught in it and tumbled down four floors. He died instantly.

'Drugs?' I said.

'No,' she said.

'Was he drinking?'

'You don't understand,' she said, 'he was doing nothing like that. He couldn't drink. He could not use drugs. He had an addictive personality. He recognised that. He was doing so well.' She was angry with me for suggesting otherwise.

Her initial problem was identifying the body. It was supposed to be next of kin. She wanted it released for burial or cremation. I said I wasn't next of kin and she said that he'd had a photograph in his possession. It had been taken somewhere there were ships in the background. I was the only person she knew of. The authorities would accept me as next of kin, they wanted rid of the body. It was apparent – from the photograph – that I had known him a long time. In any case, she said, 'he talked about you always.' I said, 'What about his family in Limerick?' There was a pause.

'Do you want to help or not?' she said.

I was standing in the hallway in Finsbury Park, shivering.

'Give me your address,' I said. 'I'll be there later today.'

There was no doubt it was Roadkill. His hair was short and he'd got heavy. He had a little pot-belly and the same stick legs. I nodded and they drew the sheets back over him. The doctor who did the autopsy told me he looked in good enough physical condition for a man of his age. This only proved how deceptive looks could be. Inside he had the organs of a man twenty or thirty years older than he was. It wasn't the fall that killed him. It was the shock of the fall. It was only a matter of time. He could have turned over in his sleep and smothered on the pillow as easily. His constitution was shot.

Then there was the question of what to do with the body. I brought up his family again. We were sitting in a restaurant. She was toying with her schnitzel, her eyes were on her plate. I remembered the way he'd turned melancholy that time on the train to Amsterdam. I told her about his father and the scanner. I was reliving it. It was a reprisal of the man I'd known, a bleached out, monochrome memory, of a train trundling through Holland. Evidently it had little bearing on her experience. She looked up from her plate. Her eyes were tear filled, opaque – what I read in them was that I was talking about the wrong man altogether. She shook her head.

'He liked to make up stories,' she said.

'He told me about a Dutch woman he lived with on a boat – are you saying that was a lie too?'

'Who knows,' she said. 'I never asked. I do know he wasn't Irish. He did very good accents. I think he may have worked in the antiques business with an Irishman in London. Perhaps that was it. He did see himself as Irish. He said his mother was Irish. Perhaps he grew to be Irish?'

'Then what was he?'

She told me his real name was Weintraub. His family were in the garment business. He was originally from Whitechapel, in the east end of London. His mother died when he was young. She said his family were wealthy. He had taken her back to Whitechapel but there was nothing left there. All the Jews were gone. He had no connection with his family. He had been disowned years before. She didn't know why. He never said. As far as she could say he came from nowhere. 'Why wouldn't he claim to be Irish?' She said those last words defiantly. I was too shocked to contradict her even if I'd wanted to. At last I said, 'What about his family. Do they know?'

'I phoned them,' she said. 'He always had his brother's number. I told them. There was a silence on the line. It was, how would you say it, like a lead balloon. They didn't say anything. Ja, they had nice manners. I gave them the number here. That was two days before I phoned you. They never phoned back. That was why I phoned you. He talked about you all the time.'

We had him cremated. She'd got hold of some kind of a secular rabbi who said a few words. There were two or three tree surgeons there and some students who knew him from the university. One of the students read some Ginsberg poetry badly, that shit about having seen the best of our generation. There were flowers and things. The sun was shining. The whole thing had an air of unreality, of the surreal about it. We went back to a bar. I was in a daze, baffled. I could hear everybody talking about someone I hadn't known at all. Someone, the woman said, who talked about me incessantly. Yet when I was asked how I knew him I could only mutter that it was all a long time ago. It felt like I was entering a plea of mitigation. It all felt like a washing machine was going off all the time in my ears. I stood out amongst them all. I didn't even have what might have been called respectable clothes. I was wearing a T-shirt and black jeans, a battered Levi jacket and the same scuffed cowboy boots I'd worn on that train almost five years before. I used to think of them as lucky.

I went with her to the Black Forest the next day and we shook his ashes loose from the urn. It was a windy day and they blew away deep into the trees.

# A Tale of Two Tickets

### Arnold O'Byrne

*P*at Ryan sat in his office looking out of the window at the traffic on the busy A5 trunk road, which connected London with Carlisle in the North of England. He was feeling at peace with himself. As the Senior Vice President in Century Engineering, the UK subsidiary of a large American multinational, Pat was the second in command and was widely expected to take the top position when the present incumbent retired next year. Pat would be seen as a safe pair of hands. Not given to making hasty decisions or taking chances, in yachting parlance he would be described as a 'steady as she goes' person. He liked to lead a structured and orderly life, with no complications. He was only known to get excited when things did not go as planned. Married with three teenage children, devoted to his wife Mary, a member of the local golf club – more for business reasons than for playing the game – a regular church goer and President of the local Chamber of Commerce, Pat was a pillar of the local community.

He reached for the ringing telephone.

'Hello, Pat Ryan,' he said.

'Howya Pat, its D,' came the reply.

Pat's heart skipped a beat. D, his young brother, was not given to making telephone calls to him. Pat's immediate reaction was that there was something wrong at home. Pat lived in Dunstable, some thirty miles outside of London, and despite living there for over twenty years he still referred to Dublin as home.

'Is everything alright?'

'Oh yes, I just thought I'd give you a call,' replied D.

That, Pat thought, was definitely unusual. Spontaneity was not in D's vocabulary. Certainly there had to be a reason for this call, and knowing D it would not take him too long to get to it.

D was Pat's younger brother and enjoyed a bachelor's life. He had brought many girls home to meet the Mammy, but when either the Mammy or the girl, or indeed both, felt the relationship was reaching a serious level, with the possibility of marriage, the girl was dropped. Mrs Ryan, their mother, prayed daily that he would find a wife. Initially, she prayed for a good Irish Catholic girl, but as time went by, and her prayers were not answered, she changed the request, first by dropping 'good', then, after some months, 'Irish' and, finally, in complete desperation, and with much soul searching, even 'Catholic' was eventually discarded. Alas, no girl was forthcoming, or if there was, D showed little interest. And why should he? As D once said, while slightly inebriated, he had a good job, no financial worries, was his own boss and could, within reason, come and go as he pleased. A wife, he reckoned, would have a serious negative impact on this current lifestyle.

D was not his real name. He had been christened Aloysius, after Sister Mary Aloysius, the nun who helped deliver him in the maternity hospital. Early on in his life, Aloysius grew to dislike his name. He was the only boy with the name Aloysius in the entire school. Pat used to tell him it could have been worse, what would have happened if she had been called Sister Mary Chrysoginus. In his opinion, Aloysius Ryan was preferable to Chrysoginus Ryan.

One day D confided his dislike of his name to the teacher who promptly told the class that, 'Alo wishes he was not Aloysius.' Within a short time this was chanted at him wherever he went. After a few months of, 'Alo wishes he was not Aloysius' he decided on a change of name and he chose the name Dee. This was after the hero in some second-rate movie that he had seen. Everything went fine for some six years until he discovered that 'Dee' was also a name for females. However, rather than change his name a second time, he simply changed the spelling to 'D'. He also felt with just one letter 'D' was much more macho.

'How is everyone at home?' inquired Pat.

'Grand.'

There followed a silence where neither spoke. Pat knew that if he could get D to break the silence first, then he would learn much quicker the real purpose of the call.

'I was wondering, any chance of getting me two tickets for the Cup Final on Saturday?'

Two tickets for the Cup Final on Saturday! That was only four days away. God, thought Pat, the Mammy would have a better chance of getting him a girl and a good Irish Catholic one at that.

'D, Cup Final tickets are like gold dust, how could I get you two, and by Saturday?'

'Sure you know a few people. Give it a try and let me know.'

With that he was gone. D was certainly a man of few words.

D was shrewd enough to know that if he appealed to Pat's sense of importance then Pat would try harder to obtain the tickets, just to prove that he did know the right people.

Pat suspected that D knew he would pull out all the stops to get him the tickets. After all, Pat mused, D was his baby brother and if he could not help his baby brother, whom could he help? Pat also had a very strong sense of family loyalty, firmly believing, and practising, whenever possible, the words of the adage 'Family comes first.' Comparing Pat to D was like comparing chalk to cheese. Pat was organised, methodical, predictable, everything that D was not.

If the Mammy was getting nowhere with her request for a wife for D, whoever was asking for divine intercession on the two Cup Final tickets had their prayers answered. Within two days of the telephone call, Pat had successfully obtained two tickets, at face value, for the game.

Another equally brief telephone conversation took place between Pat and D and it was agreed that D would collect the tickets from Pat's home on Friday. D intended to travel over to the UK by ship and take the train to London. He would then travel to Dunstable to collect the tickets. He expected to be in Dunstable around lunchtime. Pat decided that he should at least be at home to meet D on Friday when he called, so consequently he arranged to take a half-day.

On Friday, Mary, Pat's wife, prepared lunch for four, D and his friend and Pat and herself.

D arrived alone at 1.30 p.m. After the usual greetings Pat inquired,

'Where is your friend?'

'Lost.'

'Lost! What do you mean lost?'

D looked at Pat as though he was facing someone with a poor command of the English language.

'Lost,' he said with a wry smile, 'you know, vanished, gone, cannot find him.'

Pat was astounded. He had never been confronted before with somebody being lost and he was amazed at the casual way in which D appeared to be handling the situation.

Over the lunch, Pat slowly extracted from D that the friend, by the name of Pablo, had left the train at Crewe to buy a sandwich and had, in all probability, boarded the train at the adjoining platform which was going to Cardiff. D was unconcerned, firmly stating his belief that he would meet up with Pablo in London. Pablo, he claimed, would make his way to the Guest House in Euston where they had stayed on previous visits to the capital and where they intended to stay on this visit.

Before he left to return to London, Pat elicited the information that Pablo was in fact a nickname, the origins of which were unknown, and that, like D, he was forty years old. His surname was Murphy. Pablo Murphy. God, he mused, D thought Aloysius Ryan was bad.

It was approaching five o'clock when D telephoned to say that the Guest House was closed for renovation and he had checked into another one. However, as he had no way of advising Pablo of this he was going to Euston Railway Station in the hope of meeting him there. He reasoned that as Euston was the London terminal they were meant to arrive at, Pablo would make his way there.

Pat was exasperated.

'There are over eight million people in London, I have no idea how many people pass through Euston, nor do I know how many entrances and exits there are into and out of the station and my brother is hoping to find Pablo there. He must be mad,' he ranted to Mary. 'How does a grown man succeed in getting lost? I bet he was drunk. I bet they were both drunk. I wish I had never got involved.'

Mary was used to Pat's occasional excitable outbursts and knew from years of experience that it was best to say nothing. Also, she had a quiet smile to herself as she thought that he never appeared to notice her silence when he got into these infrequent tirades. She also knew that despite what he may say, if D telephoned again with a similar request, then Pat would once again attempt to help. She knew that Pat derived immense satisfaction from helping people, particularly family. She also knew that he was extra pleased that he had been able to secure the two tickets for D.

Little did they realise that the farce was going to get worse.

Some two hours later, D telephoned him again to state that he had not located Pablo, but as they had planned to go to a game that evening at West Ham, he was going to proceed there in the hope of meeting him.

By now Pat was getting more exasperated despite Mary telling him that it was not his concern and he should forget about it.

'Now I've heard everything. There will be about thirty thousand people at that game and your man expects to bump into Pablo, I can envisage them meeting –

"Hi Pablo."

"Hi D, any score yet?"

'You know,' he continued, 'these two guys must surely be the most laid back guys in the world.'

'Sure, this probably happens every time they go away,' she said.

Suddenly Pat had an idea.

'If,' he explained to Mary, 'they are both going to West Ham, then I will ask West Ham to make an announcement over the loud-speakers and arrange for them to meet up.'

Feeling pleased with himself he went to telephone West Ham Football Club.

Having explained to the West Ham telephone receptionist that he wanted a missing-person announcement made, Pat quickly put through to the announcer.

'How can I help, mate? I believe there is someone missing.'

Pat was immediately impressed with the sincerity and the warmth that the announcer exuded. Everything was proceeding well until the announcer said, 'I'm really sorry mate, your brother must be worried sick. What's the name and age of the missing lad?'

'Pablo Murphy, and he's forty.'

There was a silence before the announcer said, 'This has to be a wind up. A forty-year-old Irishman called Pablo Murphy and he is lost. Blimey, I thought we were talking about a kid.'

Pat had to use all his powers of persuasion to convince the announcer that the story was true. Having succeeded the announcer then asked, 'What's your brother's name?'

'D Ryan.'

'How do you spell that ... D E E?'

'O no, just the letter D.'

'What does the D stand for?'

Without thinking Pat replied, 'Aloysius'.

This response resulted in the announcer having apoplexy. Eventually Pat heard a sound which was somewhere between coughing and suppressed laughter. After what seemed at eternity the announcer said, 'Look mate, this has to be a wind up. A lost forty-year-old Irishman called Pablo Murphy with a friend called D which stands for Aloysius. You must take me for a right plonker.'

Pat's powers of persuasion went into overdrive and it was only after he had given the announcer his name and home telephone number and had invited him to telephone back to confirm his authenticity that the announcer appeared, albeit without much enthusiasm, to believe him and promised to make an announcement at half-time.

Again Mary had to endure the ranting.

'Never, never, never again. That man thought I was a right eejit. In fact, I felt a right eejit. I don't need this in my life. Here I am worrying about a guy I never met by the name of Pablo, when my little brother who has involved me in this débâcle is enjoying himself at a football match. Well this is the end, I am not getting involved any further and I am never, ever again getting him tickets for another football game.'

It was about ten that evening when the telephone rang. It was D to inform Pat that he had heard the announcement and had guessed that Pat was responsible. He then added that Pablo had also heard it.

'So you finally found him,' as he said this Pat felt a huge sense of relief coupled with a certain satisfaction that his efforts had been successful. Both feelings were premature and soon evaporated when D replied in a very matter-of-fact tone, 'No, when I went to the Club's office to meet with him he had been and gone. You see they made the announcement at half-time and apparently he went there immediately, whereas I waited until the game was over. I did not want to miss any of it.' Before Pat could explode, D quickly added, 'But they told me that they gave him your telephone number so he will contact you. I'll call you in about an hour to find if you have heard from him.'

Wisely, without waiting for Pat to respond, he put down the receiver.

It was some forty-five minutes later when Pablo called. He was, he said, in Kings Cross railway station. He had already tried the Guest House and had, like D, found it closed for renovation. It was only then Pat realized D had not given him the name and address of the Guest House into which he had booked. He explained the situation to Pablo and asked that he call back in thirty minutes by which time, he hoped, D would have made contact.

'Now, Pablo, I mean thirty minutes, not twenty nine, not thirty one but, thirty.'

All Pat was short of doing was to ask Pablo to synchronise watches.

D rang shortly after Pablo's call. Pat explained the situation and instructed D to go to Kings Cross and to telephone him from there.

Pablo called as he was told, exactly thirty minutes after his first call. Pat elicited from him that just outside the telephone box was a newsagents.

'Pablo,' he said, 'go over and wait outside the newsagents and when D calls I will direct him to you.'

Pat was beginning to feel better. He had a sense of accomplishment and a strong feeling that this saga was coming to a happy end.

Within five minutes D called.

'Howya, I'm in Kings Cross. Any news?'

'Can you see a newsagents from your phone box?'

'I can. Jayny mack I spy Pablo.'

'Thank God for that.'

'Thanks Pat, I'll go and get him.'

Before he had the chance to put the phone down Pat laughingly said, 'D, don't get lost between the phone box and the shop ... and by the way, enjoy tomorrow.'

'Thanks again Pat. See ya.'

All's well that ends well. Pat was feeling pretty good and, as he told Mary, he had a great sense of achievement. All was forgiven and he was glad that he had been able to reunite them and was pleased they would get to see the Cup Final.

'It is probably the only time in his life that he will get to see a Cup Final at Wembley. It is a great sporting occasion and, really, I am glad I was able to help. In fact, I would not have minded going myself. Perhaps next year.'

'You know,' he added, 'I bet I don't hear from that fellow again until he wants another favour, probably next year some time.'

He was right about one part of that forecast.

Pat had just entered into a deep sleep when the telephone rang. At first his mind did not function and although he had swung his feet to the floor, it was several seconds before he realised it was the telephone ringing. Drowsily he picked up the receiver.

'Howya Pat, it's me D, sorry if I woke you.'

Halfway between a state of disbelief and uncontrolled anger that this was happening, the only words Pat could say were, 'D, what time is it?'

'About half twelve.'

Very slowly Pat replied, 'D, what the hell do you want now? You woke me up.'

'Well you see Pablo has nowhere to sleep, the Guest House is full and there is no way I can sneak him in and all the other places around here are also full so I was wondering if you could put him up for the night.' The words rushed out from D as if he was afraid Pat would hang up and he needed to get his message out before that eventuality.

'I don't believe you. We live about an hour's drive away and you want me to go to London to collect a guy I have never met and give him a bed for the night.' As his anger rose so did his voice. 'Next you will want me to drive him back to London and then drive both of you to Wembley for the game. You have some nerve.'

'Ah no Pat, just collect him now, he can get the train back tomorrow and we will make our own way to the game.'

Pat will never know how he came to be driving down the M1 at 1.00 a.m. to collect Pablo Murphy from outside the newsagents in Kings Cross Railway Station. On reflection, he thinks it may have been the persuasiveness of Mary combined with that family loyalty trait. His anger was unabated and he was determined that when he met D he was going to give him a verbal lashing. The entire journey was spent rehearsing exactly what he was going to say. With grim satisfaction he thought that this time there would be no Mary to restrain him.

On arrival at Kings Cross he was surprised at the number of people just hanging around. As he parked the car he became aware that quite a number were prostitutes and the fact that he was solicited several times as he made his way into the station did nothing to improve his temper. He saw the newsagents shop as soon as he entered the Terminal but as he made his way towards it he realised there was no sign of D.

'Are you Pat?' On hearing the question Pat turned. He knew from the accent that the person in front of him was a Dubliner. The swarthy appearance coupled with the shoulder-length hair and the drooping moustache gave a Mexican appearance. This, he thought, had to be Pablo Murphy.

'Are you Pablo?'

'I am and I'm pleased to meet you.'

Pablo had a firm handshake and, despite his anger, Pat could not help but like him. Anyway, he reasoned, his anger was not with Pablo but with that brother of his. At that point he realised he had not seen D yet.

'Where is D?'

As Pat much later admitted, nothing could have prepared him for the reply.

'Well,' said Pablo, 'there was little point him waiting knowing you were coming to collect me so he went back to the Guest House. He said he was tired as it had been a long day.'

Pat fumed all the way back to Dunstable. Few words were exchanged between Pablo and himself as he was fully occupied with silently castigating D. He knew D had gone simply because he could not face his wrath. He vowed that no matter what, never again would he attempt to help D. Assisting D, for whatever cause, he reckoned, was a health hazard. It did not help his temper when the late night radio DJ played The Hollies singing, 'He ain't heavy, he's my brother.'

It was nearly 3.00 a.m. when they arrived at the Ryan's home. Mary extended a warm Irish welcome to Pablo and despite it being the early hours of morning, Pablo was given a large plate of chips with a steak that had originally been intended for Pat's lunch on Sunday. Watching Pablo enjoy his steak only increased Pat's determination not to assist D again. As he later said to Mary, 'This family loyalty thing sounds great but I have to seriously question it when I lose my sleep, make a journey of some 70 miles at some God-forsaken hour and then watch as my Sunday lunch is eaten by a stranger, all because of an inconsiderate brother who is probably sleeping soundly without a care in the world.'

Pablo was treated to a full Irish breakfast, which he ate with undisguised enthusiasm. During the breakfast Pat took the opportunity to enquire about the day's arrangements. After all, he thought, while Pablo's inability to board the correct rain to Crewe was the cause of this fiasco, the real problem was with D's failure to have a contingency plan. Pat's planning always involved a contingency plan and he believed anybody not having a contingency plan was irresponsible. D, he reasoned, should have planned for one of them getting lost and had a prearranged meeting-place at a designated time. If he had done this, then there would have been no need for all the shenanigans of yesterday.

While D may have understood the term contingency plan, Pablo most likely would have thought it something to do with planning for incontinence.

'Where are you meeting D today?'

'London,' replied Pablo.

Pat sighed and almost wearily said, 'Yes, but where in London.'

Pablo looked at Pat as though he did not understand the question.

'Just London. When we parted last night D just said he'd see me tomorrow.'

Pat was to say later that this was the point when he knew he did not have a weak heart, as he was positive that had he had any heart problem he would have had his heart attack there and then. This, he thought, is almost a repeat of yesterday. Two grown men agreeing to meet in London without agreeing a specific location was beyond his comprehension. Nor could he understand that the unflappable Pablo was completely unconcerned. This, he reasoned, must be faith but, he felt, there was little hope of them meeting and, certainly, his charity was evaporating. Very quickly he decided he was not going to become involved. He would deliver Pablo to the railway station, return home and disconnect the telephone. He did not share his intentions with Mary as he knew she would disagree.

Having left Pablo to the railway station, Pat returned home where, having surreptitiously disconnected the telephone, he busied himself for several hours. He was looking forward to watching the Cup Final on the television.

One hour before kick-off he settled himself in front of the TV. Mary, who had gone shopping, had prepared some sandwiches for him and he had a few bottles of lager to sustain him through the game. He liked to watch the lead up to the game and flavour some of the atmosphere: the marching bands, the interviews with the fans and various sporting persons, the so-called experts waxing lyrically about their favourite and the fans singing 'Abide with me'. He felt relaxed as he watched Jimmy Hill interviewing fans as they trooped up the famous Wembley Way to the stadium. Match tickets were waved to the cameras, 'Olé, olé olé ... Wembelee' rang out from both sets of fans and some were stopped for interviewing. Suddenly, he sat bolt upright in his chair, a half-eaten sandwich in his hand as Jimmy Hill interviewed D and Pablo.

'Where are you lads from?'

'Ireland,' they chorused.

Pat was transfixed. Against all the odds they had succeeded in meeting and he suspected from their garrulous nature that they had visited a few hostelries en route to the ground.

'When did you arrive from Ireland?'

'Yesterday,' replied Pablo, 'and we have had great craic. It has been one big adventure.'

'Will this be your first time to Wembley?'

'Ah sure,' said D, 'we're not going to the stadium. We sold our tickets for £500 each and now we're heading for the pub. We'll watch it on TV. We're quids in.'

'Yes,' interjected Pablo, 'we'll probably do this again next year.'

'Olé, olé olé ... Ireland,' echoed through the sitting-room in Pat Ryan's Dunstable home as D and Pablo were gobbled up in the swirling mass of people making their way to the Cup Final in Wembley Stadium.

# The Sand Dance

*Leo Cullen*

*(The Sand Dance: a routine performed by a trio named 'Wilson, Kepple and Betty' during the era of the Music Hall Variety Show.)*

'Welcome, ladies and gentlemen,' Nicholas Hunt announced. 'Give a big hand for "Teddy, Lou and Madame George". The reincarnation of "Wilson, Kepple and Betty".'

We were on stage. Teddy played that old mouth organ, making that reedy Eastern music. I did the Tap dance. Up the stepladder, tappety, tappety, tap, down again. My dhoti holding me tightly into the act. Teddy winked when I reached the highest of the steps. Nicholas was in the crowd, that night. Sometimes he took part on stage, sometimes he was in the crowd. The Corn Dance: sheets of cardboard held before us, we swayed like sheafs of corn. Our heads peered out through holes in the cardboard. The audience talked and drank at their tables. Audiences never did get into The Corn Dance. Sock it to them, Teddy said. Georgina turned around and twirled her bum at the tables. That meant she was facing Ted and me. He winked at her and lifting her cardboard, she shook her breasts. That was for Teddy, always that was for Teddy and I wished it was for me. Next, The Sand Dance. Georgina stepped into the wings and came back holding the sand bucket. It was one of those buckets that kids made sand-castles with on Southend beach. She sprinkled the sand on the floor. It was always the best, The Sand Dance. The audience always seemed to stir before The Sand Dance. Georgina did her sprinkling, she sashayed to the crowd and Teddy and I slipped behind the props and changed into our shifts. 'I'm getting fat, Twinkletoes,' Teddy said. But he always got in. He was sleek as a cobra. I was sleek as a cobra too.

Then we took the floor. Shuffle and sand, cigarette smoke and laughter. Open mouths of the audience. How I loved it. The Sand Dance.

*Once upon a time there were four young people who lived in the same place, or thereabouts, and these four, all of them, wanted to be entertainers. They didn't, of course, know the name for what they wanted to be. But the name was entertainer and that was what they wanted.*

Where did it all begin? How did 'Teddy, Lou and Madame George' take to the road? The names are easily explained. Lou. That's me. I am Louie Kennedy. Teddy is Teddy Holland. And Madame George is Georgina Ryan. We were having a smoke one night after work when Georgina christened herself. We were listening to a song about a 'Madame George', Van Morrison's song.

'You can call me Madame George from now on,' she announces. Nicholas Hunt capsizes off his chair in laughter. 'Chaotic far out imagination,' says Teddy. (That was in the early days, when Teddy, not Nicholas, was our manager.) From then on Georgina was Madame George.

That's the names part of it.

Once to our small town in Ireland there came the Talent Spotters. Nicholas at that time was about fourteen, about three years older than Teddy, Georgina and me. We were the same age. Nicholas was thin and fit and had black hair and at fourteen looked almost grown up.

Here is Nicholas. He is cycling into town. He feels the wind in his hair and against his knuckles as he grasps the handlebars. He sings one of his Mario Lanza songs, which he knows from his father's gramaphone. He sings at the top of his voice. He rides the High Nellie, his mother's bicycle. He speeds down the hills from the colliery. He heads for Wolfhills and if any of the fellows in that town of stuck-up cyclists say to him, 'You, from Lisnamrock, where do you think you are going in your old High Nellie?', Nicky has his answer for them: 'To win the Talent Competition. To take the first step to stardom.'

But Nicky's bike is no ordinary High Nellie. He has fitted a new saddle, new handlebars like on a man's bike, smoothly-ticking gears. On that sleek black bike, I swear, even if it was a woman's, Nicholas could have cycled across the world.

But he did have to get off and walk Lahert's Hill. You would think all the downhill momentum from Copper Cross would have got him over Lahert's Hill. It did not.

Yeah, that's Nicky alright. As he used to be, head flaming with exuberance, before he changed and became the solid one among us.

We passed Nicholas on his bike that day as he climbed Lahert's Hill. I was in the back of our car, stuffed into it along with my brothers and sisters, clutching in my schoolbag my outfit for the competition. He didn't know I had passed him. A hundred cars could have passed and he wouldn't have noticed. I told him years later. 'How do you remember these things? I remember nothing,' he said to me. Then he contradicted himself, telling me things that he remembered about me: 'The toes of your shoes curled up. I remember that from when we lined up for the Talent Competition. In my mind I had a nickname for you. Twinkletoes, I called you.' Indeed that was a name I came to be called in our troupe. 'You had a long neck, long and bare, with a head nodding on top of it full of fragile eagerness.'

Georgina. Her first memories of me? The day I went into Daly's Drapers? Would that be it? With my step-mother one day … she took me into Mrs Daly's to get me a trousers. Georgina was by the counter. 'This lad needs a trousers, Mrs Daly,' says my step-mother. 'He is leaping out of everything he has.' I must indeed have been badly in need. Why else would the swanky Kennedys have gone to buy clothes in Mrs Daly's. The Kennedys always went further afield for clothes. Is that what Georgina was thinking? She gave me an eye that day. I went into Mrs Daly's kitchen to try the trousers on. When I came out she gave me the eye again. And after that, every day at school, over the play-yard wall during break time, she gave me the eye. Then she knew she had me. Then she ignored me.

And Nicholas. When would Georgina first have noticed Nicholas? A fruit-cake on a bike. At that Talent Competition, or before? Flying down the hill into town, or if he was in town, hovering outside the shops with that way of his of making his bike stand while he stood on the pedals and twisted the wheels over and back in a rubbery dance? Did he ever get off it?

We two would have passed Georgina and her pals as they walked up town for the Talent Competition. Three Little Maids from Gay Japan. They linked arms and every time one of them stumbled they all came falling down. Georgina, Eileen Roe and blocky little Bibi Considine. Why would Georgiana have bothered to notice two boys anyway? Whenever I went near her in those days, she looked away. She knew she had me. So her interests would stray elsewhere. She would dance on the dusty roadside, as if it was the most enjoyable exercise imaginable. Or laugh with the girls. Or smirk at the big men. All that. Keeping me on my toes. And miserable. And Nicholas, a boy from the collieries. What town girl wants to take notice of the likes of him? Georgina, all pretence, suggested she didn't either.

Of the three competitors about to take first, second and third spot at Wolfhills Talent Competition, the telling of the story of the night should belong to Georgina. She was not like the boys, too fretful to witness anything of it. While Georgina preened with her girlfriends, twirled with them before the mirror of Daly's on the dark side of the street, we two boys lathered up like thoroughbreds at starting-stalls, everything happening about us in a blur.

Yet Georgina may not be a reliable teller either; in other ways she was also of a restless nature. That leaves Teddy Holland.

At this time Teddy is a small round boy not yet showing the signs of the growth that will soon make him shoot up long and lanky until in late teens he will again resume his roundiness. He and me share the same desk at Wolfhills Primary School. He does not yet know Nicholas. He knows Georgina but has little time for the relationship she shares with me. He has little time for girls. Teddy's mother is Bean uí Holland, assistant teacher at St Mary's Boys' National School. He runs all her errands but still manages time to stand back and laugh at her and at most of what goes on in town. She had a husband but he has long left. Teddy is hen-pecked, both husband and son. He evades hen-pecking by paying no attention to it. She is cultured, particularly in affairs of Irish language and traditions, and that is to her credit. She sometimes organises events in an attempt to cultivate what she sees as the cultural desert of this town in which she finds herself having to make a living to keep her son. Tonight she is the principal organiser of the Talent Competition; hopeful of recognition for the talent she nurses during school drama lessons. Teddy is charged with stage management. He pulls the curtains, operates the hall lights, dispenses and pins numbers onto the chests of competitors, lines up each act in proper sequence. He is on stage most of the time, though nobody seems to notice him. Invisibility, that is his talent.

Here is the gist of Teddy Holland's remembrances of that Talent Competition. Here is how it would come across to us, listening to him talk of it – amid great laughter – in later years:

Teddy: *Yes, Three Little Maids from Gay Japan... but only one was there to be seen. Two little maids from Gay Japan were overcome with a bout of shyness as soon as they hit the stage. They were supposed to stand behind the first Little Maid at the beginning. All three of them were supposed to be shy and to wave their fans before their faces. But Georgina Ryan forgot to be shy and the other two forgot to stop being shy and stood behind Georgina for the whole act. There's me in the wings with my mother. 'Cailíní, stand out on either side of Georgina.' She is whispering, and I swear everyone in the hall can hear her. She is making a sound, like a bellows with something stuck in the neck of it. No, I'm afraid there was only one Little Maid from Gay Japan. Stand forth, Georgina. The fat arse judges still had to give you third place. – Oh save us the tyranny of judges, but I have a problem with authority!*

*Louie, you could sing in those days. You had the legs of a skylark! A pity your voice went but at least you don't need one nowadays for The Sand Dance. I'll always remember how the rain began to pelt down just before Louie's act. It was like drums; it beat down on the old corrugated roof of our Hall. Louie sang 'The Croppy Boy' that night and I swear the atmosphere that Louie could create by his natural sad looks – was it fervour or what, for he always got it into every song he ever sang – the atmosphere was only added to by the pelting rain. It was like the drumbeat of the Yoemen for the condemned Croppy. The judges were in tears. Second place to young Louie Kennedy.*

*'I am the Dancer of Lisnamrock,' Nicholas begins, the bicycle is on the stage with him and he stands it on its back wheel. He wears white gloves and points to the heavens with one hand, the other partnering his bicycle in a sort of dance. Your jokes were not funny, Nicholas, but you were unusual: 'Come dance with me,' says Nicky to the judges. 'Or if you do not rise you shall require patches to be stitched into the bums of your trousers by your good wives. Notwithstanding,*

*I say. Notwithstanding.' Everybody was hooting with laughter at the judges.*
*They were so embarrassed they had no option but to give Nicky first place.*

*Yes, you were keen, you three competitors. You wanted it. Nobody else came*
*near. I could see it even then. I wonder was it as far back as then that I began*
*to have my plans for you?*

If Teddy Holland had plans for us, it was not until long later they came to
anything. And Teddy was lazy anyway. The Sand Dance would never have
come to anything if it weren't for Nicholas. In fact of the four of us,
immediately following that 'Talent Competition', only Nicholas went
anywhere. He was selected to go to Dublin for the National Finals. I knew
nothing of how he got on there apart from hearing people afterwards
saying that anybody having such big notions of themselves deserved to get
nothing. So Nicholas must have got nothing. But I think that we three,
Nicholas, Georgina and Louie, were united in some way after that night.
And even Teddy may have been affected. Some craving had entered our
souls. When we performed, we satisfied some hunger, only to crave for it
again within hours. I still remember how I felt that night in the Wolfhills
Hall. I felt a huge turbulence whipping up inside me and then after my act
I felt more at peace than I'd ever felt before. That single night was to create
an even greater hunger in me though. I would not be satisfied until it
happened again. And that would not happen until seven years into the
future.

∗ ∗ ∗

Copper Cross, Coalbrook, Lisnamrock, The Commons: they were windy,
hilly places. The colliery country. From somewhere up there came Nicky
Hunt. His father was not a miner but a farmer. He worked over the
ground, not under it. It was not good farm land. Cold and late, my father
always said. After the Talent Competition it was a while before I again
came across Nicholas: it was the day of a big hurling tournament final at
Ballincurry Sports. Two great teams, great hurlers.

But there was one person not interested in the hurlers and that was Nicky
Hunt. Other things occupied Nicky. Before the match, he stood at a corner
inside the gate, togged down to his waist and on a little circle of trodden grass

he danced while playing a mouth organ. He was just one of the buskers there. The other buskers played or blathered as if their whole life depended on the performance. But Nicky was different. He would stop every now and again and look around before going on. Take for instance when he saw me. 'How is young Kennedy?' he said. The seasoned performers would never pretend to recognise anybody. 'Are you going to watch the match?' I said. 'What match?' said he. So I left him there and he hitched up his trousers almost to his chest and started up another dance. But you could see he was new to the game. Not as in years to come, when he would instruct me on The Sand Dance: 'If you want to perform your act, you must belong in your act and pay no notice to people.'

It did occur to me though that I had never seen anyone dance like him before: one hand up to hold the mouth organ, the other stiffly by his side in the manner of Irish dancers; not in reverence, in fun. I wished I could be like that, whatever the word for that was. The word was 'anarchic', though I did not know it then.

When the match ended the crowd wandered among the sideshows. There was a boxing-ring. Bashing his gloved fists together at the ring's centre, a champion boxer called Denis Makem invited all comers. There were only three challengers: the main challenger who was a well-known pub scrapper from Wolfhills, then Nicky Hunt and after him a man with blonde hair.

A crowd gathered around the ring because everybody knew the local man, Bonar Hegney. Bonar had learned his boxing from his days in the army. He liked to grow his hair long now, so that it curled in ringlets on his neck, but he still held his back straight and walked in short army steps. He was married but it was said he had lots of women. When he stood into the ring, the champ eyed him for a long time. Bonar flicked punches and threw back his head to stop his long hair falling in his eyes. Still the champ did not move. He was of much lower stature than Bonar. Then suddenly, he went straight at Bonar and landed about six haymakers to his body and then one to his head. Bonar Hegney went sprawling through the ropes, a spit flew into the crowd and then I could not see him again. He was stretched out, a woman kneeling before him, her legs flung open and her wide backside cutting him off from view. A smell of crushed grass rose up. The man alongside me who knew everything about boxing said that was the only and proper way for a professional to conduct himself. Over the course of his career he would have so many challengers after him that it would wear him out if his retribution was not swift and lethal. 'He can't be hanging around and getting his face bet in by every ex-army mongrel in the country.'

Seeing how Bonar had been treated, I was worried for Nicky Hunt. In he steps, cautiously, like he is stepping on a hot cooking-range. 'He's mad,' a man said. The crowd closed in around the ring. The champ carried on the same as last time. Eyeing Nicky, girding his togs round his waist. And what is Nicky doing? Dancing. Dances up to him, up to his face and quickly skips away again. We all waited for the champ to pounce. And he did. But Nicky, like a light-footed kangaroo, simply skipped out of his way. Then he laughed. The champ made another lunge. Nicky skipped away again and laughed again and the champ, carried by his forward lunge, found himself on the ropes. It was Nicky's chance to give him a thump, or a clip at least, on the side of his ear. But not Nicky, it seemed Nicky was not interested in hitting. Dancing, that was his game. While the champ tangled with the ropes, Nicky had the ring to himself. He put his hands to his side, Irish dancing style. 'La la, la la, la la la la la la,' he sang out his steps. The crowd had become silent. 'Crazy young lad,' somebody said. 'He's for it.' Suddenly it dawned on everybody that Nicky was for it.

The champ charged again. This time he held his arms wide so that Nicky would not escape him. 'Champ is leaving himself very open,' somebody said.

'That's 'cause he knows that young fella won't hit him; that young fella is capable only of dancing,' somebody replied.

I saw the look on Nicky's face. It was a look I would often, in aftertimes, see: a lightening around the eyes, a glimpse forward at some distant possibilities, a daring, the beholding of a vision. I would see that look when he would dream up routines for The Sand Dance.

He let fly with his left. He connected. He didn't connect hard, almost pulling away his glove as he struck – it was like the effect of a cat as it claws back having struck its quarry. The champ shook on his mountain feet.

'That young lad is running out of places to run to,' a man said.

It was as if Nicky had heard him. Because he suddenly capitulated. He stood his ground on the champ's next charge and one, two, one, two, he was on the ground, his legs crumbled like kindling. The champ stood above him, spat on his gloves and the next contender, the blonde man, entered the ring. I had to go home then. The car was ready. I did not know how Nicky got home. He told me in future years: 'On my bike of course, how else did you expect?'

'Why did you box him?'

'Something to do.'

Another story was Georgina. How could I have managed to see anything else in the sportsfield with Georgina there? She was wearing a cardigan and her little brothers had it stretched to a string from pulling at her. Hot and prickly, I always felt in myself when Georgina was about.

Georgina on the day of the sports: with Ger, her father. And how many of her little brothers in tow? Seven, a small hurling team. Links of a chain, looped to Georgina, the big link. Ger loved hurling. He pointed out famous hurlers to the kids and they hung from the rope that marked off the sideline, bringing it down as they fell on the grass. 'Daddy I have no straw for my drink. That's not fair, my straw is broken.' Orange crush around their lips. They didn't care about hurlers, or hurling.

Georgina didn't care about hurling either. Not one bit. I did, but Georgina was too close for me to maintain any interest. We were separated only by some grown-ups. She was pretending to be minding the children. I felt exposed. It was a bare countryside up there by the colliery. Not a tree grew up there. Not one word did we say, not one step closer did we take. But that was what you did. You just hung about in the excitement of being boy and girl friend. Yes, that was just another of those days when I claimed Georgina and Georgina claimed me. Nicky Hunt – he would have stepped towards her. Yeah, but only if he decided upon it. Once he decided upon it, Nicky would have done anything. But he made no decisions regarding women. Not then. They did not enter into his world. He got in the boxing ring. Georgina's father said, 'See him. He is a wild young man. He has the spring of a hurler. He should be a hurler. And not making a fool of himself by boxing Denis Makem.'

Teddy Holland on the day of the sports: assisted his mother on the lorry where the Irish dancing competition was being held. He set up the public address system. He made tea for the musicians. He winked at those he knew in the audience. Smirking and smoking cigarettes, he tried to subvert the authority of the judges. But the dancing competition could not have run without him.

$$* * *$$

I didn't see much of my future Sand Dance partners for a long time after that. 'I am your friend, young Kennedy,' Nicholas Hunt says to me one day we meet in Wolfhills. Yeah, Nicholas is my friend. I go to boarding school. Teddy goes to boarding school. Georgina goes to boarding school. Five years. Nicholas stays at home and works on his father's farm. All this time Georgina is my girlfriend. So I imagine. Though I don't see her. Then Georgina gets her Leaving Cert. I get my Leaving Cert. Teddy gets his Leaving Cert. And what does Georgina do? She and Nicholas Hunt; they elope to England together.

And then no contact. For at least two years no contact with any of them. Until our moment. Our moment of reunion. How did it come about? Very simply: A July day. July 1st actually, wet. I had come to live in London. Everything was very green in London that year. A man, busking at the Underground entrance on Hyde Park corner. A girl, passing the hat for him. I approach from one entrance. Another man approaches from the other. Bang. Recognition. The busker, dancing and playing a banjo, was Nicholas. The girl was Georgina. The man coming from the opposite entrance was Teddy Holland. Bang. Explosion. We skittered about the tiled floor. Teddy produced a mouth organ. We took off on an impromtu dance routine. It lasted fifteen minutes. Fifteen minutes of forgetfulness and remembrance. Fifteen minutes at the end of which we found ourselves holding a full silver collection. Says Teddy: 'This is an ordained moment. I have an idea. We should perform an act together.' We should resurrect an act he had seen in a movie. They were a trio: *'Wilson, Kepple and Betty.'* They had, back in old times, performed a routine called 'The Sand Dance'. Supposed to be how natives had once danced in the colonies, it was really a send-up.

'Come with me,' says Teddy. 'Let me tell you my idea. The Sand Dance was made for you three.' That was the day he took us to the Wimpy Restaurant on Oxford Street and ordered chicken and chips for all. I never pay, says he when we finish. We all bolt for the door. It is raining. Change jangling in our pockets, we run and run until, sick with laughter, we can run no farther. We are panting, leaning against one another. Spurts of blood are splashing down Georgina's legs. I see blobs of it run from beneath her dress, mingle with rivulets of rain.

'Oops, my friendly visitor,' she says. Suddenly, in my mind, something dissolves: an image, an ideal, a phantom person, which, without realising, I have for years been cultivating. A real person, real Georgina, stands there in its stead. I am in love with her. It is breathtaking how quickly it has happened. I look around. We are all in love with one another.

* * *

*The time we went on the Outreach.*

Teddy got us on Outreach which was run by some government department. We travelled to schools and old citizen's residences. This one was in Harringay. We thought we would be performing in a dining-room or big community room. It turned out to be a tiny lounge and the audience numbered about twelve people and a tiny Jack Russell terrier. The inmates moved their chairs forward so that we were restricted to about three shuffling paces in each direction. Nicholas said, as he always did, 'The show must go on.' I got to know the wallpaper intimately. The pattern was boat, train, airplane. Repeated. Between acts we had to stand against the wall in order to give room to members of the audience who got up to do their turns. A gentleman was doing his Stanley Holloway monologue, 'Sam's Christmas Pudding', when the Jack Russell escaped from its owner. My first shock of its whereabouts was the cold, wet touch of its upreaching nose against my bare thigh inside my shift. I yelled in terror and jumped until I must have hit the low ceiling. Total collapse of the 'Sam's Christmas Pudding' turn, I thought shamefully, but no, the man went on with it to the end. Why did that evening turn out to be such a success? Our elderly audience was wonderful. We joined in their singing 'California here I come...' We applauded them, they applauded us. Going home in Nicky's van, Madame

George said it was nice that people got a chance to express themselves. I loved how she could say a thing like that.

* * *

*Our very first show.*

I didn't remember what exactly he said but it was in Hackney and our changing room was in the toilets and there we were, standing in that strange silence and emptiness that immediately followed a show, when in he walked. I was hanging up my dhoti and pulling on my trousers. What was it about him – a perfect stranger and yet he was like somebody I had met before. But who? Where? I was looking at my narrow shoulders in the mirror and thinking how well suited was my physique to The Sand Dance when his face came from behind me. He pumped my hand up and down. He told me how grateful he was. He said other things but I wasn't really listening. He wore a camel coat and combed his fair hair back over a balding patch. His skin was shiny. There was a look of something in his light blue eyes, a dreaminess, an unhappiness. It's his eyes I remember. It struck me that somewhere in his life something had gone wrong. He was speaking and I was already forgetting what he was saying while at the same time wishing that I could meet him again. I thought I would. I liked him and wanted to talk more to him. He was a man for whom I could do a lot of good, I thought. But I never saw him again. Then others were backstage; people we knew, our friends from the pubs. The girls. Jenny Dalton. Jenny said she wet her knickers laughing. Pat O'Carroll, big flowsy Pat who wore a stripey dress that looked more like a circus tent, Pat said the same. And little Ursula Gorman, hair fringed Cleopatra style, she too wet herself. I had an image of a baby Ursula, her nappy wet and sopping. Funny thing was, when we were on stage I had not heard laughter. Some constant noise was in the background of my head but I was not there. I was concentrating on my steps, holding with the music, concentrating like never before. Keeping my nerve, as Nicholas had instructed me. I heard no laughter. Now laughter was all around me. Teddy shook his head gravely at the girls, 'Ladies, The Sand Dance is no laughing matter.' That sent them into further peals. Every table we sat at, all night, every drink we were toasted with, they said, 'We laughed and laughed.' And Teddy said laughing was not the object of the exercise. Artistry, Teddy said. The theatre of the absurd was not a laughing matter but a serious business. And I wondered if he really meant what he was saying because as far as I was concerned, to make them laugh was all and everything. Roars of laughter, heard during the performance only as background, had now returned and were filling my head, filling my whole body with warmth and light. To make people laugh. That was what I had been created for. It made them feel so good. It made me feel like God. I was powerful.

Or I was nearly powerful.

That man I had met after the show, our very first show, the man who I thought I could help – I couldn't. I did not see him again. But others, just like him, would keep turning up through the years of our show, would keep pumping my hand in gratitude and then would go away. All through The Sand Dance years I would see them, from that very first day when we performed in Hackney. And I would not be able to help them. (Mind you, sometimes fellows came backstage and shouted at us and said we were depraved. We didn't mind. Madame George just loved it then. She made her arms into a garland above our heads. Made of our troupe a union. Sometimes we even raised money for charity. Once, in Harlesden, we performed our Sand Dance to the air of 'The Mighty Quinn' – 'Come on without, come on within ... ' and had the audience in a frenzy of movement on the floor.)

* * *

For two years we performed The Sand Dance. At the beginning, when Georgina was the girlfriend of Nicholas. Then, when Nicholas had his injury (miscalculating on a high table one night on a shaky stage) and became a different person almost overnight, became our manager and coached Teddy to take his role. Then, after Georgina left Nicholas. Until one day, when she said she was going to live with Teddy. And that was the day I left The Sand Dance. I walked out. But all through those Sand Dance days I would have met that handshaking man backstage or somebody like him. Only now, when I go to see a really good act, a really original act like our Sand Dance, do I remember what he said about us. In his exact words: 'A sharing. A shared flight of the spirit: that's what I love about you four.'

The Sand Dance beat me.

# The Fortune Teller

*Cathy Kelly*

Stanley Maguire hadn't planned on renting out the upstairs office. A large, L-shaped room on the floor above Maguire's Travel, the office had just been vacated and Stanley had finally decided that the time had come to extend his travel agent empire onto the second floor. The architect had already drawn up the plans and Stanley could see himself in a spacious office overlooking Main Street, with cool green walls and a couple of cream leather couches perhaps, for valued customers to sit on. It was time to make a statement about the success of Maguire's Travel.

And then the woman had come into the travel agency and asked him, in a quiet but somehow steely way, if she could rent the office out for a couple of weeks. Stanley had meant to say no, he'd done his best, in fact, but the words wouldn't come. There was something about her smiling round face and those warm brown eyes that made him lose the run of himself. No had become yes.

'No bother at all, Sister,' he'd said, because she had a look of a nun about her with her tidy grey hair and the sober navy suit. Sure, what harm would it be to have a nun in the place for a while. He even heard himself offering to send the cleaner up to give the office a good spring clean.

'Thank you, Stanley,' she'd said, clasping his hand. 'You're a kind man: I can tell.'

Stanley Maguire, who hadn't told her his first name, beamed like a schoolboy even though it was at least thirty years since he'd graced a schoolyard. It was only when she was gone that he realised that she hadn't told him her name or what she wanted the office for.

\* \* \*

The girls in Maguire's Travel were fascinated when the small card went up above the doorbell for the upstairs office.

Madame Lucia: fortune teller.

'I thought Himself was going to turn it into a posh office,' said Carmel, who'd worked in Maguire's longer than anyone else and who'd had it up to the tonsils with men and their empires. 'Wait till he comes back from his holidays and sees this. I suppose she'll be some flamboyant type who'll stick exotic lights in the window and have a stream of lunatics dropping in and out.'

But there was no stream of lunatics. There was only the neatly-dressed figure of Madame Lucia herself going in and out quietly during normal business hours. Flamboyant was certainly not a word that could have been applied to her.

Between customers, Carmel, Gwen and Becky discussed how they didn't trust fortune telling. Carmel didn't even read her horoscope anymore.

All the magazines had told her that Geminis and Libras were a good match, but she and Michael had fought like cats and dogs and now Michael was back living with his brother while Carmel had their apartment to herself. She was thirty-four and her mother kept making snide remarks about how living with a man before marriage hadn't been the gateway to anything but ruin when she was a girl.

'When you come to your senses, your old room is there for you,' her mother, Phil, said at least once a week. Carmel knew she couldn't afford to pay the rent all by herself for much longer but neither could she face living with her mother again. Phil wore her bitterness like an Olympic medal. It was the only thing she'd been left with when Carmel's father had walked out on her thirty-two years ago. Phil had seemed almost triumphant when Michael had moved out of the apartment. History repeats itself, she'd said. Under the circumstances, Carmel had no interest in hearing that red was her lucky colour or that Saturday was her best day of the week. Such frivolity didn't cut any ice with her anymore.

* * *

On the third day, Gwen decided to risk it.

She was ready for Madame Lucia, she told her colleagues confidently. Fortune tellers were canny and could read clothes, handbags and jewellery with as much skill as they could supposedly read the cards. Gwen's good leather handbag and her engagement ring would have given the game away.

She'd left her handbag and the ring with Carmel and she'd taken off her travel agent uniform jacket, so there'd be none of that 'I see you going on a foreign holiday' malarkey. Madame Lucia would get no clues from her.

Upstairs, lemon aromatherapy oil was heating in a small burner and the air was redolent with scents of somewhere far away. Madame Lucia sat at a table with a crystal ball in front of her. She smiled silently at Gwen who sat down politely and looked into the crystal ball too. They both gazed at it for ages. Gwen did her best to see whatever it was that people saw in them. Fog or swirling mist. Wasn't that what you were supposed to see? Gwen tried hard but all she saw was a fat globe that smelled strongly of the window cleaner her Gran was always using. Madame Lucia was not a million miles away from Gwen's Gran, now that she thought about it. Sensible grey cardigan, cream blouse buttoned up to the neck, a kind smiling face and not a jangling gypsy earring in sight. She even had the same sort of gold-rimmed glasses Gran wore but without the gold chain. Behind the glasses, Madame Lucia's eyes flickered but she said nothing. Could Madame Lucia see something? Maybe it was all a con.

'You'll be married within the year,' said Madame Lucia. 'I see you in … Australia, I think. Yes, that's it.'

Gwen rolled her eyes. So much for fortune telling. She and Brian were going to Sardinia on their honeymoon.

'No, Australia,' Madame Lucia said firmly, as if she could read Gwen's mind.

Gwen blinked.

'I know you've booked somewhere else but it'll be Australia in the end. There's a bit of a shock coming and you have to make a decision but I think you'll take the right road. It's all for the best, really. You're a strong girl.'

'What about other things, money, family … ?' Gwen wanted more than this limited vision of the future.

'You came to ask me about love,' said Madame Lucia simply. 'That's what I saw for you.'

'I didn't say what I came to you for ...' began Gwen, but she stopped. Because she had come to find out about her and Brian. Not that she'd have admitted it to anyone, even her closest friends, but there was something not quite right. Brian was so distant these days. He looked uncomfortable when she began going through her wedding notebook, listing all the things they'd done and all the things they still had to do. Gwen was worried about the wedding cake. Was it unlucky to have a pyramid of profiteroles instead of the traditional fruitcake?

Madame Lucia smiled, a kind granny-ish smile. 'You'll do what's right,' she said.

'Well?' Carmel and Becky were curious when Gwen arrived back at work.

'Oh, you know, the usual rubbish,' said Gwen, searching in her handbag for her mobile phone. She might just send Brian a text message.

Gwen and Brian met in Mario's Coffee Shop after work. Brian had pulled a sweatshirt on over his plain bank cashier shirt and tie.

'What's up now with the wedding of the century?' he said, gloomily stirring two fat sugars into his latte. 'Don't tell me: the florist can't get the exact shade you want for the roses and everything's going to be ruined.'

Gwen looked at him, hurt.

'How can you say that ... ?' she began, and then stopped. He was right. All they ever talked about these days was the wedding. Gwen had dreamed of her wedding day since she'd seen Barbie resplendent in her meringue of crispy lace.

'You're fed up with all this wedding stuff, aren't you?' she said.

The question took both of them by surprise.

'A bit,' he admitted. 'I feel as if I'm stuck on a roller-coaster and I can't get off.' Brian looked at Gwen to see how she was taking this. She wasn't gasping with shock or anything, so he took the plunge. 'I always thought it would be nice to get married on a beach or somewhere simple. Without all the fuss.'

Gwen thought of the elaborate plans for a wedding feast that was going to cost a fortune and which made her break into a cold sweat when she thought about the inevitable drama of the table plans. Imagine her wild uncles sitting beside Brian's beautiful but shy cousin? Or Brian's brother telling risqué jokes as best man, jokes that would shock Gran and make her reach for her heart tablets?

'If we had a quick, tiny wedding, just for immediate family, we could use the money we've saved for a huge holiday. Like ...' she searched for a place '... Australia. We could dive off the Great Barrier Reef, see Sydney, Melbourne, Perth, everywhere.'

Brian didn't say anything. He didn't have to. The huge smile lighting up his face said it all.

\* \* \*

Becky passionately believed in fortune tellers. She always had, but she couldn't say that because the girls would tell her to give it a go, and if Madame Lucia took one look at her, she'd know. Becky was terrified that someone would find out. She still had the money, hidden in an envelope in her desk under a spare pair of tights so that anybody seeing the tights would know this was her personal drawer, and wouldn't look any further. Because €2,000 was a lot of money and anyone with half a brain would realise that Becky, the office spendthrift, could never have saved that much in her life.

She hadn't meant to take it, she really hadn't. She had never stolen as much as a notebook from the office supply box but the day that Stanley Maguire forgot to put the money in the safe, was coincidentally the same day Becky received the awful letter from the credit card people.

How could she owe them that much money? Yes, she'd bought the shoes and that long suede skirt that everyone admired so much but, surely she didn't owe nearly two thousand?

She'd added it up with shaking fingers on her calculator. Incredibly all those small amounts of money (€19.99 for sunglasses that were almost exactly the same as the ones all the Hollywood stars had; a yoga video; a new wallet) managed to add up to the same heart-stopping total on the bottom of the statement.

Which made it seem like fate when Stanley, who turned absent-mindedness into an art form, had opened the safe to put the morning's cash in and had left one wad of notes on his desk. He'd gone out to lunch then and Becky had picked up the money to give it to him later but somehow, once her fingers touched the cool, sleek notes, she'd known that this could solve all her problems.

Only it hadn't. Guilt burned her soul like the fires of hell and she hadn't had a decent night's sleep since.

'I know you don't believe in fortune telling,' said Gwen, who looked utterly delighted with herself since she'd called off the wedding, 'but Madame Lucia is different. She knows things. And she doesn't tell you bad things; only good news.'

What if you didn't have good news to tell, Becky thought miserably.

There was a lull in the office at eleven and Gwen urged Becky again.

'Go on, I bet you won't believe what she'll tell you. Look at me and Brian and how it's all worked out for the best.'

\* \* \*

Becky kept her glasses on. She only needed them for the computer but she thought that if she had a protective layer of glass between her eyes and the piercing gaze of Madame Lucia, the fortune teller mightn't see the guilt and the misery behind them.

'There's no need to be nervous,' said Madame Lucia pleasantly when Becky sat down, clasping and unclasping her hands anxiously. Easier said than done, Becky thought. She tried to breathe deeply but all that came out was a shaky, shuddering breath.

'It's not the end of the world, you know,' Madame Lucia remarked, staring into her crystal ball. 'Life tests us all every day: little temptations to see what kind of people we are. And you know what sort of person you are, after all. A good one.'

Becky's eyes brimmed. She wasn't a good person, she wasn't. If she had been, she'd never have been tempted by the money.

'You should talk to someone about a possible debt,' Madame Lucia continued. 'Pay off a little a week, that sort of thing. The banks are happy once you're paying something.'

Becky realised the fortune teller was talking about the credit card bill. She didn't know about the other money.

'Spring cleaning,' added Madame Lucia.

Mystified, Becky looked at her.

'The office hasn't had a good spring cleaning for ages. You'd be amazed at how things can fall down into drawers and filing cabinets and get lost. A good spring clean will soon restore everything to its rightful place.'

Her words sent a little jolt of excitement through Becky. Of course. It had been months since the office had been given a good sorting out. The back office was always cluttered with paper and Stanley's desk had a paper mountain as big as Everest on the floor behind it.

A wad of money could easily have got lost in the depths of this mountain. A wad of money that nobody would ever suspect had been hidden in Becky's drawer for a month.

'You'll talk to the bank, won't you?'

Becky beamed at Madame Lucia. 'Yes. Thank you, for everything.'

She bounced down the stairs, her mind racing. She'd ask Stanley if she could order some new filing cabinets while she was at it. A proper spring clean was definitely a good idea. Just because they'd all been busy lately didn't mean that standards should slip.

* * *

Carmel's asthma flared up half-way through Becky's office spring clean. 'There might've been money behind Stanley's desk, but there's nothing but dust in that corner,' she wheezed as Becky cleaned like a woman possessed.

Becky had already filled two bin bags and had come up with a new office code of conduct for dealing with duplicates of documents already on the computer system.

'If we back up the files on disc, then file the discs, we needn't keep any hard copies,' Becky announced.

'I'm going out for some fresh air,' Carmel said.

Outside, she looked at the door that led to the upstairs office. Why not, she decided. She had a few minutes to spare.

She didn't waste time staring at the crystal ball. She eyeballed Madame Lucia, who gazed back with a quiet intensity. Then, Madame Lucia took Carmel's hand and gently turned it over so that the palm was up.

Her unmanicured hand was cool and firm and Carmel felt some of the tension leave her.

'You're carrying someone else's pain,' Madame Lucia said matter-of-factly. 'It's not your burden. You have to let it go before you can live your own life.'

Carmel held her breath. This was unexpected.

'There are two good men in your life. One is far away but he's never forgotten you. He prays for you.'

'He can't,' said Carmel, shocked. 'My father's gone, he left years ago. He's never written, he doesn't care.'

'He does and he has,' insisted Madame Lucia calmly. 'The other man cares deeply for you too, but there is this … ' she paused, considering, 'this guard around your heart that keeps him away. It's the pain you're carrying, the other person's burden. You have to let it go.'

Carmel was still trying to take in the first bit of information. 'What do you mean, "he has"?' she asked slowly.

'He has written to you,' Madame Lucia replied. She squeezed Carmel's hand, this time in comfort. 'This is good news for you,' she said. 'This is a new beginning and you are in charge of it. You, not anybody else, not someone who is angry with the whole world.'

It was such a good description of her mother that Carmel smiled wryly. 'What should I do?'

Madame Lucia's mouth relaxed into a smile. 'That's up to you.'

Carmel's mother was polishing the brass on the door when Carmel walked up the path. Everything in No. 9 The Crescent was polished to within an inch of its life. Phil used to say it was because that waster hadn't left her much and she had to look after it. Carmel tried to imagine what it must have been like for her mother all those years ago. Alone with a small child. Had that hard shell been her only defence?

'What brings you here?' demanded Phil, as if Carmel never visited instead of coming home at least twice a week.

'I wanted to talk about my father,' Carmel said evenly. She never called him Dad.

'What about him?' Her mother kept grimly polishing.

'About the letters.'

The old yellow duster stopped moving.

'How did you know?'

'That doesn't matter. I want to see them.'

She waited outside until her mother emerged with a large manila folder crammed full of envelopes, some open, most untouched.

'I didn't want him in our lives anymore,' her mother said in a small voice, handing the folder over.

Carmel said nothing: she'd become good at that over the years. When Phil raged against Carmel's father, Carmel had learned to hold her tongue until the anger was gone.

'Where are you going?' asked Phil now as Carmel walked down the path, holding her precious cargo of letters.

'Home,' said Carmel pleasantly. 'I'll talk to you later.' There was no point in recriminations or bitter words. As she knew, that type of thing got you nowhere in life.

* * *

The most recent letter was dated the previous Christmas. Her father wrote every Christmas, despite never having had a reply in thirty-two years of writing. He'd worked it out, though. He knew his wife would never forgive him for walking out.

'I hope that one day she'll give you these letters so that you know I've never forgotten you,' he wrote. 'I would love to see you but you would have to want to see me and you might not, because I left. Your mother was a hard woman to live with but I should not have left you. I was young and stupid, and I regret that every day of my life.'

He lived in London, a city Carmel had visited many times, never knowing that her father lived just off the Hammersmith flyover and kept a picture of her as a baby in a frame by his bed. When she'd read the last letter, she'd phoned Michael, who'd arrived over immediately and hugged her tightly as she sobbed for all those lost years. Michael said she should write to her father. But Carmel wanted to visit him. Now, immediately.

'I'd love you to come with me ... ' she said hesitantly, not knowing if Michael would want to be involved any further because, after all, she'd pushed him away and they'd split up.

'Why don't we go tomorrow?' said Michael, holding her tightly.

* * *

Stanley's holiday in Florida had been fantastic.

'We had the holiday of a lifetime,' he said ruefully, patting his belly and remembering the pancake breakfasts he'd grown to love. 'Two weeks isn't enough, though. Two months would be better.'

He was delighted with the cleaned-up office, and even more delighted with the recovery of the missing €2,000.

'Fair play to you, Becky,' he said. 'You've worked hard on the place and I like the new disc filing system. I suppose you'll be looking for some of that two grand as a raise?'

'No,' said Becky quickly.

He was less pleased to hear that Gwen wanted three months sabbatical to go to Australia.

'Ah Gwen, what'll we do without you?' he complained. 'Anyhow, I thought you'd booked The Central Hotel for a big wedding?'

Gwen grinned. 'We've got it all worked out. Carmel has had five applications from people looking for holiday work now that the college term is over, and she and Becky say they can cope if we take one person on.'

'Where's Carmel?' Stanley suddenly realised that his office manager was missing.

'She had to go to London with Michael,' said Gwen. 'Something came up.'

'I thought she'd split with Michael?' Stanley was getting very confused.

'It's all back on,' said Becky.

Well, Stanley didn't know what to make of it all, but if the women were happy, sure he supposed he was happy too. He looked at his watch. Half nine. He had a meeting later with the architect about the office upstairs. It was time to get the Stanley Maguire – The Empire plans back on track. Then, he remembered that kindly woman who'd wanted the office for a couple of weeks.

'Is the nun still upstairs?'

All the phones went at once.

'She's not a nun,' said Gwen, leaping to answer a phone.

'She's a fortune teller,' Becky added, before saying 'Hello, Maguire's Travel, how can I help you?' in her professional voice.

Stanley went out onto the street, then in the door of the upstairs office. He marched up the stairs, feeling the weight of those extra pounds from two weeks of pancakes for breakfast. There was nobody there, just a table in the centre of the floor with a chair on either side of it. A small card on the table caught Stanley's eye and he picked it up.

On one side was inscribed a child's prayer to a guardian angel and on the other, was a picture of an angel, all flowing robes and wings, hovering on a cloud. Stanley smiled to himself and put the card in his pocket. Fortune teller indeed. He knew she was a nun. Anyhow, she was gone, God love her, and it was back to work in the real world.

# Liam

*Maura O'Neill*

*The* first time I saw him he was sucking his thumb and rubbing a fingernail of wool on just the right spot under his nose. This was his 'figgle' he would tell me later. It helped him sleep.

When my sister, Clare, became ill on her second pregnancy we all decided to lend a hand. I was Liam's godmother so I offered to take him for a few weeks. We had expected that once the baby was born everything would return to normal. I suppose, looking back I had an ulterior motive, thinking he would be a companion for Kate, my six-and-a-half-year-old. So I got the spare room ready next to my daughter's and thought about what it would be like to have a second child in the house, for a few weeks anyway.

Kate asked if she could stay at home from summer camp that day to welcome her cousin, who was a year younger than her. The whole idea of having a boy in her house both fascinated and bewildered her. She wasn't keen on boys. 'They are smelly and don't know how to play,' was her verdict so far on the opposite sex. But she was willing to give Liam a chance. She forfeited the last day of camp and got ready to meet her cousin. His dad, Phil, dropped him off, literally, barely turning off the car engine. He was worried that his son would ask too many awkward questions about why he had to have a sleep-over at his aunt's house. 'You be a good boy for Aunt Mary and ring whenever you want or if you feel lonely. Mammy will be fine in a few weeks and you can come home and see your new baby brother or sister. Okay Liam?' He didn't answer, nor did he look up at this dad, but just concentrated instead on a hole he was defiantly making with his toe in the loose gravel which surrounded our house. A quick awkward hug and his dad drove off leaving us in a haze of dust. 'Typical,' I thought to myself, finding old resentments and grudges swelling up inside me. When the air cleared the little boy just stood there waiting for God knows what.

I went over and tried to be as cheery as I could. 'We are delighted you are going to stay with us for a while Liam. You have grown so much since I last saw you. Kate has been dying to have someone to play with this summer.'

She hovered carefully in the wings, waiting for her chance to take control. 'Would you like to see my animals?' He really had no choice in the matter as she already had him by the hand leading him to the small wooden shed where her guinea pig and rabbits were. In the meantime, I went into the house with his bag, anxious about what lay ahead. It had been nearly a year since I saw my nephew. Life always kept my family so busy. We tended to find too many excuses too easily for not visiting each other. Maybe deep down that is why I was so keen to help this time. It was my way of making up for not phoning more often, for not keeping in touch. I suppose I was hoping to reopen those precious communication lines our mother used to talk about so much when she was alive. What would she think of her family now, I wondered.

'Mammy, where are you?' Kate came running into the house.

'Upstairs,' I shouted down.

'Bring Liam up to see his room.'

I heard her go out to him but there was no reply.

Slowly and with heavy step he came up the stairs and peered into the room. He still hadn't said a word since he arrived.

'Well, what do you think? You can change it around any way you like. Kate is next door and myself and Uncle Noel are just across the landing if you need us in the night.'

I came over to him and put out my arms to give him a hug but he just turned and went down the stairs.

I whispered to Kate to keep an eye on him. She grew tall with the responsibility and loved every minute of this new importance which had been thrust upon her. Suddenly the fact that her cousin was a boy didn't seem to matter any more.

When Noel came home that evening he made a fuss of our young visitor with plans to go fishing and have adventures in the nearby forest. But nothing seemed to bring any sort of reaction from Liam. I looked at him wistfully as he just sat at the table, moving food around his plate, not able to eat. For one awful moment, I just wanted to pick him up, put him in the car and drive him back home to his Mam and Dad. But that wasn't going to happen. I bit my lip, put on a smile and asked if anyone fancied ice-cream. My eyes were on Liam hoping that maybe this would be something which would bring a smile to his face. But he just sat there, head down, staring at his plate.

Kate perked up and told him that if he liked he could chop up a carrot for Lassie the guinea pig and get some lettuce for the rabbits. They got up from the table and organised the animals' tea then off they went to feed them.

I watched as my daughter took charge yet again. She had an uncanny knack of knowing what to do if someone felt down or sad. My six-year-old was growing up. Contented with her day's activities she decided that she would go to bed at nine o'clock on the dot, just in case Liam got lonely in the night.

The three of us made the climb up the stairs saying our prayers as we went, our routine every night. We looked out at the moon and noticed long brush strokes of a deep red in the night sky.

'Red sky at night, shepherd's delight,' sang Kate.

'If it is a fine day tomorrow, Mammy, can we let the animals out?' she pleaded.

I said I felt it was better we let Liam decide what we will do tomorrow. She agreed, nodding.

When they got into bed I offered to read a story but they looked done in so I snuggled them both and said good night. I left on a night-light and Liam turned his head slowly and whispered thank you and then turned into the wall to go asleep. I waited at the door, listening, hoping to hear deep, contented breathing of children heading off to the wonders of their dreamworld. Then from Liam's room, I could hear a soft scratching noise. I crept in quietly and asked him if he was warm enough. He nodded. I wondered if he had a cuddly toy he liked to snuggle up to. Kate had her kangaroo. But he just said that he always had his 'figgle'. When I asked him to tell me about it he showed me how his little fingers would gently pull at his blanket, gathering little bits of fluff. I watched as he put his thumb in his mouth and began his ritual, gently and rhythmically rubbing the wool across his face. 'My mam told me she used to suck her thumb when she was small,' he confided in me.

'We're like twins,' he said proudly.

I tucked him in and kissed him goodnight.

My footstep down the old wooden stairs was slow and deliberate as I tried to quel the need to cry, for my godchild, my sister, for the times when we hadn't been there for each other.

I found myself reaching for the phone and dialling my sister's number, something I hadn't done, unselfconsciously, for a long time. We talked, giggled, wallowed in times past as sisters and friends, a warmth and ease drawing us closer than we had been for a long time. The next day was bright and warm. I waited anxiously for noise from upstairs but there was no sound until 10 o'clock. Then down they came. Liam seemed happier. Kate was in full bustle mode and told him that she could make her own breakfast. Afterwards it was out to the animals and there they played for most of the day.

Liam was beginning to find his own voice and to feel more at ease. As the days wore on, he and Kate were getting closer and closer. His dad phoned him one night and I overheard him talking about the animals and how much he loved helping Kate to care for them. My sister's condition had stabilised but there was no news yet. I spoke to her and could hear her loneliness for her son and her worry about her unborn baby. She was at home and spent the time looking out at the trees in her garden hoping that somehow nature would hear her prayer for a healthy baby and bring her family back together again. 'Liam has become a real friend for Kate, so don't worry about him, Clare,' I tried to assure her.

The days slipped by warmed by the summer sun and fairytale skies of blue.

A routine had developed between the two young cousins by the end of the second week. I, the adult, was excluded. I couldn't possibly understand the complexities of taking care of Lassie the guinea pig, not to mention the rabbit sisters, Floppy and Susie. They chatted incessantly, coded, guarded, secretive. Always busy, animals had to be fed, grazed, hutches cleaned, no time to dilly dally with a boring adult.

Then one morning, a cry, a scream, brought that adult into their world, running, breathless with panic. What has happened? Is there much blood? Who is injured? Please God don't let it be serious.

I reached the shed in a state but desperately trying to look calm, collected. My daughter's face turned to me when I got to the door. She was sobbing convulsively, her little body shaking. Words were falling from her lips but all I understood was her hand pointing to her guinea pig's house. I gasped, please don't let it be her pet. She is only six. I don't want her to know the pain, the sadness, the loss which death brings, not yet, not at this age.

She couldn't move. I looked into the cage and there was the little body of her beloved pet.

'Her eyes are still open,' she blurted out, in some hope that maybe Lassie was still alive.

Drawing her close to me, holding her tightly against me, I gently told her that Lassie had died during the night.

'Mammy, I don't want her to be dead', she sobbed.

'What did I do wrong?'

'Nothing my darling, it was just her time, she lived a good life and was 73 in guinea pig years,' I explained.

She wanted to look at the body, closely, definitely. I hesitated but she insisted.

Out of the corner of my eye I noticed Liam standing, watching, waiting. Suddenly I felt like an intruder. This was their secret place. I stood back and he took Kate's hand and gently stood beside her as she looked into the cage one more time. He spoke to her softly, in whispers, she nodded, hair covering her face, shoulders hunched, shuddering. She turned to me, tears still falling and said she wanted to have a funeral for Lassie when Daddy came home. I hugged her, held her and kissed her. Liam and I brought her into the house and we all sat down. We talked about the funeral arrangements. I was sent to get a pillow case in which the body would be laid. Then I was dispatched to find Lassie's coffin. I presented a number of boxes, among them a shoe box and a chocolate box. The shoe box was though to be the most dignified.

All this time Liam sat protectively by Kate's side. I heard him tell her not to worry that Lassie is in heaven now and that she is happy. This seemed to comfort my daughter but every now and then the whole sadness of her guinea pig's passing became too much and I would take her in my arms and rock her, saying, 'My darling, my darling.'

By the time Noel came home I had already warned him of Lassie's death. Kate ran into his arms and Liam, as always, stayed close to his cousin but allowed her to be sad with us too. She decided she wanted to have the burial that day, before the sun went down, when the sky was glowing and golden.

In the meantime, we just sat around talking about Lassie and what we remembered of her. Liam joined in as naturally as if he had lived with us forever.

Just as the funeral was to get underway, the phone rang. It was Liam's dad. I held my breathing expecting the worst.

They had arrived at the hospital an hour ago and Clare was in labour. His voice quivered with the strain of not knowing, of feeling totally helpless. He promised to ring as soon as there was any news. For the first time I sensed what my sister saw in this man, my brother-in-law, her husband. I told him to take care and give our love to Clare.

When I put the phone down, Kate and Liam were outside discussing where the grave was to be. I hesitated and decided not to say anything about the call. Let's get Lassie's funeral over first, I thought to myself.

Meanwhile, the sun was beginning to slowly sink behind the trees at the edge of the cornfield. The night sky was a furnace of colour, gold and deepest red.

The children and Noel were already outside. I was instructed to bring out the pillow slip. Liam held the box while Kate and her dad went into the wooden shed to get Lassie's body. The two rabbits, Floppy and Susie were uncharacteristically still, sensing something had happened.

Noel placed the body gently into the pillow slip and Kate helped to lay Lassie gently into the coffin. Then Liam walked over to Kate's side, Noel went ahead as the undertaker, I was the last in the funeral procession.

We walked out to the edge of the cornfield next to our house. The grave had already been decided on earlier in the evening by the two cousins. The hole dug, the body was placed into the earth. Kate looked at me, she was crying again, 'Mammy will you say something?' I thanked Lassie for all the fun Kate had with her.

Just as I finished, trying to think of something else to add, Liam started to talk. 'Bless Lassie and keep her safe in guinea pig heaven. Help her to make friends and to be happy. Thank you Lassie for letting Kate and me play with you. We miss you.'

Silence.

Nobody spoke until Kate wanted a special stone from her treasure onto the grave so she would remember where it was. There were more tears and then the small procession went back into the house.

Everyone was tired but nobody was able to sleep. Kate was still very upset. I tried to help her to think of nice things like a giant bowl of her favourite ice-cream, swimming on her holidays, but it didn't work.

Then I heard Liam getting out of bed and coming over to her. I got up to let him talk to her.

'Kate, you know what I do to help me sleep?'

'No, what?' she asked, curious. 'I suck my thumb, but that's not the best part. If you get your fingers and rub them on your blanket, like this, you can get some wool off the blanket. Then rub it on your face when you suck your thumb and it's really nice. Try it.'

Kate plucked at her blanket and got her bits of fluff. She stuck her thumb in her mouth and then tried to rub the wool on her face.

'Nice isn't it?' Liam said enthusiastically.

'That's my figgle, it helps me to sleep, especially when I miss my Mam and Dad.'

Kate thanked Liam and then remembered why he was staying with us. She asked him was he lonely for his Mam and worried about her? They talked into the night about his new brother or sister, about his Mam, about her Lassie. I left them to it, hoping that soon the phone would ring and it would be all over.

About an hour later I came back upstairs to see if they were alright. Liam was just about to get into his own bed. I had looked out the window coming up the stairs and saw the most wonderful golden sun, sinking beyond our cornfield. I called the two to look out and see how beautiful it was.

'Look,' said Liam, 'red sky at night, shepherd's delight. It's going to be a nice day tomorrow, we can let the animals out.'

Then he stopped, remembering Lassie. He said he was sorry, he forgot. But Kate said it was okay, they still had the bunny rabbits to mind.

With that the phone rang and it was Liam's dad. Clare had had a beautiful baby girl and both were just fine. I cried I was so glad, Liam ran down the stairs and Kate after him.

We all danced, jumped up and down. Liam talked to his Dad who said he would come to collect him the next day. When he put the phone down we all decided we were hungry.

'Pizzas and cokes all round to celebrate your new sister, Liam,' I suggested. 'My favourite treat,' he smiled, hair flopping over his eyes. Kate gave him a hug. Promises and pacts were made that night, sleep-overs planned. Kate was to visit to see her new cousin and Liam, of course, had to be kept up to date about Floppy and Susie.

As the sun disappeared I looked up at the sky and knew tomorrow would bring an abundance of delights for us all.

# Golden Feathers

*A modern retelling of an old Irish fairytale by*
*Catherine Ann Cullen*

*S*ean, a small, pale boy of six, is lying in bed. Sunlight, streaming through the window, picks up the blue, green and gold shades of the threadbare patchwork quilt that covers him.

'I'm fed up being sick. I wish I could go outside and do things like the other boys and girls,' Sean says, thumping his pillow crossly as he watches the children play outside his window. 'I can't even do something for you, Mam, like going to the shops or helping in the garden.'

'Ah, but you can do something for me,' his mother smiles, as she smoothes down the quilt. 'You know I love to hear you singing while I'm working in the house.'

'What good is singing? I want to do things and go places! I want to grow up and change the world! Singing's not going to change anything.'

'Isn't it? Well, I think that when you do anything with love, it changes things,' his mother says, sitting down on the side of his bed. 'When I was a little girl, my mother made me this quilt, and I've often thought about all the love she put into it. Even when I was sick in bed, I used to have the most wonderful adventures, just imagining that the quilt was a magical country.'

Sean looks at the quilt as she speaks, and her voice seems further away. His mother kisses him and plumps up his pillow before she goes out of the room. A feather is dislodged from the pillow, and it floats down onto the quilt. Sean picks up the feather and holds it in his hand. It is golden. He sees the spot in the pillow where the feather has come from and there is another golden feather peeping out. He begins to pull feathers out one by one, until there is a little heap of gold on the quilt. The sun makes the feathers gleam as if they are alive. Suddenly the heap stirs, and a golden bird with a silver beak emerges, smoothing down her ruffled feathers.

'Sean, you must help me,' the bird says in a silvery voice. 'I have come to ask you to take the road to the Green Kingdom, where a young boy is destined to become prince. I did not think it would be a young boy wearing blue stripy pyjamas, but with magic, you can never be sure.'

'You're the most beautiful bird I've ever seen, and I'd love to help you. But I can't leave my room – I haven't been out of bed in weeks!'

'To get to the Green Kingdom,' says the little bird, 'all you have to do is follow me into the fields of the patchwork quilt. Like this.'

The bird perches on Sean's hand and he suddenly finds himself walking over a blue mountain that, a few minutes ago, was the hump made by his knees under the bedclothes. The bird tells him that the road will take him to the palace, and that he will not see her again until he has come to the end of a long journey. But she promises that she and her friends will help him whenever they can. She sings:

> Golden feathers, silver beak,
> The old king weeps, and what does he seek?
> Bring him the thing that will bring back laughter,
> And you will be prince of the land thereafter.

Then she flies away, leaving Sean to walk through his patchwork quilt land until he comes to the palace gates.

The guard on the gate looks sad, and the guard at the door looks sad, and all the staff and courtiers in the palace have long faces, too. As Sean nears the throne-room, he hears the sound of weeping, and when the door of the room opens, he sees that it is the king who is crying as if his heart would break.

Sean asks the king why he is sad, and the king tells him that only one thing will make him happy – the Golden Bird who once sang so beautifully outside his window. The bird has gone away, and the king believes it is because his own two sons, Festus and Celsus, have been so wicked and cruel that they have brought unhappiness to his subjects and to the bird itself.

Sean feels sorry for the king. He doesn't like to say that he has seen the Golden Bird, but he tells the king that the bird he seeks cannot be far away, and that he will do his best to find it. The king looks a little happier. He tells Sean that in his country, music is the most precious and magical thing of all. He also says that he has promised his kingdom to the person who can return to him the Golden Bird.

*Golden feathers, golden wings,*
*Find me the Golden Bird who sings,*
*My throne and my kingdom and riches untold,*
*To whoever can bring me the bird of gold.*

The king's two sons, an unpleasant-looking pair, are listening to this. They are not going to stand by and allow any of their father's kingdom to be given away, so they announce that they themselves will go to find the bird. Sean offers to go with them to help. The brothers laugh at him, but they let Sean walk down the road with them. After all, if he does come in useful, they can take the credit.

In a short time they reach the edge of a forest, and there they meet an old man who asks them to help him to cut some logs. The brothers refuse rudely, but Sean chops the wood until it is all done, while the brothers sit on a log and make fun of him. In return for his help, the old man tells Sean how to find the road to the Golden Land, where the bird can be found. The only way into the land, he says, is to climb the highest apple-tree in the Green Kingdom, where hundreds of birds build their nests. The tree is in this very forest, but anyone who has ever tried to climb it has been pecked at by the birds and has been so bruised and shaken that they have had to come down again. The old man gives Sean a wooden barrel and a rope, which, he says, will come in useful on the journey. Sean thanks him politely and the two brothers follow him into the woods.

Before long, there is a tremendous clamour of birds squawking and singing. The three follow the sound to an enormous tree, which is weighed down with giant apples. There is no doubt that this is the tree that will lead to the Golden Land. Sean suggests that he and the brothers tie the rope to the barrel, throw the rope over the highest branch they can reach, and use it to haul each other up into the tree in the barrel.

Festus climbs into the barrel first, but as Sean and Celsus raise him up, the birds peck and screech so loudly that he shouts to be pulled down again.

Shaken, he climbs out of the barrel and Celsus teases him as he climbs in for his turn. But he fares no better, for no sooner have the others raised him three feet in the air than a huge apple falls on his head, and several smaller ones begin to rain down on him. Roaring in pain, he is lowered down, and Sean goes to climb into the barrel in his turn.

The two princes laugh at him. 'How will a boy in blue pyjamas succeed where we fine princes have failed?' they sneer. But Sean is determined, and the brothers, winking at each other, promise to wait for him under the tree if he makes it to the Golden Land. As they raise him up, the birds chirp kindly at him. He thinks he hears from far away the Golden Bird's song:

> *Golden feathers, silver beak,*
> *The old king weeps, and what does he seek?*
> *Bring him the thing that will bring back laughter,*
> *And you will be prince of the land thereafter.*

And in the golden leaves of the tree, he imagines he sees the Golden Bird itself. He soon finds himself at the top of the tree, where a golden road unfolds before him. He hasn't gone far when he comes to a row of stables. The young stable-girl greets him kindly, and he asks if she knows where the Golden Bird is kept. The stable-girl tells Sean that the bird has been captured by the King of the Golden Land, who lives at the other end of the kingdom, across three islands and across three seas. She offers to help Sean by letting him choose any horse from her stables to speed him on his journey.

The horses are all so enormous that Sean is afraid of them, so he picks the smallest he can find, a poor-looking white mare. The girl smiles. She says he has chosen her very best steed, but that only by singing to the mare will he discover her true power. Sean climbs onto the mare and sings to her:

> *Come little mare, and be my guide,*
> *Together to the Golden Land we'll ride.*

The mare answers him in a human voice, and tells him to look between her ears, and he will be able to see for miles. On the mare's back, Sean crosses three seas and three islands, until finally they see the golden turrets of the castle of the Golden Land rising before them. At the gate of the kingdom is a mean-faced guard, who looks them up and down, and laughs.

'Er – we'd like to see the King of the Golden Land, please,' says Sean. But the guard does not hear him.

'There's no point in asking me anything. I've stuffed my ears with cotton wool just in case anyone ever starts singing around here, because there's nothing I hate more than the sound of music. But if it's a bird you're after, you're not the first and you won't be the last to fail in your quest. You might have dressed a bit more sensibly for the job, though.'

The guard stands aside, sniggering at Sean's pyjamas. But Sean thanks him politely, and rides on to the palace.

The King of the Golden Land is a giant who does not seem too happy to see Sean. He keeps the Golden Bird in a cage beside his throne, although the bird has not sung at all since she was brought to the Golden Land. The giant swears he will force her to sing – for every kingdom needs music. Every day, his servants bring a barrel of apples from the highest tree in the land for the Golden Bird, but she eats nothing.

The giant tells Sean that he will never be able to steal the Golden Bird, because the giant never sleeps. But when Sean says he will do anything to get the bird, the giant, grinning, promises to give him what he wants on one condition. For three days in a row, the giant will hide, and Sean must find him. Then, for the following three days, Sean must hide, and the giant must not be able to find him.

So, for the first three days, Sean asks the little mare to help him find the giant:

> *Over the green and under the blue*
> *Lies all that is false and all that is true,*
> *Come little mare, and be my guide,*
> *Show me a place where a giant might hide.*

On the first day, the giant is disguised as a barn full of grain, on the second as a mountain covered in trees, and on the third as a storm-cloud in the sky. But some features of the giant are obvious in these three if you look closely at them, and the mare helps Sean to see them clearly.

However, the giant does not have the same success in finding Sean. On the first day, the trusty mare helps the boy to transform himself into a flea on the giant's horse, and the giant rides home at the end of the day seething with rage, and singing,

> *By all that is bad and all that is base,*
> *Tomorrow I'll find your hiding place.*

On the second day, the trusty mare transforms Sean into an eyelash on the giant himself, and the giant rides home at the end of the day, boiling with rage and screaming,

> *By all that is bad and all that is base,*
> *Tomorrow I'll find your hiding place.*

Finally, on the third day, the little mare changes Sean into a pip in the middle of an apple on one of the trees in the giant's orchard. Towards evening, when the giant has almost given up hope of finding Sean, he comes upon the tree where Sean is hiding and plucks the very apple inside which our hero is concealed. He bites into the apple and Sean is so afraid of being eaten that he cries out, and he is discovered. The giant is triumphant, and Sean cannot persuade him that he has beaten him by bettering him on five occasions out of six. The giant insists that the bargain was that Sean had to win all six challenges, and he locks him into the stables with the mare.

'If only I could get out of here! If only the giant would fall asleep!' says Sean in despair. 'Then, maybe I could steal the Golden Bird. Little mare, is there anything that might put a giant who never sleeps to sleep?'

'I don't know. And I've used up all my magic helping you to hide,' says the mare. 'How are people put to sleep in your country?'

'Well – mothers and fathers sometimes sing lullabies to their children to put them to sleep,' Sean says, a little doubtfully.

'What a pity it is that the Golden Bird will not sing, for perhaps then the giant would fall asleep, and we could steal the bird,' replies the mare.

Sean is thoughtful. 'I can sing,' he tells the mare, 'but I wonder how I can get to make music for the giant.' He begins to sing as loudly as he can, and eventually the giant asks where the music is coming from. When he finds out, he orders that Sean be brought before him to sing. Sean pretends to be unwilling, but when he gets before the giant he begins to sing softly and sweetly, all the lullabies he can remember.

At the first song, the giant's head begins to nod. At the second, he calls for his favourite blue blanket, and begins to suck his thumb. Then Sean sings the third lullaby –

*Golden feathers fall and rise,*
*Golden sleep close up your eyes.*
*Silver stars and moonbeams take you*
*Till the golden morning wake you.*

– and the giant begins to snore. And when the giant falls asleep, all his courtiers fall asleep, too. Sean seizes the Golden Bird in its cage, leaps onto his mare, and rides off triumphantly. But as the three reach the palace gates they meet the guard who has stuffed his ears with cotton wool – the only person who has not heard the music. The mare leaps the gates as Sean clings to her back, the golden cage clutched in his hand. But the guard roars out, 'STOP, THIEF!' so loudly that he stirs all the sleepers.

The giant wakes with a jerk. When he hears what has happened, he flies into a rage and sends three armies after Sean. All the birds of the air have joined Sean and his friends to fly with them, and the three armies behind are delighted to have such a clear indication of where the runaways are. All they have to do is look up in the air and they can follow the path that Sean has taken. But when they reach a fork in the road, all the birds of the air go one way, leading the three armies away from Sean and his two friends, who take the other road. As Sean gallops to the end of the golden road, he passes the stables again, and the stable-girl comes out to meet him.

'I may look like a stable-girl, but I was enchanted by the giant, and am really the Princess with One Crown. And your little white mare is the Princess with Two Crowns. Take me with you on the mare's back, and you will soon see us both as we really are.'

Sean takes the stable-girl on his mare, and when they get to the place where the top of the great apple-tree is poking out from a gap in the golden road, Sean dismounts from the mare and helps the stable-girl to jump down beside him. Then Sean calls down to Festus and Celsus, who he can see are still waiting beneath the tree.

'Send down the Golden Bird first!' the brothers cry, and Sean puts the bird in its cage into the barrel, and the brothers haul it down.

'Now, come down yourself!' Festus and Celsus call.

'The king's sons have never shown me any kindness yet,' Sean tells the stable-girl. 'I don't know if I can trust them to bring me down safely, so I will test them before I let them try.' So, instead of climbing into the barrel, he plucks a huge apple from the tree and puts that in instead. The brothers pull the apple half-way down the tree, then let go the rope so the barrel and its load dash to the ground and splinter into a million pieces. The brothers stroll away, laughing, carrying the golden cage, and singing mockingly:

> *Golden feathers, silver beak,*
> *The old king weeps, and what does he seek?*
> *Bring him the thing that will bring back laughter,*
> *And you will be prince of the land thereafter.*

Night is falling and it is too dark for Sean and his friends to try to make their way down the tree, so they resolve to wait until morning. As the mare, the stable-girl and Sean curl up to sleep, the fields around the tree curl up to cover them like a quilt.

In the morning, the quilt unfolds again, and with the help of the stable-girl, the mare and all the birds of the air, Sean manages to get down the tree. When their feet touch the ground, the mare and the stable-girl are transformed into lovely princesses, and so the three of them walk along the green road to the palace. The sad-faced guards stand aside to let them pass. They hear the sound of weeping, and the three enter the throne-room to see the king crying beside the cage of the Golden Bird.

'Why are you sad, Your Majesty?' asks Sean. 'The Golden Bird that you longed for is yours at last!'

'Since my two brave sons brought back the bird yesterday, she has not sung even one note,' sighs the king. 'All the wise men and women in the kingdom have tried to make her sing, but in vain.'

'Let me try,' says Sean, and he gently opens the door of the cage. The Golden Bird leaps onto his hand and at once begins to sing even more beautifully than before:

*Golden feathers, golden wings,*
*The true prince comes and the true bird sings,*
*Hail to the heart that will bring back laughter,*
*Hail to the prince of the land hereafter.*

The king's face breaks into a smile. 'How has this happened?' he asks, and when he hears the full story, he grows angry with his two sons, and commands that they be brought before him. The brothers swagger in, but when they see Sean, they begin to tremble. They fall down before him and beg for his forgiveness. Sean asks the king to pardon them.

'I have found two beautiful princesses, one for each of them to marry, if the brothers will promise to be good and faithful from now on,' says Sean.

'You are too kind to my wicked sons,' answers the king, 'but they have learnt nothing, and they must be punished. Festus and Celsus, you will spend tomorrow picking a barrel of apples from the highest tree in the land for the Golden Bird, and if the other birds peck you and the apples fall on your heads, it will be only what you deserve.'

The brothers spend the next morning picking the apples, and at noon, Sean creeps up to see how they are managing. He sees that the brothers are pecked and bruised, tormented by all the birds of the air and the apples falling like rain from the tree.

'If it wasn't for Sean, this would never have happened to us,' Festus says, darkly. 'No matter how many apples we pick, the barrel does not seem to get any fuller.'

'When we get home, we will make Sean's life a misery,' agrees Celsus, and Sean tiptoes away, shaking his head.

At evening Sean returns to the tree. The two brothers are black and blue from the falling apples and the pecking birds. While Sean watches, a small bird falls out of a nest in the tree, right beside Celsus's foot.

'Perhaps we should put it back in the nest,' says Festus.

'Why should we save it?' asks his brother. 'The birds have done nothing but peck at us all day.'

'If we were kind to them, like Sean is, maybe we would fare better in the world,' says Festus.

'If we are kind to the birds, we will have to be kind to Sean too, for he has brought us two beautiful princesses, even though we were cruel to him,' says Celsus, a little puzzled.

'When I think about it now, I'm sorry that we tried to kill him. Even though my arms are aching from the birds, my heart is aching even more. If we had been kinder to him we could have helped to make our poor father happy,' Festus says sadly.

Together, the two brothers pick up the little fallen bird and put it gently back in its nest. Suddenly, the other birds begin to sing instead of squawking, and they help the brothers by shaking apples into the barrel. In a trice, it is full.

Sean comes out of his hiding place and the brothers embrace him and beg his forgiveness. The three of them carry the barrel back to the palace. The king agrees to pardon his sons at last, and the two smiling princesses take their hands.

The king invites Sean to live with him in the palace for as long as he wishes, where the king can listen to the singing of the Golden Bird, while Sean rules over his kingdom:

> *Golden feathers, golden wings,*
> *The true prince comes, the true bird sings,*
> *Hail to the heart that has brought back laughter,*
> *And hail to the prince of the land hereafter.*

The king smiles and says that at last his palace is a real home, with the sound of singing and music in it. Sean thanks the king, and asks that two castles be built in the fields beside the palace for the two brothers.

Sean goes up to the tower at the top of the palace to look over his kingdom, and as he looks down at the fields, they seem to look just like the patchwork of his quilt back home. His eyes rest on the blue mountains, and they seem to shift a little, as if a boy's knees were under them. As he turns around, the pillars and walls of the tower begin to look like the pillows on his bed. Something tickles his nose, and he sneezes. He opens his eyes, and on the quilt before him lies a white feather.

'I hope you haven't been pulling feathers out of your pillow, Sean,' his mother says. 'I thought I heard you humming to yourself, but when I came in, you were asleep.'

'I'd like to sing for you, Mam,' Sean says. 'I was just practising a new song while I was closing my eyes. A lullaby for putting grown-ups to sleep.'

'There, now, and I thought singing was no use,' says his mother, teasingly, as she sits down beside him.

Sean grins, and imitates his mother's voice. 'Except when it's done with love,' he says, teasing her back. His mother puts her arm around him, and he sings:

> *Golden feathers, fall and rise,*
> *Golden sleep close up your eyes,*
> *Silver stars and moonbeams take you,*
> *Till the golden morning wake you.*

His mother closes her eyes and smiles as he sings. Sean opens his hand and looks at what he is holding – a golden feather that gleams in the sun as if it is alive.

# Nasty Nick

## John Scally

Once upon a time there lived a man named Nicholas. He was a tall, thin man with long hands. He always seemed to wear an ill-fitting, black suit with an old sky blue scarf draped around his neck. His once-dark hair was slightly silver now, but the ice-blue eyes set in a craggy face and fringed with the blackest lashes were the same as when he was a teenager. He had a habit of looking deep into other people's eyes and then into some unseen place. He always said what he thought, sometimes with disastrous results.

He lived in a lonely house on the side of a mountain by a rutted grass track which led to the tiny village of Whitepark. His house was cheaply furnished. Congealed grease of dinner stuck to plates in his kitchen sink, the porridge dish from breakfast was dry on the draining board. In the corner of the kitchen was a wash-stand with a soapdish, basin and a pitcher jug so topped up with water that a fly could drink out of it.

He was the best shoemaker in all the land. People came from far and near to have their shoes made by him. The king always wore shoes carefully crafted by Nicholas's magic hands.

But Nicholas was a sad and bitter man. Ten years previously, on Christmas Eve, his wife and three children had been drowned in a boating accident. A sketch of his wife was displayed religiously on his mantelpiece. It whispered to him the secrets of loss and heartache. He felt like a stone had crushed his heart.

Although he had a special talent he was not a little feared because of his fierce temper and his rough manner with people. The nickname his neighbours gave him was Nasty Nick, though no one would dare call him that to his face.

The weeks before Christmas were always his busiest time of the year. As the winter dawned and with the rain coming through the holes in the roof and the wind howling through many of the many gaps in the walls he needed money badly. He worked eighteen hours a day, seven days a week, because he had a big contract to make new boots for all the soldiers in the king's army.

One evening, six weeks before Christmas, he had a visitor. She had curly white hair, a very cross face, brown eyes and a false smile. She was a doctor's daughter and that most reviled of species in the locality, a 'blow-in'. No humility and precious little humanity could be diagnosed in her as she looked down her nose in a conscious glow of superiority while she spoke to her neighbours. Nicholas eyed her with disfavour when she came into his home. In a voice much too loud for his liking she introduced herself: 'My name is Mrs Frida Fruitcake. You've probably heard of me. My husband, Freddie, owns the biggest bakery in the town. We were featured in *Goodbye* magazine last month. You *must* know of us.'

In an increasingly cross voice Nasty Nick answered, 'Madam, I've never heard of *Goodbye* magazine. It seems to me that you are a fruitcake by name and nature. I can't afford to waste my time listening to an old bore like you talking rubbish. What do you want?'

Mrs Fruitcake didn't really notice just how angry Nasty Nick was and continued in an excited voice, 'My darling Freddie has been working hard all year. I would be obliged if you would make him a nice snug pair of slippers for Christmas. They would be lovely for him on the cold nights. I'd pay you handsomely of course.'

Nasty Nick shouted at her in a voice as loud as thunder, 'Do you think I can afford the time to make silly slippers for a man with such a stupid wife? Have you any idea how many pairs of boots I have to make for the king's army? How dare you waste my time. Get out of my sight at once.'

Mrs Fruitcake was so terrified by Nasty Nick's outburst that she was sobbing like a baby. She raced out the door faster than an Olympic runner. Nasty Nick followed her out and slammed the door after her so hard that the hinges nearly came off. He got back to work muttering under his breath about the stupid woman with the stupid name.

Suddenly he stopped in his tracks. He heard a faint knock on his front door. He scratched his head. Then there was a slightly louder knock on the door. Nasty Nick was fuming. He said in a whisper, 'If it is that Fruitcake woman again I'll kill her.'

Then in a very angry voice he said aloud, 'Come in.'

A small, slim woman walked in. She had a small nose and shiny, black hair touching her shoulders. By her side was a little boy. He was a shy seven-year-old who was incapable of seeing evil in others. Although his nose was a little lumpy, his teeth crooked and his eyebrows too dark, he still almost had the face of an angel.

In a soft, sweet voice the woman said, 'Good evening sir. I know you are a very busy man and I'm really sorry to bother you. My name is Siobhán O'Grady … '

Nasty Nick gruffly butted in, 'Are you anything to the late Captain Lennie O'Grady?'

For a moment it looked as if the woman was about to burst into tears. Then she took a deep breath and said in a whispery voice, 'He was my husband.'

Nasty Nick shook his head, 'I'm sorry for your loss. I was saddened by the news of his death in the great war seven years ago. People say he was the bravest soldier ever to wear the king's uniform.'

Siobhán smiled weakly, 'It is kind of you to say that sir. My son Lennie here wasn't even born before his father died. I've found it very hard to put food on the table for little Lennie since but now I've taken on a second cleaning job and at last I can afford to buy some nice things for him and I'd really like you to make him a new pair of shoes for Christmas. The poor boy has never … '

Nasty Nick stood up from his chair and waved his hands as if he were holding a hot coal. His voice was like a growling dog, 'Madam do you have any idea who you are talking to or what you ask? Do you think I can afford the time to make silly shoes for a little boy? Have you any idea how many pairs of boots I have to make for the king's army? How dare you waste my time. Get out of my sight at once.'

Mrs O'Grady nearly jumped out of her skin with fear. Her face was white and she fought vainly to hold back the tears. She struggled to keep calm as she said, 'I'm sorry for bothering you. I wouldn't ever trouble you again. Come with me little Lennie.'

Siobhán walked to the door. Little Lennie kept looking back over his shoulder as he almost ran with her. Ten years of pain had poisoned Nasty Nick's blood and hardened his heart, but there was something about that little boy's sweet innocent face that touched him deep inside and he had never seen such a beautiful woman as the fair Siobhán. He felt bad because he had been so horrible to this beautiful woman and this sweet child. Yet he was shocked when he heard himself say, 'Stop. Come back.'

Siobhán walked back slowly with her son behind her repeatedly tugging at her coat and whispering ever louder, 'Mama no. Mama no. Mama let's get out of here. Let's get out of here, Mama.'

A look of terror came in his eyes when Nasty Nick walked over to him and raised his hand. Little Lennie almost wet himself as he looked up at this giant of a man. The shoemaker nearly smiled as he said, 'Relax boy I don't eat children. Wait a second. I'm not promising anything mind but maybe I might be able to do something. Little boy let me have a quick look at you again. Oh stop crying. Okay call back to me Wednesday evening at seven and we'll see.'

Siobhán took her son away not really understanding why Nasty Nick changed his mind. As they left the shoemaker's house night had fallen early but the shroud of snow reflected a light that gave eerie life to hedges and house, and by a celestial miracle night was transformed into day. Only a cow lowing in a distant field shattered the spell of silence. Siobhán and Lennie plodded up the pathway, through the thickening snow-storm, leaving big, deep footprints in the fresh snow. Lennie was hoping for his first white Christmas. All previous seasons of goodwill had only brought heavy showers of icy rain, which were swept over the village by gusts of bitter wind. The days had been dark and dreary.

'Drat it. Why didn't I just send them packing especially as I hate Christmas,' thought Nasty Nick to himself as soon as the door was closed. All the same, there was something about that little boy.

He went into the kitchen and picked up an old piece of paper and started scribbling furiously on it. In spite of himself a small smile crept over his face when he saw the finished design for little Lennie's new shoes.

The next Wednesday evening Lennie didn't want to go back to Nasty Nick he was so scared of him but his mother made him. The shoemaker had his measuring tape ready when they called. He looked quickly at the boy's boots with an expert eye. In a surprisingly soft voice he said, 'Little Lennie I want to see you here every Wednesday evening for a fitting till Christmas Day and on Christmas morning you will call here on the way to Church to collect your shiny shoes.'

Each Wednesday the fair Siobhán and her son faithfully visited Nasty Nick and on each visit little Lennie's eyes grew wider as he saw new shoes taking shape. Although he never said much to Nasty Nick little Lennie began to like the shoemaker and for his part the shoemaker started to look forward to their visits. As the weeks passed the visits got longer and longer as the fair Siobhán got to know Nasty Nick much better.

Two days before Christmas they had the final fitting. Little Lennie was not as excited as he expected because he had no present for his mother. What could he get her because he had absolutely no money? Lennie was the biggest football fan in history. He had picked mushrooms all summer to get the money to buy himself a new football. It was his pride and joy. He decided to go to Mr Golden's second-hand shop and sell his football.

Mr Golden was an anorexic figure with long hands and the kind of exuberant nasal hair from which it was difficult to tear one's gaze. He once boasted that never once in his seventy-three years did he break a custom, and custom was the only law of the imagination. He was a gifted story-teller, talking in a way that was delightfully descriptive and wickedly insightful of human foibles. He had a great way with horses. In Whitepark if a man's horses liked him it was always his best character reference. Any quarrels that flared up in his shop were quickly nipped in the bud. Memories were long in the hills, and tastes of ancient feuds lingered. Mr Golden might be old but he was vigorous enough still. He had a way of mollifying awkward customers; as silent as the stones which surrounded him on this bleak mountainy landscape. He was like a sponge; he said little but absorbed everything. The rheumatism which often crippled him was playing up again in the cold weather. It was not sufficient to stop him working, just enough to cloud his days with a tetchy temper.

Mr Golden explained he didn't sell footballs but when Lennie told him the full story he agreed to make an exception. As Mr Golden was a kind man he paid the boy a high price for it. Lennie rushed out to the clothes shop nearby and bought a beautiful new blouse for his mother. Her greatest treasure was a beautiful silver locket his father had bought for her a few weeks before he died, but she was too poor to afford a new blouse to show it off properly. Now she would get the chance.

The next day Mr Golden was shocked to find Lennie's mother walking into the shop. She wanted to sell her locket. Mr Golden refused to take it at first but then she explained that she needed the money to buy a pair of football boots for Lennie so that he could play on the school team. Mr Golden again paid her a high price but he shook his head sadly after his happy customer had left.

Later that evening Mr Golden called to the O'Grady's home. He handed Lennie back his football and his mother her locket and a basket of fruit. Their eyes nearly burst with the shock. Siobhán insisted on cooking Mr Golden a delicious hot supper and he stayed for hours talking.

As Mr Golden was saying goodbye to his hosts, Nasty Nick was feeling anxious because his only cow had decided to bring her new calf into the world just then. Self-sufficiency was the thing for Nicholas; cash outgoings were kept to a minimum. As he went outside a lone robin was hopping on the window-sill in search of crumbs. The sticks on the ground were earthy, glittering with the night frost. The cowhouse was warm, smelling strongly of milky breath. Nick had wriggled his toes and rubbed his gloveless hands to keep warm in the cold of early night. The stars were like holes in God's carpet which allowed the eternal light to shine through. Nick tiptoed in his shiny boots avoiding heaps of cow dung in the stable. A hoar frost lay on the fields and the hedgerows were hung with the lace trimmings of what seemed to be a thousand spiders' webs. His neighbour's cattle were huddling under creeping hedges, staring vacantly up at the slate-grey sky with their tired eyes, as they churned the day's grass. The trees seemed to be standing and shivering together, hugging bare limbs and grumbling about the cold. A few tattered leaves made a flimsy blanket on the frozen earth. Two hours later the proud mother was licking her calf. The calf had a red spot on his white face, so in keeping with the season Nicholas decided to call him Rudolf.

For the first time in ten years the shoemaker had made a huge effort to make his home ready for Christmas. Cards, showing people walking about snowy landscapes, decorated the walls. On the top of his big Christmas tree was a tin foil star. There were little silver balls, lights like tiny stars and pale-coloured tinsel threaded among the branches. Round the bottom were boxes of presents done up in pretty paper tied with red ribbon.

When the knock came on his door on Christmas morning he raced to answer it. Nicholas was almost dancing with excitement and anticipation. The butterflies were going mad in his stomach. He opened the door and walked back visibly shocked. For a moment it looked like he had lost his voice. Finally, in squeaky speech he said, 'Please forgive my manners. Come in. I was expecting somebody else.'

As a group of carollers walked in Nicholas said, 'I would be honoured if you would sing for me. Please.'

After they sang a beautiful version of 'Silent Night' Nasty Nick said, 'My, that was wonderful. Hang on a second.'

He went back into his kitchen and started rooting in one of the cupboards. He came back with a fistful of money and handed it to the oldest man in the group. The man's mouth opened with surprise, 'But Nasty Nick … I mean Nicholas you've become so generous.'

Nasty Nick replied, 'I've had a great lesson in the last few weeks. I've been reminded that the greatest Christmas gift of all is the present. From now on I will live each precious day as if it were my last. For the first time since my family died I'm going to have a happy Christmas.'

As the carollers left, Siobhán and little Lennie walked in. Nasty Nick was smiling like a child in a sweet shop as he greeted his two visitors, 'Well at last the big day has arrived. Oh, happy Christmas by the way.'

Siobhán answered with an even bigger smile, 'Happy Christmas.'

Nasty Nick presented the new shoes. Lennie grabbed them and proudly displayed them to his mother, before trying them on.

'Oh little Lennie they're perfect. You've done an amazing job Nicholas. Thank you so much. I've never seen anything so lovely. They must be the eighth wonder of the world!,' said Mrs O'Grady with awe in her voice.

Nasty Nick made a little bow and said, 'It was my great pleasure.'

Siobhán winked up at him, 'Little Lennie has something for you. It's not much.'

Lennie handed the big man a beautifully wrapped parcel, 'Happy Christmas Nicholas. Mama made them for you.'

Nick opened the Christmas paper and pulled out a pair of woollen gloves and a woollen cap with Nicholas written on it as well as a Christmas card. He turned away and wiped the tears toppling in steady streams down his cheeks. Then he said in a choking voice, 'It's been ten years since anyone gave me a present. Thank you so much little Lennie and you too, Siobhán.'

He quickly took two boxes from under the Christmas tree and presented one each to his guests.

Siobhán's voice was a mixture of surprise and delight as she said, 'Oh Nicholas you shouldn't. You're much too generous. We'll save them for later. This has been our best Christmas ever but we're going to be late for Church. I'm sorry Nicholas thank you for all you have done for little Lennie, for both of us. Have a great Christmas. Come on now little Lennie.'

Little Lennie chirped in, 'Bye Nicholas. Thanks.'

There was sadness in his voice as Nick said, 'Happy Christmas.'

Siobhán and her son rushed for the door. Just as they are about to go out Nick shouted, 'Stop. Siobhán there's something I have to say to you.'

The small woman walked towards the big man with a puzzled expression. Lennie followed behind. Nick took Siobhán's hand and said, 'You are the fairest of all God's creatures. Make me the happiest man alive and be my wife.'

Siobhán almost staggered with confusion. A lifetime seemed to be crowded into the space of a second. For a few moments the only sound that was heard was the ticking of the grandfather clock.

Then Lennie butted in and said, 'Oh Mama, say yes. You love him and he clearly loves you. What could be simpler? Say yes and make the three of us very happy.'

His mother turned first to the boy, 'Oh Lennie are you sure about this?'

Lennie said, 'I've never been more certain of anything in my life.'

His mother smiled shyly as she said, 'Oh Nicholas I would be honoured to be your wife.' Their eyes met and a warmth went through her that Siobhán had not felt before.

The big shoemaker went on his knee and pulled out a ring from his pocket and put it on Siobhán's finger, 'Wear this always and know that I will love you forever.'

His wife-to-be said, 'I will always love you Nicholas.'

All three exchanged hugs. Nick looked up to the sky and smiled, 'God has indeed answered my Christmas prayer. I'm the luckiest man in the whole wide world.'

As the bells boomed out from the village church Siobhán said breathlessly, 'Oh my gosh. Look at the time. We are going to be late for Church but in the circumstances I think God will understand. Nicholas why not come with us and join us after for Christmas dinner. It's very simple but …'

Nick stopped her, 'There's no meal I'd enjoy more nor no place I'd rather be.'

Nick took both Siobhán and little Lennie by the hand and they walked out. Across the fields the houses glittered, the light from their candles like jewelled pin-points in the darkness. It was bitterly cold as they left the shoemaker's. Little Lennie's breath was coming out on to the cold air like puffs of steam from a kettle. A few swirling snowflakes drifted onto his head. All three felt very happy, though now the snow was making white carpets on their heads. The whole sky seemed to be filled with dizzy, dancing snow.

Three weeks later Nasty Nick and the fair Siobhán got married. Little Lennie was both the page boy and the best man. The next Christmas morning a taller Lennie was back in Church but this time he was accompanied by his new twin sisters Roisín and Katy. To mark the occasion his step-father presented a gift to every child in the district. The next Christmas he presented a gift to every child in the whole country and the following year to children everywhere. Gradually he became even more famous for his love of children than his wonderful skills as a shoemaker. Within a few years everyone forgot that his nickname was once Nasty Nick and soon he became known far and wide by his new nickname, Saint Nicholas.

# About the Contributors

Catherine Ann Cullen received a distinction for her M.Phil in Creative Writing from Trinity College, Dublin in November 2001, for *Taboo*, a collection of sonnets on the breaking of taboos in myths and fairytales. She is a former RTÉ producer and the author of *The Magical Mystical Marvellous Coat* (Little Brown, 2001) and Thirsty Baby (Little Brown, April 2003), both children's books in verse. She won a second prize in the Brendan Kennelly International Poetry Competition in August 2001, and was shortlisted for the Francis Ledwidge Poetry Award in December 2001. She is currently working on an animated feature film in verse, *The Marsh King's Daughter*, and a series, *Walt and Wisteria*. Her first book won a NAPPA Gold Award for Poetry and Folklore from the American Parents' Association, was chosen as a Borders Bookshops original Voice Book, and was a Boston Book-Show, 'Cream of the Crop' book. 'Golden Feathers' will be produced as an animated feature by Tim Fernee and Rocket Animation in 2003.

ଔ

A native of Tipperary, Leo Cullen now lives with his wife and family in Dublin. He is author of *Clocking Ninety on the Road* to *Cloughjordan and Other Short Stories* and an acclaimed novel *Let's Twist Again*. Last year he was awarded a bursary in literature from the Arts Council of Ireland. His poetry and short stories have been published widely. His work has been broadcast on BBC, RTÉ and Lyric FM.

ଔ

PJ Cunningham's book of short stories *A.N. Other* was one of the publishing surprise successes of last year, striking a chord with an audience who readily identified with his portrayal of small-town life and the activity of the GAA. Married with five children, PJ is a native of Clara, Co. Offaly and now lives in Bray, Co. Wicklow. He works in Independent Newspapers where he is sports editor of the *Irish Independent*. He is currently writing a second book of short stories and a novel.

CB

Born in Omagh, Co. Tyrone, Martina Devlin now lives in Dublin where she works as a columnist for *Ireland on Sunday*. She won a Hennessy Prize for her first short story and went on to write two bestselling novels, *Three Wise Men* and *Be Careful What You Wish For*. Her third novel, *Excavating Venus*, will be published next year.

CB

Anthony Glavin was born in Boston but moved to Ireland in 1974. A former editor of 'New Irish Writing' in the *Irish Press*, he has published two collections of stories, *One for Sorrow* (1980) and *The Draughtsman and the Unicorn* (1999), and a critically-acclaimed novel, *Nighthawk Alley*. His forthcoming novel is entitled *Something to Write Home About*.

CB

Dermot Healy was born in Finea, Co. Westmeath but now lives in Sligo. His collections of short stories include *Banished Misfortune*, which won two Hennessy Awards and the Tom Gallan Award. His novels include *Fighting With Shadows* and *A Goat's Song*, which won the 1994 Encore Award for the best second novel. His collections of short stories include *The Ballyconnell Colours*. He has edited two journals, *The Drumlin* and *Force 10*.

CB

Cathy Kelly is one of Ireland's most successful writers with a series of bestselling novels to her name, including *Someone Like You* and *What She Wants.*

ଔ

Brian Leyden lives in Co. Leitrim. His first collection of short stories, *Departures,* appeared in 1992, followed by the novel *Death and Plenty* in 1996. His most recent publication is *The Home Place* published by New Island Books, 2002.

ଔ

Kevin McDermott was born in Dublin where he lives with his wife and their three children. He has written two novels: *A Master of the Sultan* (1997) and *Watching Angels* (2000). He has written extensively for radio.

ଔ

John MacKenna's early publications were about local history. It was the publication in 1992 of his first collection of short stories, *The Fallen and Other Stories,* that first catapulted him to the forefront of Irish writing – a status confirmed when the book won the prestigious *Irish Times* First Fiction Award. Three years later came his second collection of short stories, *A Year of Our Lives,* which advanced still further his growing reputation. His first novel, *Clare,* was based on the life of the Romantic English poet, John Clare and his other novels are *The Last Fine Summer* and *A Haunted Heart.*

ଔ

Marisa Mackle lives in Dublin and Spain. Her first novel, *Mr Right for the Night,* was a number one bestseller. Her second novel, *The Happiest Couple in Ireland,* will be published next summer.

෴

Arnold O'Byrne, former Managing Director of Opel Ireland Ltd, is well known for initiating the successful Opel sponsorship of Irish soccer in 1986. His main interest is his family but he also has a keen interest in soccer and he is an Honorary Life Member of the FAI. He is known to occasionally write verse, which he describes as a form of relaxation. His ambition is to find the time, and the nerve, to write his autobiography.

෴

Joseph O'Connor was born in Dublin. He is a serial writer of number one bestsellers, including *The Secret World of the Irish Male, The Salesman* and *Inishowen.* He has won a glittering array of prizes, including the Hennessy New Irish Writer of the Year Award.

෴

Maura O'Neill teaches English and French in a secondary school in Co. Kildare. She doubles up as a presenter with RTÉ radio and as a columnist with *The Sunday World.* She is currently working on her first novel.

෴

Micheal O'Siadhail has published ten collections of poetry, which include his latest, *The Gossamer Wall* (Bloodaxe, 2002), as well as *Hail! Madam Jazz* and *A Fragile City* (Bloodaxe, 1999) and *Our Double Time* (Bloodaxe, 1998). Awarded an Irish American Cultural Institute prize for poetry in

1981 and the Marten Toonder Prize for Literature in 1998, he has read and broadcast his poetry widely in Ireland, Britain, Europe, North America and Japan.

♋

Meeghan Piemonte lives in Boston, Massachusetts. She graduated from Trinity College, Dublin in February 2002 with an M. Phil. in Creative Writing. She is now back home, teaching English.

♋

Suzanne Power is a former journalist whose first novel *Lost Souls Reunion* was published by Picador to critical acclaim earlier this year. She is currently working on her second novel.

♋

Kate Thompson was catapulted to stardom as one part of Ireland's most famous love triangle in *Glenroe*. She then turned her considerable talents to writing and was an instant success with four bestselling novels to her credit to date: *It Means Mischief, More Mischief, Going Down* and *The Blue Hour.*

♋

John Quinn, from Ballivor, Co. Meath is an acclaimed RTÉ presenter and producer, with a number of award-winning documentaries to his credit. He has published a number of books including four books for children, one of which – *The Summer of Lily and Esme* – won the Bisto Childrens' Book of the Year award in 1992.

♋

John Scally is a native of Roscommon. He is the author of a number of bestselling sports biographies including *Raising the Banner*, the official biography of Ger Loughnane. His most recent book is *Sporting Foot and Mouth*, a compilation of funny sports quotations.

ଔ

Kathy Sinnott almost caused a seismic shock in Irish politics when, after two recounts, she came within six votes of taking a seat from Fianna Fáil in the 2002 General Election. She is the mother of nine children and campaigns for the rights of those with disabilities.

ଔ

Peter Woods was born in London but grew up in Monaghan. He now lives with his wife and children in Dublin. An acclaimed documentary-maker, he is currently working on his first novel which will be published by New Island Books.

Another New Title from Blackwater Press

# Sporting Foot and Mouth:
## Hundreds of Funny Sports Quotations

*John Scally*

The truth is stranger than fiction and often funnier. This collection of sporting quotes provides an entertaining tour of the minds of some of sport's greatest artists as well as some famous people who may know little about sport but are always good for a quote. Sometimes their words are way more entertaining than their achievements.

Anyone who is anyone in sport may find themselves quoted here in their scurrilous, unguarded, rude or humorous moments.

The great and the good, the wonderful and the woeful are all here: from Ger Loughnane to Woody Allen; from Charlie Haughey to the Queen Mother; from Jack Charlton to Groucho Marx; from Mohammed Ali to Brian O'Driscoll, from Pope John Paul II to Spike Milligan and from Robin Williams to Jimmy Magee.

'For some men at least in the match between football and sex, football will always scrape home on goal difference.'

*Joe O'Connor*

'I played rugby once. Then I discovered that you had to run with the ball so I gave it up.'

*Garret FitzGerald*

'The real problem with the foot and mouth epidemic Pat was that you didn't get it.'
*Ted Walsh to Pat Spillane*

'I'm still trying English.'
*David Beckham, asked if he was learning Japanese for the World Cup.*

'Someone threw a petrol bomb at him and he (Alex Higgins) drank it.'
*Frank Carson*'

It is a pot pourri of double entendres, satirical quips, unintentional puns and foot-in-mouth disease from the tongues of sport's elite – reading pleasure for the madly mischievous and wickedly warped.

*Available in bookshops nationwide*